Shivers ran u

A night owl hooted in th

"You sure smell good," he said, catching her off guard.

"Just castile soap," she said hoarsely.

"I can smell your hair all the way over here."

"I washed it last night."

"Bet it's soft, too."

"Oh, I don't know. It's just hair."

He looked over at her then. "Mind if I smell it up close?"

"I—" She swallowed. "I guess I don't mind."

He leaned toward her, his bare chest rubbing her
shoulder because she wore her batiste nightgown
without sleeves. Tilting his head, he buried his face in
the hair at her neck and inhaled.

Of course that breath had to come out, and when it did,
the moist warmth fluttered against Ellie's ear and her
neck and shoulder. Goose bumps broke out on her flesh.
"Yes," he whispered, a soul-deep sound....

Dear Reader,

Autumn is such a romantic season—fall colors, rustling leaves, big sweaters and, for many of you, the kids are back in school! So, as the leaves fall, snuggle up in a cozy chair and let us sweep you away to the romantic past!

If you haven't discovered Cheryl St.John by now, you're in for a treat. Whether writing historicals or contemporaries, Cheryl's emotional, slice-of-life stories will warm your heart. In *The Doctor's Wife,* scandalous secrets are revealed but love triumphs when a waitress "from the other side of the tracks" marries a young doctor in need of a mother for his baby girl.

Branded Hearts by Diana Hall is another Western chock-full of juicy surprises. Here, a young cowgirl bent on revenge must fight her feelings for her boss, an enigmatic cattle rancher. Jacqueline Navin returns with *Strathmere's Bride,* an evocative Regency-style romance about a darling duke who suddenly finds himself the single father of his two orphaned nieces, and in dire need of a wife! And don't miss *Briana* by bestselling author Ruth Langan. In the final book of THE O'NEIL SAGA, a feisty Irish noblewoman falls in love with a lonely, tormented landowner, who first saves her life—and then succumbs to her charms!

Enjoy. And come back again next month for four more choices of the best in historical romance.

Sincerely,

Tracy Farrell
Senior Editor

P.S. We'd love to hear what you think about Harlequin Historicals! Drop us a line at:

Harlequin Historicals
300 E. 42nd Street, 6th Floor
New York, NY 10017

CHERYL ST. JOHN

THE DOCTOR'S WIFE

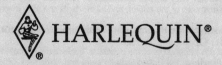

HARLEQUIN®

TORONTO • NEW YORK • LONDON
AMSTERDAM • PARIS • SYDNEY • HAMBURG
STOCKHOLM • ATHENS • TOKYO • MILAN • MADRID
PRAGUE • WARSAW • BUDAPEST • AUCKLAND

ISBN 0-373-29081-0

THE DOCTOR'S WIFE

Copyright © 1999 by Cheryl Ludwigs

Books by Cheryl St.John

Harlequin Historicals

Rain Shadow #212
Heaven Can Wait #240
Land of Dreams #265
Saint or Sinner #288
Badlands Bride #327
The Mistaken Widow #429
Joe's Wife #451
The Doctor's Wife #481

Silhouette Intimate Moments

A Husband by Any Other Name #756
The Truth About Toby #810

Silhouette Yours Truly

For This Week I Thee Wed

CHERYL ST.JOHN

is the pseudonym for Nebraska author Cheryl Ludwigs. Cheryl's first book, *Rain Shadow,* received nominations for *Romantic Times* and *Affaire de Coeur* awards and for the Romance Writers of America's RITA Award. And her Silhouette Intimate Moments title *The Truth About Toby* won a reader award from Wisconsin RWA's "Write Touch" contest.

Cheryl has served her Heartland RWA chapter as president, vice president, program director, Published Author's Network liaison and conference committee chairman.

A married mother of four and a grandmother several times over, Cheryl enjoys her family. In her "spare" time she corresponds with writers and readers, and she would love to hear from you.

Send a SASE to: Cheryl St.John, P.O. Box 12142, Florence Station, Omaha, NE 68112-0142.

This story is dedicated to the most supportive and
talented group of ladies I've ever had the pleasure of
knowing: the other Harlequin Historical authors, lovingly
dubbed "The Hussies." I will not name each one here,
because I might inadvertently miss someone and have to
cringe later, but you know who you are.

What I want you to know is how special each of you is
to me and how proud I am to be published among the
ranks of such gifted and professional writers. Thanks for
the laughs. Thanks for the tears.

Special thanks to my diligent and gracious editor,
Margaret Marbury, who always makes certain that I've
written the best possible book.

Prologue

Florence, Kansas, 1879

A shimmering silver moon spied upon the girl's halting, labored progress as she crept through the stand of midnight-cloaked cottonwoods, their long-fingered branches snagging her threadbare dress and scratching her bare arms. She held the tiny shawl-wrapped bundle protectively against her breast and stopped often, fighting the trembling that shook her exhausted limbs and the weakness that threatened her ability to reach her destination undiscovered.

Another spasm racked her belly, and she fell to her knees, curling herself around the bundle and whimpering soundlessly. A cloud momentarily obscured her vision, or perhaps she blacked out, but too much time had passed when she could once again see clearly enough to move forward through the frosted moonlight and into the sleeping town. Quickly, she found the alley.

A cat yowled, startling her, and she nearly stumbled again. She gripped her concealed burden and hurried on. Finally, she came up behind the house she'd been heading toward with single-minded purpose. No light shone from the eyelike windows, the occupants having long ago retired.

The girl watched the house enshrouded in darkness for several minutes, torn with what she must do and what her heart and her body rejected as unendurable.

The infant moved against her breast, a helpless, tiny creature needing more care and protection than she ever could hope to give it. The feeble movement tore at her heart, but prodded her forward.

Once crouched in the concealing darkness at the corner of the house, the precarious safety of this rash plan struck her hard. What if no one came to the door? What if a dog or a wild animal was first to reach the mewling infant, who still bore traces of her blood?

Exhaustion hammered at her nerves and her thoughts, but fear pushed her forward. There was more chance for survival here than where she'd come from. A rock bit into the cracked sole of her shoe, and she picked up the stone, testing its size and weight.

She pressed her nose into the shawl, inhaled the musky scent that pierced her heart anew and resolutely placed the wrapped child on the wooden porch floor, a safe distance from the back door, yet in plain sight.

Without a lingering touch or a backward glance—by sheer force of will—she slipped back into the shadows, hobbled into the alley and steadied herself against the rough wooden side of a toolshed.

In the shadows of the porch roof, she couldn't see the shawl or the remnant of her heart that lay within. The vigilant moon illuminated the glass-paned windows of the house. She stared heavenward for a full minute, garnering strength, purpose…courage. Then, with a prayer for accuracy and the last shred of stamina she possessed, she took aim and directed the rock with a skill born of desperation.

Breaking glass shattered the fragile silence of the night. Her lacerated heart hammered against her ribs.

Her vision blurred, then cleared.

A yellow light came on in the house.

An eternal minute passed.

Another.

With an echoing creak, the back door opened. The long black barrel of a gun preceded a tall man dressed only in trousers. He took a wary step forward. Then stopped.

Cautiously, he nudged the bundle on his porch with the rifle barrel. The trembling girl who watched didn't breathe, and her heart stopped.

Finally, miraculously, after glancing around, he knelt and touched the shadowy bundle with his free hand. His voice carried across the backyard, the words of astonishment indistinguishable. Another light came on behind him, and a robed woman appeared, silhouetted in its gentle radiance like a delivering angel.

As soon as the woman fell to her knees on the porch, the girl's heart resumed a frantic beat. She turned and fled into the night, the silvery glow of the silent moon the only witness to the deed that would forever scar her soul.

Chapter One

Newton, Kansas, 1885

Up ahead, the locomotive whistled a long, urgent warning that roused the sluggish passengers. The chugging train swayed and slowed, and the tired travelers jerked forward in their seats. Stockmen, herders, businessmen and women gathered belongings and children and prepared to step from the car.

Elianna Parrish clung to the handle of her one small battered satchel, and allowed impatient travelers to move ahead. She was in no hurry. She'd been on a three-day pass and didn't need to report back to her job at the Arcade Hotel until morning.

The melancholy feeling that always accompanied her on returning from a visit with her two younger brothers washed over her like the claustrophobic taint of unwashed bodies and cigar smoke that filled the railcar. Even though she traveled to see the boys each time she could get a pass from her job, she missed them terribly. The Heaths, who farmed a few miles outside Florence, tolerated her visits and put on as if they were actually fond of the boys.

Ellie knew better. For the past year, her brothers had been laborers, expected to perform the tasks of men while receiving stingy meals and lumpy bunks in the barn. Ellie's high hopes of immediately getting them out of there had faded as quickly as the vaporous smoke from the train's engine. She hadn't been able to save enough to get herself a place, let alone provide for Benjamin and Flynn.

A portly man with a smelly stogie clamped between his stained teeth jostled her, and she stepped away.

Resentment built in her like a head of steam. Why, for once in their cheerless lives, couldn't the boys have a decent home? They deserved to know the security of a home and family before they were completely grown.

Like her.

Passengers filed out ahead of Ellie, and she waited her turn patiently. Finally, the eager crowd moved forward, and she stepped out into the sun. A dry prairie wind kicked up dust that filled her nostrils and caked her teeth. She squinted and worked at keeping her dress down around her ankles.

Several men stood on the platform, scrutinizing the arrivals. Ellie identified the fakirs, the Monte men and sneak thieves immediately, and skirted them while they made their moves on the businessmen who looked as though they had money lining their pockets.

"Come to see the city by gaslight, did you, little lady?" A man of medium height in a dusty brown suit cut off her departure.

"Pardon me," she said, and attempted to move around.

"Here to see the elephant, hmm? A lovely young thing like you should have an escort." Deliberately, he prevented her from passing.

She met his small gray eyes directly. "I'd appreciate it if you'd get out of my way."

His eyes widened at her bravado. "Well, la-di-da, don't she take the whole biscuit?"

The throng of passengers converged on the hotel restaurant, jostling Ellie and the man to one side. Once again, she tried to move around him.

"You're gonna wish you was nice to me."

Ellie stepped back in an attempt to move another direction, but succeeded only in stumbling. A sharp yelp pierced her ears and, too late, she glanced back. She'd stepped on a small dog. The leashed animal jerked away frantically, tugging its smartly dressed female owner off balance, and the three of them lurched off the edge of the platform.

Ellie landed with her bag under her side and her arm twisted beneath it. Pain shot up the limb, and she cried out.

A handful of concerned men leaped down from the wooden platform, and a porter came running.

"Oh, my gracious!" Sitting up from her delicately sprawled position and blinking at her surroundings, the pretty young woman fanned herself with a lace hankie. She cradled the dog to her generous breasts and spoke obnoxious baby talk into its panting face. "My darling sweet pea, are you awright?"

The whining dog darted its tongue in adoration over her chin.

Those who'd run to their aid stood mesmerized, watching the woman croon and the rodent-faced canine bathe her face.

If her arm hadn't hurt so badly, Ellie would have laughed. Instead, she sat up. Racking pain shot through her arm, and she bit back a wail.

One of the gentlemen awoke from his reverie and transferred his attention. "Are you hurt, young lady?"

"My arm," she replied with a grimace.

"Could be broke."

"I'm sure it is."

"We'd best get you to the doc's."

Ellie moved to stand and nearly fainted.

"Stay put," the stranger said, extending his palm to stop her. "I'll get my wagon."

She nodded and gratefully leaned back against her lumpy bag. It took three grown men to assist the other young woman to her feet and lead her to the stairs. The sun beat down mercilessly, and the wind blew dust across Ellie's face and clothing. Belatedly, she glanced around, already knowing she wouldn't see hide or hair of the con man who'd brought on this whole fiasco.

Her arm throbbed. The scorching sun beat on her shoulders. Perspiration trickled between her breasts, and her blouse stuck to her itchy skin. She blinked back tears of frustration and pain.

After what seemed like an hour, the Good Samaritan returned and, with as little jostling as possible, assisted her into the back of his wagon.

A woman and small boy sat up on the seat beside him. He called to the team and guided the wagon through the rutted streets, reining in the horse before old Doc Thornton's place.

The chalkboard beside the door had had Back at Three scribbled on it since Ellie had first come to Newton six months ago.

After banging on the door and shuffling from one foot to the other, the man stepped to the edge of the boardwalk and took stock of Ellie in his wagon bed. "Doc must be out."

Passed out. Or down at the Side Track Saloon, more than likely. Ellie squinted down the dusty street. It was common knowledge that the old doctor spent part of his days and most of his nights with his belly pushed up against a poker table.

The woman on the wagon seat turned. "Take her to Doc Chaney's, Clive."

Clive squinted at Ellie. "You trust the young doc?"

Working in the Arcade Hotel, Ellie had overheard all the suspicions and mistrust directed toward Newton's newest physician. His youth and modern practices gave the long-time Cottonwood Valley residents pause. Local gossip had it he'd even been unable to save his own wife's life.

"Harvard University cost the man a king's fortune, Clive. Least he can do is set the poor girl's arm."

Any doctor was better than none—or one who was drunk, Ellie reasoned. Every minute with this pain seemed like a day. She blotted a perspiring cheek with the sleeve of her uninjured arm. "I—" She held back a grimace. "I agree with your wife, sir."

He vaulted back up onto the wagon. A few minutes later, they pulled alongside the boardwalk fronting Miss Eva Kirkpatrick's Dressmaking Shop, and the man helped Ellie from the wagon and into the alley. A hanging wooden sign and a steep flight of stairs led to the doctor's quarters above the seamstress's shop. At the top of the stairs, Ellie gritted her teeth and feared she might faint.

Sunspots swam in her vision. Her head grew light. The stranger caught her before she tumbled down the flight of stairs.

Ellie's arm throbbed. A monotonous pounding in her head matched it, beat for beat.

She cracked her dry eyes open a slit and discovered it was nearly sundown. An oil lamp had been lit near the bed where she lay, casting a golden glow on the brown-haired man who looked up from the thick book he'd been reading.

"Hello," he said, a friendly smile lighting his comely features. "How are you feeling?" Lamplight glittered from the earpieces of the gold-framed spectacles he wore.

She looked away from his too-direct eyes. "My mouth tastes like I ate a pile of buffalo chips."

He laughed, and the deep-chested sound almost made her want to smile, too. "I have some fresh water for you. Can you sit up?"

Before she could object, he slid a strong arm behind her back to help her sit, leaning in so close she could smell the starch in his white shirt and the sun-fresh scent of his hair. She fought the uneasy feeling that washed over her and made her want to scuttle away from him.

He propped a pillow behind her and released her. Her aching left arm hung uselessly in a sling, a plaster-of-paris cast holding her elbow in a bent position against her midriff. She glanced from her swollen fingers up to where the sleeves of her good traveling jacket and the blouse beneath had been cut away in an irreparable fashion. Mentally, she weighed the cost of making new ones against doing without.

"I had to cut them away to get to your arm."

Realizing she'd been frowning, she ran her glance over the rest of her clothing. "My skirt and shoes have gotten your spread dusty."

"Never mind that. Here."

Ellie realized what she'd said, took note of her surroundings and, with a start, realized she was lying on a bed. The long narrow room held an examination table, glass-fronted cabinets for medicines and equipment, and a washstand and basin. A pleated curtain could be pulled across the back sleeping area where she lay. The creeping discomfort that had started earlier spread through her chest.

"You were out cold," he explained, as though reading

her mind. "I was afraid to leave you on the table for fear you'd wake up and fall off. Now drink this."

Ellie drank thirstily and finished, touching her tongue to her lip. The doctor's warm gaze rested on her mouth, and Ellie's face grew hot. She brought her fingers to her cheek, noting the travel grime had been washed away.

"I took the liberty of washing your face and hands," he explained.

Her cheeks burned at the thought of him touching her without her knowledge. Discomfort constricted her throat.

"Cleanliness is important," he supplied.

"Yes, I know," she managed to get out. Working in the dining hall, she'd had plenty of instruction on cleanliness.

"You have a nice, even break." He set the glass aside. "I heard a little about your accident from Clive Sanders."

"Who?"

"The man who brought you in."

"Oh."

"He got you here before it swelled much. That was fortunate. Otherwise I'd have had to wait to put the cast on."

"I'll have to thank him. How long will I be like this?" she asked, dread sinking into her pores. Her disability wiped the other thoughts from her mind.

"In that cast? Several weeks at least. It will heal as good as new, I promise."

The severity of the situation struck her full force. "But that's impossible. I have to be at work tomorrow morning."

"I'm afraid *that's* impossible," he countered.

"Oh, dear."

"Is there someone to come for you? Parents? A husband?"

She shook her head.

"Where do you live? How will you get home?"

"I live in the dormitory behind the Arcade."

"Ah. Well, I can see that you get there safely."

Ellie's meals and room were provided as part of her pay. What would happen if she couldn't work? She had only small savings started toward the day when she and her brothers could live together again. Spending it on room and board until her arm healed would take it all.

Ellie closed her eyes and bolstered her purpose. She couldn't afford to lose that money. She couldn't afford to lose her job. The boys were depending on her to secure a place to live and bring them to Newton. She would work with one arm if she had to.

Cautiously, she swung her legs over the side of the bed and angled her hips to reach the toe of one shoe to the floor. "How much do I owe you?"

His brown-eyed glance traveled thoughtfully from her face to her arm and back again. "A dollar ought to cover the supplies and my time."

"I'll bring it tomorrow."

"I can set up an account and you can pay whenever you like," he offered.

She faced him with her chin raised. "I will pay you tomorrow."

"That'll be fine, Miss..." His voice trailed away, waiting for her to supply the rest.

"Parrish," she said, turning her gaze away and using the name she'd fabricated to obtain a job. "Elianna Parrish."

"Miss Parrish," he said. "Clive left your bag here. I'll carry it to the dormitory. Or I can fetch my buggy if you don't think you can walk."

"I can walk. Of course I can walk." She got off the bed, but her legs were rubbery, and the motion set her arm to aching something fierce.

He must have seen the pain reflected in her face.

"I'll leave this with you." He took a tiny bottle of white

powder from a cabinet and slipped it into the pocket of his neatly pressed shirt, drawing Ellie's attention to the way the fine ivory fabric encased a broad chest. She looked away quickly, surprised with herself for noticing. "It'll help you sleep tonight. Take only one teaspoonful in a glass of water every six hours."

He picked up her shabby bag and his stylish hat and held open the door.

Ellie walked out ahead of him, gripped the wooden banister with her right hand and prided herself on limping down all the stairs without groaning aloud. Her hip hurt like the very devil, too.

The young Dr. Chaney strolled beside her, tall and lean, his boot heels thudding on the creaky boards. He greeted an occasional passerby with a courteous lift of his hat. In the fading sunlight, she sneaked a sideways glance at his profile, his warm brown hair shot with streaks of gold. Once, when he turned his face down to hers, she had a good square look into his dark-lashed brown eyes.

Finding herself in the company of a respectable and handsome man was disconcerting. If he knew who she was and where she'd come from, he wouldn't risk being seen with her on the street. But then no one in Newton knew who she was, and she intended to keep it that way.

She pretended, for the length of time it took them to get to the hotel, that she was a young woman just like any other young woman in Kansas, and that this handsome man with the gentle caring manner and warm eyes was a friend.

She wondered what it would be like to have a friend like Dr. Chaney. Someone who'd been to college and traveled and aspired to an important profession. Someone who was smart and compassionate and smiled easily. They reached the door of the dormitory and, tight-throated, Ellie dismissed the lofty thoughts. "Thank you, Dr. Chaney. I'll bring your payment tomorrow after I go to the bank."

"Can I carry this bag in for you?"

"Only to the courting room. No men are allowed on the girls' floor."

"Okay."

She opened the door, and he followed her down the corridor and into the room where several young women sat playing board games and entertaining guests. A few of the girls glanced up and acknowledged Ellie with wide eyes.

"What happened to your arm?" asked her roommate, Goldie Krenshaw, quickly crossing to Ellie.

The interesting cast and the handsome doctor were too much of a distraction for the others, too, and they crowded around. Ellie made quick work of the story of her misfortune, and the girls sympathized.

Diplomatically, Dr. Chaney excused himself from the bevy of chattering females. Ellie watched him leave and experienced a strange sensation akin to loss and anticipation. No one except Mrs. Conner, a schoolteacher in Florence, had ever been so kind to her, so...respectful.

Of the few Florence citizens who knew her, half looked down their noses and whispered about her. The other half pitied her. She'd rather bear scorn than pity any day.

Surprised murmurs broke out among the females, and Ellie turned to find the doctor had returned. An odd little catch tugged in her chest.

"I almost forgot." He took her hand and pressed the bottle of medicine into her palm.

Ellie jerked back her tingling hand. "Thank you."

He frowned. "Every six hours."

"I remember."

"Goodbye, then."

"Bye."

The looks on the other girls' faces were far from pitying.

She was accepted here. She'd worked her way up from the pantry to the dining hall, just as they had. The Arcade hired men and women from all over. A few of her co-workers were locals, but most were from other parts of the country. Ellie had given a false name and asked a gentleman in Florence who'd known her mother to falsify references. Since she knew infinitely more about the man's leisure activities than did his wife and neighbors, he'd complied.

Goldie carried Ellie's bag to their room and helped her change out of her ruined traveling suit and into a flannel gown. Goldie had come from Indiana, and like many of the girls, sent much of her pay home to her family. Her fondest wish, also like most of the girls, was to meet and marry a Western man.

The two got along well because both stayed to themselves. Until Goldie became especially homesick, and then Ellie would cheer her up by popping corn and setting up the cribbage board.

This night, Goldie returned to the courting room, and though it wasn't yet bedtime, Ellie took a spoonful of Dr. Chaney's bitter-tasting medicine and climbed between the covers. Her trip and her accident had combined to leave her exhausted.

She turned from her side to her back and adjusted her arm in several positions until the medicine started to work and the pain turned to a dull ache. As she always did to get to sleep, she gave her mind over to thoughts of Benjamin and Flynn, and imagined what life would be like when they were all together. She'd do whatever it took to make a home and a family for them. They'd all been without love and security far too long. Ellie meant to change that. The boys deserved it. She deserved it.

She'd taken care of her brothers her whole life—diapered them as babies, cut their hair and kissed their skinned knees. She'd grown a small tobacco patch and sold cigars to the men who patronized the saloons in order to buy them food and shoes. Her brothers were as much a part of her as the grieving heart that ached in her chest at every thought of their being apart from her.

Benjamin had turned fifteen last winter—soon he'd be a man. The first thing she'd noticed when they met her at the station in Florence had been the new shirt and trousers she'd saved to buy him. Planning for the boys and providing for them eased her loneliness while they were separated.

After the state workers had discovered the three of them living in an old shack and condemned it, forcing the boys to go live with the Heaths, Benjamin at fourteen had become aloof.

Ellie never had much of an opportunity to talk to him alone. Perhaps he'd felt as helpless as she had, but he was even younger and more helpless to do anything than she to protect Flynn.

Flynn was nine, good with animals, handsome and quick to laugh…when there was something to laugh about.

Tears spilled from the corners of her eyes, slid down her temples and grew cold in her hair. Flynn had always pretended hurts so he'd get hugs and kisses, then he'd break into a grin and she'd let him think she'd been fooled. This morning he'd been too self-conscious in front of the Heaths to kiss or hug her when she left. She'd climbed aboard the train with a space as big and hollow as the Santa Fe railroad's roundhouse gaping in her heart.

Getting drowsy, Ellie took out every sweet memory she'd saved and gave them to herself now as a gift. She had to keep her memories fresh. Had to keep them vivid.

There were too many ugly ones crowding in from the bleak outskirts to let the good images fade or diminish.

Ugly memories. Shameful memories. Pictures so dark and black and oppressive they could only surface at night in her sleep, when she couldn't consciously keep them at bay.

Secrets nobody but Ellie knew.

And wished to God she didn't.

"How's that fine son of yours, Caleb?"

"Nate's just fine, thank you."

"It's so unfortunate that your wife died so young. Such a pretty young thing, she was. And it's so sad that the boy will grow up without a mother."

Caleb listened to Mabel Connely's heart for the third time in as many days, and ignored the depressing thoughts she continually rattled on about. From her two-story house on Broadway and Main and the front window of Miss Libby's Tea Room, she made it her business to know the comings and goings of everyone in Newton. She never wasted a minute in sharing the latest bits of gossip or admonishing the citizens from her boundless perspective.

He didn't need anyone to remind him of his situation, or that of his son, unless they had a solution. Caleb had been trying to figure out a plan for taking care of Nate for weeks.

Mabel smelled of mothballs and the garlic she'd obviously eaten for lunch; an evil combination. "Your heart sounds just fine to me, Mrs. Connely."

"Well, it's not, I tell you. It beats like a triphammer when I come in from hanging laundry. I have to sit on the back steps and rest in the shade. Why, your stairs out there were nearly enough to put me in my grave." She plucked a rumpled damp hankie from the sash girding her enormous waist, and waved it beneath her bulldog chin, stirring the humid air with mothball scent. "Any doctor worth his salt would have an office on the ground floor."

Caleb leaned back against a wooden cabinet, folded his arms across his chest and leveled his best wiser-than-his-years look on her. He had a sneaking suspicion that she'd started coming to him because she wasn't hearing what she wanted from old Doc Thornton. She was one of only a dozen patients who'd been visiting him regularly, and he'd probably lose her business once he spoke his mind.

"I'm sure it seems that strenuous activity is putting strain on your heart," he said.

"Land sakes, yes!" she hastened to agree. "I told Mr. Connely yesterday that I was going to need some help with housework."

"I don't think help with housework is the solution."

"Why ever not?"

"It's not the work that's straining your heart, it's the extra pounds you're carrying around."

"Why, I never!" She fanned the hankie frantically.

"You're going to have to push away from the table a little sooner and take off that weight. Do some walking. Cut out Joe Hintz's custard pies."

Mabel Connely blustered, her face turning red and her posture indignant. "My mother was a large woman, Caleb Chaney." She scolded him as though he were ten again and she'd caught him playing a Halloween prank. "We're big-boned people."

She hefted herself down from the examination table.

"Didn't your mother die young, Mrs. Connely?" he asked.

"Only forty-nine." She touched the hankie to her quivering lips. "God rest her soul."

"All the more reason for you to take care right now and do something about your situation before it's too late."

"Why, that's preposterous!"

"Not at all. A lot of health factors are passed down from our parents. Ending up overweight or with a weak heart is a chance like blue eyes or big ears."

She snatched up her reticule and marched to the door. "Your impertinence is unbecoming, young man. Good day."

"Come back if you'd like to discuss a menu."

"Humph!"

She yanked open the door and Elianna Parrish, who'd been about to enter, nearly flew into the room, her good hand riveted to the doorknob. She released it quickly and caught her balance, turning to watch Mabel huff and puff down the steps.

Turning back, she cast enormous violet eyes his way, a curious expression lighting them from within. There were mysteries in those haunting eyes, a softness and a sadness that made him want to offer protection and comfort.

"A disgruntled patient," he explained.

"Oh." She closed the door and stood just inside. The plain brown skirt, which she wore with a crisply pressed high-collared blouse neatly tucked in, showed off her tiny waist and girlish figure. He hadn't noticed yesterday, because she'd been wearing a jacket. And he'd concentrated on looking at her as a patient.

Today it was more difficult to see her as only a patient. He wasn't sure why. Maybe because he'd walked her home and seen where she lived. Maybe because she'd flitted through his dreams last night. Maybe because his last caller had been Mabel Connely.

"How's the arm today, Miss Parrish?"

"My fingers are black and blue," she said, stepping forward and showing him.

The faint scents of soap and clean hair drifted to his

nostrils. She wore no artificial floral or powdery smells, but her skin and clothing exuded their own pleasant feminine scent. He checked a sudden urge to place an arm around her shoulders and offer his strength. "Can you wiggle them?"

She demonstrated.

He touched her darkened knuckles gently, but she drew the hand away quickly. When he looked up, tears shone in her luminous eyes, and immediately regret pierced him. "Did I hurt you?"

She turned her face aside and shook her head. With her right hand, she reached into her pocket and withdrew a silver coin. "Your dollar."

Caleb accepted the payment she placed in his palm without touching him. "I'll get you a receipt." He scribbled the amount on the pad on the counter, dropped the coin into a drawer and handed her the paper.

"Thank you. And thank you for tending my arm."

"You're welcome. Did the medicine help?"

She nodded.

She avoided his eyes for several seconds. He asked, "Can you tell me what's wrong?"

Her mouth pressed into a firm line. She looked up, but her gaze rested on his tie, then meandered past his head to a chart on the wall. "Mr. Webb—the hotel manager—won't let me work until the cast is off and I can carry trays."

"I think that's wise," Caleb said. "You could reinjure yourself trying to do too much."

"He's only worried I'll get in the way and be a nuisance. He won't even let me help in the kitchen or pantry."

"I'm sorry." He didn't know what more to say.

She took an unconscious step toward the table where he did his bookwork, and her fingers stroked the back of his wooden chair. The sight started an ache deep inside him. "I can stay two weeks without paying for my room and meals. After that I'll have to pay, or eat and sleep somewhere else."

"What about family?"

She angled her chin over her shoulder uncertainly.

"You said last night you had no parents, but isn't there anyone who can help?"

She shook her head and drew her hand away from the chair.

The silver dollar in the drawer weighed on Caleb's conscience. After her reaction to his mention of credit yesterday, he knew better than to offer to give it back to her. "I know most of the families in Newton and on the surrounding ranches," he said. "Maybe we can find someone to take you in for a few weeks."

"Do you think I can take the cast off sooner?"

"No." His reply was firm. "Especially not with the type of job you do. That bone needs time to knit firmly."

She nodded halfheartedly, as though she'd known what his reply would be, but had needed to ask anyway. For the first time, her wide violet eyes rose directly to his, and their intensity and vulnerability surprised him. Her pride held her so straight and taut, he imagined she'd snap in a stiff wind. "I won't be a charity case. If you can find someone for me to stay with, I'll work for them. I can do anything I'm shown how."

"I'm sure you can."

"I'm strong, and this arm will be better soon. I heal fast. I never get sick."

"You don't have to sell me, Miss Parrish."

A rose-tinged blush lent her ivory skin becoming color. "No. Of course not."

He wanted to turn away from the instinctive desire to

ease whatever pain he read in her eyes, but he couldn't. "I'll start inquiring today."

She nodded and moved toward the door. "Thank you, Dr. Chaney."

A clatter of boots pounded up the stairs and Ellie moved back out of the way just before the door flew open and a young man burst into the office. "Doc! There's a fire out at the Bowman place! Come on!"

Chapter Two

Caleb checked his medical bag for salves and bandages, grabbed his hat from its hook and thundered out the door and down the stairs behind the fellow who had a wagon waiting on the street.

Robert Bowman had died of influenza last winter. Joanna Bowman had stayed on at the farm alone, and Caleb felt an affinity with her now, since they'd both lost their mates. Only a few weeks ago, Caleb had delivered her stillborn baby boy. How much more hardship could the woman bear?

Townsfolk were saying she'd either have to find herself a man to take over the farm or get work in town. Caleb had taken her a few supplies on his last visit.

He didn't realize until they were almost to the Bowman property that he hadn't excused himself from the Parrish girl before running out of his office. He hoped she'd forgive his lack of manners.

Ghostly wisps of gray smoke curled into the sky, pointing out what little remained of the charred house. The dry air carried the acrid stench of soot and ash. Held together with aged wood and dry newspaper, the structure must have gone up like kindling.

The few neighbors who had seen the smoke and come to help stood around a frighteningly limp form on the ground. Alarm knocked along Caleb's spine. He jumped down from the wagon before it rolled to a stop and bolted toward the gathering. The men and woman parted to give him room.

Joanna lay unconscious on a soot-covered blanket, her fair lashes and eyebrows singed. Her face and hands were bright red and blistered, and her clothing had been singed.

Caleb ticked through the possibilities in his mind. She wasn't burned that badly, but the condition of her lungs could be fatal. He bent to listen and was grateful to hear her heart beating faintly. "Who got here first?" he asked.

"We did," Sylvia Quinn said with a tremor in her voice. "Elmer saw the smoke from our west field and we came as fast as we could. She was already out here."

"Was she awake? Did she cough?"

"Coughed something terrible at first, the poor thing," Mrs. Quinn said, a little sob tearing from her throat. "Like she couldn't get any air. I didn't know what to do for her."

One of the other women cried softly, then turned and looked Caleb over skeptically. "Is she gonna die?"

Caleb turned Joanna on her side and pounded her back as hard as he dared. Someone behind him gasped.

Joanna coughed and gagged up black mucus. With his heart pounding frantically, he breathed a grateful sigh and eased her to her back. Efficiently squeezing ointment onto gauze pads, he covered her face and hands loosely, trying to distance himself from the patient. He worked at trying not to think of her tears the day her husband had died or of her grief when she'd seen her lifeless baby. Getting too close to his patient wouldn't allow him the level head he needed to think and work.

"She doesn't look good, Mrs. Douglas," he answered

finally—and frankly. "I'm going to take her back to town with me." At the same time he tried to see Joanna Bowman as a patient who needed his medical training and his clearheaded decisions, he wondered what he would do with a patient in this serious a condition in his small, rented office.

Elmer Quinn helped Caleb lift Joanna into the back of the wagon, using the blanket as a stretcher. Caleb fought the apprehension that gripped him. What if she didn't recover?

He looked up into pale gray eyes swimming with tears. Clella had endured many of the same hardships as Joanna. They were neighbors, friends. With a pained look of regret in her eyes, she stepped away from the wagon.

Caleb's worried gaze took in the neighboring farmers. One by one, they turned away and started back to their homes. Resignedly, he climbed into the wagon bed and settled beside the badly injured woman.

The wagon rumbled toward town. Caleb shielded Joanna's loosely bandaged face from the sun with a feed sack. He'd wanted to be a doctor. He'd asked for the responsibility of caring for the health and well-being of the community.

This woman depended on him, and he'd do the best he knew how to see that she pulled through. Caleb studied her still form and fought uncertainty. He'd never doctored anyone this badly burned. He wasn't certain any treatment would help her.

So much rode on every patient he treated. If she died it would feed the mistrust the community harbored toward him. He wasn't a miracle worker. And that was what he'd have to be to prove himself to the people of Newton.

Gazing skyward, he prayed for a miracle. What if he couldn't save *her,* either?

* * *

He got help carrying Joanna up the stairs and placing her on the bed in his office. He treated the burns methodically, knowing they were not the problem. The smoke and heat she'd inhaled had damaged her lungs, and he knew of no way to correct that.

It was a blessing that she remained unconscious. Even when he pounded her back to force up the black mucus, she fortunately remained unaware. He made sure she stayed that way by giving her laudanum every few hours.

He glanced over at the cot he'd purchased and set up in case he ever needed to stay the night. It looked as if he'd be staying.

He hadn't thought about food, about leaving, about anything except seeing to Joanna's care since he'd brought her here, so the sound of footsteps on his stairs brought him back to reality.

The door opened, and his silver-haired mother, in one of her best dresses and hats, entered his office, a flannel-wrapped bundle in her arms.

"Mother!" he said with surprise. His father followed on her heels, a handsome figure in his fashionable serge suit.

"When you didn't come to the ranch for Nate, I got worried," his mother said with a frown.

"I'm sorry. There was a fire today. Joanna Bowman is here. I've been working on her burns and trying to make her comfortable."

"Oh, how awful," his mother said, clucking sympathetically.

Caleb crossed the distance and took his three-month-old son from her arms. "Hello, little man. Were you missing your daddy?"

The blue-eyed baby smiled a toothless smile. Caleb's heart constricted with the painful reminder of his blue-eyed wife.

"We have the cattlemen's dinner tonight, Caleb," his father prompted from near the doorway.

"And we're going to Florence to visit Patricia tomorrow," his mother added. "I reminded you yesterday."

"You did," he agreed, "and I didn't see a problem until this happened."

His mother eased toward the door. "Well, it's too late to make any other arrangements now."

It dawned on him then that his parents intended to depart and leave Nate here with him. "Wait a minute."

His mother brushed lint from the front of her smart jade dress. "What, darling?"

They had been nothing but helpful since Leila's death. His mother kept Nate nearly every day while Caleb ran his practice. Their own children were grown and gone, and she'd passed middle age years ago. She and his father deserved this time to spend with each other, and with the other ranchers, to go visiting if they chose. He couldn't bring himself to object to their leaving his own son with him.

They'd wanted him to take over the running of the ranch. All he'd ever wanted was to be able to heal people. He'd made his choice in choosing a profession that demanded his time and energy, and he had to accept the consequences.

His sister, Patricia, wanted Nate to come live with her, and she made no secret of her desire to raise him. Caleb knew the boy needed a mother. But Nate was the only part of Leila he had left, and he loved him. He couldn't give him up. He would have to make do, no matter how difficult.

"Have a good time." He managed a more gracious sentiment than he felt.

Three hours, four diapers and a regurgitated bottle of goat's milk later, he placed the sleeping Nate on the cot and checked on Joanna. She had a fever and her breathing was so shallow he had to check her pulse to assure himself she still lived. He cleaned and rebandaged her burns and, with stoical persistence, succeeded in getting some water through her blistered lips and down her throat.

He'd never spent a longer night than the one that followed.

The next afternoon, Ellie climbed the stairs to Dr. Chaney's office. That noon in the hotel kitchen, she'd heard the talk spreading through Newton that the young doc had a seriously injured patient to tend. Skeptics were taking bets on how long the woman could hang on. The doctor wouldn't have had any time to inquire about a job for Ellie, so she'd decided to pay him a call and see if he could direct her somewhere. Perhaps he'd need some help himself today.

She knocked on the door and waited. It opened a moment later. The rumpled young doctor stood before her wearing the same clothing he'd worn the day before. His cheeks showed a day's growth of reddish brown stubble, and his hair looked as though he'd run his fingers through it in lieu of a brush.

But more startling than the abrupt change from his previously impeccable appearance was the infant cradled in the crook of his white-sleeved arm. Her curiosity at the flannel-wrapped baby wasn't easy to hide.

Ellie stared at the tall, dark-haired doctor and the rosy-cheeked baby who frowned owlishly and blinked back, a glistening drop hanging from his lower lip.

"Miss Parrish," the doctor said, stepping back. "Is your arm all right?"

"Well, it's still broken. But it's no worse." She glanced around, noting the curtained-off section she knew hid the bed, amazed that his first thought had been concern for her. "How's your patient?"

He sighed and ran a hand through his hair, demonstrating how he had achieved its disheveled appearance. "Not good."

She could plainly see how difficult this was for him. "I'm sorry."

He took note of her expression and nodded. "I apologize for running out yesterday. I didn't realize until later that I hadn't excused myself or even said a word to you."

"You had to think of the supplies you needed. I didn't think a thing of it, honestly. I appreciated the way you took care of me right away. I'm sure your other patients do, too."

He made no comment, probably wondering why she'd come.

"I came to offer help."

He stared at her curiously, and she wondered if she'd said the wrong thing. She hadn't meant to offend him.

"I heard about your patient. I can't work at the hotel, as you know, and I didn't have anything to do. I thought perhaps..." The thought faded away. Coming here had been a foolish thing to do. "I'm sorry. I don't know what I was thinking." She turned toward the door.

"No, wait!"

Slowly, she turned back.

"I do need help."

Ellie's gaze swept the healthy-looking infant. He had wispy dark hair and a cherubic pink mouth and darling nose. He leaned back in the crook of the doctor's arm and stared up at his father, his eyelids growing heavy.

"I forgot to make arrangements for Nate while my parents went out of town. Do you know anything about babies?"

The child's eyes had closed, his lashes lying against his rosy cheeks. His relaxed fists lay nearly touching his ears. Her heart contracted. Against her will, she thought of other babies, remembered cries and curses and the sick, indescribable, suffocating feeling of being a part of something unspeakable...and the terror of being helpless.

A wave of shame gripped Ellie's vitals for a full thirty seconds, and she feared she'd either cry or throw up. Pain so great she worried she'd never be able to keep it buried rose in her heart and squeezed the breath from her.

Immediately, she dropped her gaze to the floor and willed her emotions into control. She could never let anyone see she carried a burden so dark and ugly there was no hope for it.

"Miss Parrish?"

She had a purpose, and she was a strong person, not given to fits of emotion or moved by attacks of regret.

"Miss Parrish?"

Miss "Parrish" was a continual reminder to her that she wasn't who he thought she was.

"You can call me Ellie." Even her voice was strong.

"Okay...Ellie."

Her real name on his lips made her heart catch oddly, and she tamped down her reaction. She raised her gaze to his warm brown eyes and hated the flutter in her chest.

"Could you take care of Nate for a few days...maybe a few weeks?" he asked.

Ellie glanced from his earnest face to the baby and back, wondering with a little jolt of apprehension where his line of thinking was headed.

"I didn't sleep last night," he said. "Joanna requires all my attention right now. And with Nate...well, I can't neglect either one."

Ellie nodded, whether in understanding or in recognition of what was coming, she didn't know.

"I'd be willing to pay for your services while you're unable to work in the dining hall. It doesn't take a whole lot of experience to learn to change and feed him. And if you should have any problems, I can help you."

Experience? Ellie'd had enough experience taking care of babies and children to last her a lifetime. She hadn't planned to do it again. Ever.

"He's not heavy. I'm sure you can manage with one arm."

She could do it *blindfolded* with one arm, Ellie thought, not too graciously. "I don't know, Dr.—"

"I'll pay you. Whatever you were making at the Arcade. More. You can work for me until your arm is healed and you're able to go back to work."

Exactly the opportunity she needed. But not the job she'd hoped for. Ellie made the crucial mistake of letting herself look at the baby again. His bow-shaped mouth made tiny sucking motions. So helpless. So small and yet so demanding. Dr. Chaney wouldn't ask this if he knew her. He wouldn't ask if he knew her family. He wouldn't ask if he knew about another defenseless little baby....

The doctor sat tiredly on his desk chair then, shifting the infant to his lap so that his head lay cradled in the man's huge palm. The tenderness in that movement, in the way he looked down at his son, shot something raw and painful through Ellie's chest. Neither of her brothers had ever had an adult concerned for their well-being.

He looked up. "Am I expecting too much?" he asked. "It's a lot to ask to care for a stranger's child—"

"No," she replied, cutting him off. "I can handle him." Her mind raced with questions. "I don't know about doing his laundry," she thought aloud, glancing at her bruised fingers.

"I send the laundry out," he said simply.

"Oh."

"I'll get you a room at the boardinghouse for the time being," he said. "Since you can't stay in the dormitory while you aren't working at the hotel. All his things are at my house, and I keep a goat for his milk. You can stay there with him during the day—well you'll probably have to stay there until Joanna...until this situation is resolved."

She nodded, not willing to question this stroke of luck. Not only would this situation relieve her of having to pay for her room and board after next week, but she would make additional money in the meantime! Ellie didn't see how she could turn down such a proposal. She made up her mind with a new spark of determination. "I'll take care of him until my arm is healed and I can go back to the dining hall."

The infant roused and puckered his forehead in a scowl. He found his fist and noisily sucked on his knuckles.

"Looks like he's hungry—again," the doctor said. "I'll run over to Mrs. Ned's and rent you a room. Her place is clean. Do you have much to move over there?"

She shook her head.

He stood and crossed the room. "Here's a bottle for him."

Ellie stood, unprepared to be left alone with Nate so soon. She glanced from the doctor's somewhat relieved expression to the baby, whose face was rapidly growing red. She hoped he was hungry and that his displeasure wasn't an indication of her new charge's temperament.

What had she gotten herself into? She didn't even want children of her own; caring for someone else's was bound to wear her down. "I can go to my room later and pack a bag," she said in acquiescence.

"You can do that after he's fed and I get back," he said matter-of-factly, rising with the baby. She expected him to drop the baby into her arm now that she'd agreed to the task, and prepared herself, but he seemed inclined to keep him cradled against his chest. "Can you make a list for me to drop off at the mercantile? I'll have the things you need delivered."

She nodded. Ellie had never met a man like Dr. Chaney. Yes, he had the gentle, caring bedside manner one would hope for in a doctor, but he also showed an even, good-natured temperament and was the most agreeable man she'd ever known in her limited, but jaded experience.

Dr. Chaney finally handed her Nate. His minimal weight rested comfortably against her breast, and she looked down into his tiny innocent features. Nothing in the world compared to the delicate feel and smell of a baby. Against her will, against everything she'd told herself and believed, something inside her instinctively softened and stretched toward the infant she cradled. Tears stung her throat and she had to clamp her lips in a tight line to keep them from quivering.

Blinking rapidly, she followed the doctor to the door, experiencing a moment of panic.

"I'll be right back with a room key," he said. "I doubt that Joanna will even make a move or a sound. She's resting as comfortably as I can make her right now."

Ellie met his eyes. He'd be right back. All she had to do was give Nate a bottle during his absence. She nodded with more confidence than she felt.

He left, closing the door behind him.

Ellie looked down into the baby's trusting blue eyes. Her lack of confidence wasn't in her ability to meet Nate's needs. Far from that. She didn't doubt she could take care of him properly. This baby would flourish under her care. The only one at risk here was Ellie herself. She reinforced the chinks in her armor with a deep breath.

Against her better judgment, she slowly raised him, slowly lowered her face to Nate's downy head, and with her heart beating in her throat, breathed in the unique smell of him.

Her eyes closed, and a deep-seated, never-forgotten ache blossomed afresh in her heart.

What had she done?

Chapter Three

Just as the doctor had predicted, the badly injured woman never moved. In the silence, Nate sucked his fist noisily. Ellie warmed him a bottle, propped him on a table with a blanket at his back and fed him, gazing into his trusting blue eyes.

Though he was a healthier and sturdier infant than she had ever held and fed, he was still so helpless, so defenseless and completely reliant on someone to love and care for him. That utter dependence frightened Ellie, who'd seen and experienced things no child ever should. Things no adult ever should.

She studied his chubby cheeks and the creases at his wrists and elbows, comparing him to the scrawny babies her siblings had been. Resentment built in her anew, but she banished it with the discipline she'd established to retain her sanity.

Nate might be well-fed and clothed, but he'd lost a mother, she reminded herself.

"I'm sorry about your mama, little fellow," she said with a catch in her chest. "If she'd lived...I wonder if she would have loved you. I wonder if she would have sung lullabies and held you close."

One corner of the infant's wet mouth released the rubber nipple and quirked into a smile. Her heart softened. He made a gurgling sound and reached for her face. Ellie slipped a finger into his fist and he clung tightly. Tears burned behind her eyes.

She remembered Benjamin as a baby...Flynn...a sister once, too. The child had been born after Benjamin, had slept beside Ellie on a pile of rags on the floor. A cold winter and lack of food had exposed them all to sickness, and the baby girl hadn't been strong enough to survive.

Ellie had often wondered, sometimes raged at a questionable God for allowing babies to be born to people who didn't want them, who didn't love them or take care of them.

Nate finished the bottle, and she carried him to a chair and sat him up in her lap. He leaned against her breast contentedly, and she supported his back with her cast. She recalled nights of listening to her brothers' bellies growl with hunger while she ignored the gnawing, hollow ache in hers. Here was a child who would never have to experience hunger or neglect. Ellie envied him. She rejoiced for him. He burped and she chuckled.

Dr. Chaney arrived, out of breath and looking more tired than ever. He held out a key, but her good arm was filled with his son, so he placed it on the nearby desk. "Your room is on the second floor at Mrs. Ned's boardinghouse. Do you know where that is?"

She shook her head.

"It's just across from the park on Broadway."

"I can find it."

"We'll have to arrange for someone to help you carry your things over. How is Joanna?"

"She didn't make a sound. I checked on her a couple of times, but I didn't know what to do for her."

"She's sedated." He moved to the other end of the room to check on the motionless figure. "I've done everything that can be done." He glanced back at Ellie. "I suppose we should get some dinner."

"Dr. Chaney—" Ellie began.

"Caleb, please."

She stood and carried the baby to the end of the cot where the woman lay, frightfully still and silent. "Why don't I just go ahead and take Nate to your house? I can stay with him until you come home—whenever that is. It will be one less thing for you to worry over. I promise you he'll be safe with me."

He studied Ellie briefly, and a frown crossed his weary features. Was he having second thoughts about her? She swallowed against the fear that he would change his mind. "Have you eaten?" he asked.

His words eased her worry and amazed her. His thoughtfulness in the midst of his weighty problems caught her by surprise. She had to gather her thoughts. "I—I'll stop and get something on my way and I'll have something sent for you," she said at last.

He nodded gratefully. "Thank you. It would be a relief for me to think of nothing but taking care of my patient. I have no idea when I'll be able to leave here. If you should need anything, I have accounts at Swensen's Grocery, Hintz's Bakery and Dymond and Arnold's Drugstore. There is food in the pantry. A young fellow delivers ice each morning." He studied his son, then glanced back at Ellie. "Do you know how to milk a goat?"

"I'll manage it." She'd milked cows and goats in the dark of night, stealing milk for her brothers.

He reached into his pocket and brought out a leather thong, slipping off another key. He went for the one he'd placed on the table, used his strip of leather to tie them together, and handed them to her.

"Head north up Main Street. When you get to Seventh, it's the third house to the east, on the north side of the street. Mrs. McKinley is my neighbor, and she'll help you if you need anything."

His fingertips brushed her palm as he placed the keys in her hand. She wrapped her fingers around the keys and stepped away quickly. "We'll be just fine."

"Thank you, Ellie."

She lowered her gaze from his uncomfortably. "You're welcome."

He packed a few things into a bag. She slung it over her shoulder and tucked the keys safely in her reticule. He took Nate from her and hugged him gently.

The vision of the tall, strong man embracing the baby with such tenderness affected Ellie in a disturbing manner she couldn't have explained. For one thing she'd never seen a man show affection for a child before. And for another, the only treatment she'd ever received from the male gender ranged from indifference to cruelty.

His enormous palm swallowed Nate's fuzzy head and he pressed his lips to the boy's hair.

Ellie's stomach quivered.

He raised his gaze and met hers.

Her heart skipped a series of beats and her breath caught. Embarrassment blistered her cheeks.

Studying her openly, he handed Nate back. Ellie carefully avoided the doctor's eyes.

"Wait a minute," he said.

Her heart thudded uncomfortably.

He opened a cupboard and produced a cap, which he tied on Nate's head while Ellie studied the wall. He was so close, she could smell the outdoor scent of his hair and the medicine he'd been using on his patient.

"There," he said. His voice startled her, and she felt foolish.

She turned to the door quickly and carried the baby down the outside stairs. Nate squinted at the sky from beneath the hat's brim.

Relief flooded Ellie. Her plan to get away from the office and the doctor had been successful. She'd worked with the hotel manager and several of the male kitchen helpers at the Arcade, but she hadn't been in closed quarters with them, nor had she suffered their company without others present.

"Well, let's get your father some food and then find your house," she said and set off at a brisk pace. At the Arcade, she ordered a meal sent to the doctor's office, then continued on her way.

The third house on Seventh Street was a lovely two-story, the open shutters and the front door painted a fresh bright green against whitewashed siding. Fragrant red roses climbed an arbor trellis that arched above the gate Ellie passed through. Did this grand house really belong to the young doctor?

She approached slowly, climbing the porch stairs while glancing about. She fitted the key in the lock and the door opened silently. The scent of beeswax drifted to her. The dim, cool interior beckoned. Ellie stepped into the foyer.

She'd never felt so out of place. She couldn't remember ever being in a house this grand. The only home she'd ever visited had been the Heaths' rustic farmhouse, and she'd never been invited past the kitchen.

A small foyer held a highly polished piece of walnut furniture that served as a bench, mirror and hat rack. Ellie blinked at her reflection holding Nate, feeling as though she had entered a castle.

On a desk inside the next room she noted a scattering of envelopes addressed to Dr. Chaney, which confirmed that this was the right place.

Upholstered furniture had been grouped around a brick fireplace, and the flower-papered walls were lined with shelves of books. In awe, Ellie studied the titles on the spines. She'd been in the library in Florence, but she hadn't known people actually owned so many books.

Perhaps if she was very careful with them and had all of her other chores done, Dr. Chaney wouldn't mind terribly if she sat in here and read some of his books.

In the kitchen, she admired the nearly new cast-iron stove with a well for water and a shiny copper kettle atop a burner. On another wall, an enamel pan beneath a pump held unwashed dishes. Ellie placed Nate on a braided rug long enough to raise the pump handle a few times. She stared in amazement at the burst of water that gurgled and spurted across the soiled plates and pans.

The only indoor pump she'd seen had been in the hotel. What lavishness! The doctor must be wealthy beyond imagination!

An oak chest with heavy steel hinges caught her attention next. She opened the latch and cool air drifted across her midsection and up her face! Ellie reached in and touched the ready supply of butter and milk, finding them surprisingly cold. Amazed, she closed the door securely.

She picked up Nate and investigated a well-stocked pantry, a dining room without furniture, and then, with her shoulders and good arm aching, she made her way up the open front staircase.

Caleb's bedroom was easy to find. A simple brass headboard stood against the wall, a faded quilt adorning the unmade bed, which had huge coil springs and a thick mattress. A hat and jacket hung on wall hooks, and a new black leather satchel sat against a wall.

Ellie spotted the cradle and walked toward it. The massive head- and footboards were carved with chains of spiraling ivy. Ellie studied the masterfully crafted wood.

"My goodness, Nate. You must sleep like a prince in this cradle." She placed him in his cradle, noting his damp clothing, and stretched her aching back and arm. "We'd better find you some dry clothes."

A nearby chest of drawers held crisply starched shirts and celluloid collars. Ellie shut the drawer quickly and opened another. To her relief, she found a pile of delicately embroidered garments with neatly pressed hems and ribbons. "You even dress like a prince," she said. "Prince Nate. Is your name Nathan? Nathaniel? I'll bet it's Nathaniel." Getting his clothing off with one hand wasn't too difficult, but it took some maneuvering to fasten the pins and get his flailing arms into sleeves.

He gurgled cheerfully throughout the process, and Ellie had to grin. She was grateful when he fell asleep, and she could explore the rest of the house. Washing the dishes was a challenge, but pumping the water right there was such a luxury that she heated water both for washing and rinsing and had the job done quickly. By the time she'd set the spacious kitchen straight and carried in more wood for the stove, Nate was awake and howling.

She changed and fed him, then tugged a rocking chair out onto the porch where she sat and rocked him. She would get herself something to eat soon. The sweet scent of roses wafted across the porch, and Ellie closed her eyes and listened to the birds in the hedge and the sound of the train in the distance.

At the Arcade, the girls would be setting up for the arriving passengers, and the overbearing kitchen manager would be shouting directions and criticizing the table settings. Ellie felt as though she'd been given a lovely gift by being able to enjoy the evening, sitting here and resting. Yesterday her broken arm had been the worst thing that could've happened...today, well today it almost seemed like a favor—as long she ignored the dull throb.

Maybe this wasn't going to turn out so badly after all. As long as she could keep her distance from the man who had hired her, everything was going to work out just fine. She and Nate were going to get along fabulously.

More tired and discouraged than he'd ever been in his life, Caleb made arrangements with the undertaker and waited for the man to come for Joanna's body.

Three days. And during that time he'd never really had any hope. In his heart he knew no doctor could have saved her. She'd been too far gone. But he'd dreaded her death, not only because of the loss of a life, but more selfishly, because of the reaction of the townspeople.

Dr. Chaney had lost another patient.

After Joanna was gone, he wiped all the surfaces with disinfectant, cleaned his instruments, stripped the bed and carried the huge pile of laundry down the block.

Wearily, he walked home, regret and frustration churning in the pit of his hungry belly. Doctors couldn't save all their patients. People died; it was a fact of life. His treatment hadn't killed her. He had eased her suffering and made her death merciful, but he drew no comfort from those facts.

Fresh guilt ate at his already depleted conscience. He hadn't seen his son for three days. Caleb glanced up at his house.

The brick walkway and stairs had been recently swept.

The front door stood open to the late afternoon breeze, and through the screen wafted the smell of freshly baked bread. His mouth watered and his stomach growled.

An odd, welcoming feeling settled around him. For months he'd come home to a closed and empty house; this was the first time since he'd bought the place that it seemed as if someone lived here.

He entered the foyer and listened to the unfamiliar, but welcome sounds of habitation. A feminine voice beckoned him to the kitchen.

"Hello?" he called.

Ellie glanced over, her wide gaze startled, and recognition flared. "Dr. Chaney!"

Nate had been tied into the wooden high chair with a white dish towel, and the girl was standing on a chair, wiping the fronts of the cupboards.

When he saw Caleb, his son grinned and banged his palms against the wooden tray.

Immediately Caleb untied the knot that held him and raised the baby into his arms. He smelled good—healthy, like milk and baby and life. Caleb kissed his head and laid his cheek against Nate's soft hair, regretting the time spent apart. Nate needed parents. For the thousandth time, he suffered distressing thoughts of this precious boy living day after day without a mother.

"Your—your patient?" Ellie asked, carefully climbing down from the chair.

Caleb carried Nate to the open back door and gazed out across the lawn. Soon everyone would know. "She died this afternoon."

"I'm sorry."

"Yes," he replied. "Me, too."

"I baked bread," she said. "And there's ham."

"That sounds good." He kissed Nate again, placed him back in his chair and got the ham from the icebox.

"Let me do that for you," she said, bringing a loaf of bread to the table.

"Which one of us has two good arms?" he asked, and sliced a hunk of ham.

She backed away, and he felt her watching him fix his meal. It seemed strange to have her there, in his house, in his kitchen, but her presence was comforting, especially knowing that he needed to sleep and that she'd be here for Nate. Nate looked fed and happy. She'd obviously been managing quite well.

"Have you had any problems?" he asked, sitting and biting into the sandwich he'd made.

"Not really," she said.

"You milked the goat with one hand?"

She nodded.

Her puzzling yet appealing combination of strength and vulnerability intrigued him. That couldn't have been easy. "The place looks cleaner than I left it," he said. "That wasn't part of the deal."

"Nate's not very demanding," she replied, turning and rinsing out the rag she'd been using. "I've had more time than I'm used to."

"How long have you been at the Arcade?"

"Only a few months."

"What did you do before that?"

She hung the cloth over a wooden rack to dry. "I—um— I worked in Florence."

"Doing what?"

"The same things I'm doing now."

Did she have a hotel job there? he wondered. He realized he was wolfing down his food and paused.

"Would you like a bath?" she asked.

Caleb glanced down at his rumpled clothing. He had changed his shirt once, but other than that he'd only washed his hands and face. She'd obviously noticed. "I would love a bath."

Immediately she started pumping water.

"You can't lift that," he said, getting up but not wanting to step too close to her in case he smelled as bad as he felt. She had a kettle nearly full.

"I can as long as I don't get it too heavy," she replied, and moved it to the stove.

He sat back down and watched her heat the water and pump more. He carried the full pails and dumped them into the metal tub on the enclosed back porch. Each time he came for the water, she stepped well away from him and waited for him to perform the task. Once she had the kettle boiling, he carried that, too.

"This is warm enough," he said. "Just enough to take the chill off."

She backed away. "I'll take Nate for a walk."

"There's a pram in the carriage house," he told her. "The key's on the peg by the door here." He pointed.

Deliberately walking around him, Ellie took the key and removed her apron as she approached Nate. He must really smell bad, Caleb thought sheepishly.

She left and he collected toweling and a slab of soap and removed his clothing. The water felt wonderful to his tired body. He soaked and concentrated on relaxing his muscles and not thinking about the past few days. He'd done his best, and he would have to take satisfaction in that. There was nothing more he could have done. Nothing anyone could have done. If only his best had been enough.

Ellie pushed Nate in his handsome black baby carriage, chastising herself. It had never crossed her mind, after the day she brought Nate to the house, that the doctor would have little opportunity to leave his office even long enough to eat or order food. She hadn't considered his situation, and she now regretted her lack of concern. She should have seen that he had meals sent regularly. She should have taken him clean clothing.

The late afternoon breeze grew cool. As Ellie strolled, she turned her thoughts to familiarizing herself with the nearby streets and homes.

Nate fell asleep and she grew tired, as well. She pushed him home. A woman waved from the porch next door and Ellie waved back hesitantly before maneuvering the pram up the porch stairs backward and entering the silent house. She stopped and listened.

The doctor must have gone up to bed. She'd taken the liberty of moving Nate's cradle into a bedroom with her the first night. Dr. Chaney would have an uninterrupted sleep.

First, she'd see to dumping the tub of water. She'd done it for herself the night before, so she knew she could handle it. She left the baby sleeping in his pram in the hallway, and hurried through the kitchen.

Ellie stepped onto the back porch and drew up short, her breath catching in her chest. Dr. Chaney lay fast asleep in what had to be cold water, his dark hair washed and air-dried in dishevelment, his chest and shoulders bare above the rim of the metal tub.

Ellie stumbled back into the kitchen and flattened herself against the wall, her heart pounding, embarrassment warming her face and neck. She took several calming breaths and considered what to do.

She couldn't leave him there, could she? How could she go about her evening knowing there was a naked man in the tub? Would he catch cold? She should do something, she was sure. But what?

"Dr.—" she began, but her voice didn't work. "Dr. Chaney?" she called tentatively. No response. "Dr. Chaney?" Louder that time.

"M-m-what?" he replied, his voice low.

"Sir, I think you'd better get out of the tub and dry off. It's late."

Water splashed.

Ellie jumped away from the doorway.

"Oh, my!" He groaned, and water splashed again.

Ellie's heart pounded and she dashed to the hallway, pushed Nate's pram into the parlor and closed the doors. She perched on one of the wing chairs, pressed her right hand to her hot cheek and glanced around.

Good Lord, she'd walked in on the doctor in his bath! He hadn't known she'd looked upon him, but she knew it! Would he figure it out? Would he realize she'd hurried back there and seen him? How would she face him again?

She glanced around, working to still the panic in her chest and distract her thoughts. Her gaze caught on the volumes on the shelves. She still hadn't read one of the doctor's books.

Ellie concentrated on standing and walking. Blindly selecting a heavy book, she carried it to the cushioned window seat and settled it in her lap.

She drew a deep breath and opened the cover. A line drawing of a man's bare chest and muscled upper arm sprang out at her. There were words on the page, too, but her already befuddled mind closed in on the drawing. It looked very much like the doctor's chest, but this flat black-and-white drawing held none of the life or dimension his had. In reality the skin was sleek and smooth and appealing, with intriguing shadows and…

Ellie slammed the book shut.

Gray's Anatomy.

She practically ran back to the shelf to replace the book. The image was burned on her mind forever. Covering her face with her hands, she could still see his supple skin and muscled shoulders. *Concentrate,* she told herself.

This time, she focused on studying the titles and, finding one that seemed innocuous enough, she settled down to read.

There were no pictures, and the story was about a man who took a voyage on a whaling vessel. After a time she lit a lamp and curled up in one of the comfortable upholstered chairs. She'd been reading for hours by the time she looked up and realized how late it had grown.

She used the privy and closed up the house. The doctor had dumped the bathing tub, and it stood upended beside the back door. Avoiding thoughts of him, she fed Nate, then carried him upstairs to his cradle. Once he was settled for the night, she changed into her nightgown.

There was no lock on the door, so as she'd done the previous nights, she dragged a straight-backed chair from the corner and wedged it beneath the knob.

Ellie climbed into the bed and pulled the sheet up to her neck. A bed. Sheets. Regular meals. Water and soap and books. Numerous things she would never take for granted. They were worth the anxiety produced by having a man so near. Weren't they?

It was just this one night that she had to stay near him. After this she'd sleep in the room he'd rented, but for now there was no choice. The doctor was too tired to care for Nate if he should wake tonight. Ellie had everything under control. And she had nothing to fear from Dr. Chaney. She was earning her pay by caring for Nate.

The baby woke once as he had the previous nights, and

Ellie carried him down to the kitchen to prepare him a bottle. She had to lay him on the rug while she lit the lamp, and he cried in earnest. "I'm sorry," she said softly, coming back to bend and rub his tummy. "I'll pick you up as soon as I get your bottle ready."

"I'll take him."

Ellie's heart flew up into her throat at the voice behind her. She let out a startled cry and straightened.

"Didn't mean to scare you," the doctor said, moving closer.

Ellie backed away, and his dark gaze followed her. Wearing a full-length shiny dark robe that was belted at his waist, he picked up his son and looked at her with his forehead creasing in puzzlement. "Go ahead," he said. "Prepare the bottle while I hold him."

Ellie jerked herself into action, stoking the fire and warming milk with trembling fingers.

"Do you want me to take him?" she asked.

"I'll feed him. You go back to bed."

She placed the bottle on the table, rather than hand it to him. "His cradle is in the room I'm using."

"He can sleep with me until morning."

She nodded and moved to leave.

"Thank you, Ellie."

She paused in the doorway.

"Not just for this," he said from behind her. "But for every day since the fire."

"I—I haven't done much really."

"You've given me peace of mind where my son is concerned. That's a lot in my book."

"Well…" She wasn't sure how to respond. She couldn't remember the last time someone had thanked her. "You're welcome, I guess." But she felt as if she was the one who should be thanking him. She'd been on the edge of hunger and homelessness again, until he'd offered a solution.

"We'll talk tomorrow," he said.

Talk about what? She ran upstairs and barricaded the bedroom door, sitting on the edge of the bed in the dark.

Ellie glanced at the empty cradle in the darkness, finding she missed Nate's company.

She sat for several minutes trying to remember for sure how old she was. She was certainly old enough to handle her life and have a conversation with a man. She wasn't a helpless child any longer. She wasn't a young girl with no means to help or protect herself.

She was an adult. And as an adult she could work and provide for herself and make choices about her life. And she'd made plenty of choices. She chose not to enslave herself to a man. She chose not to bring any more defenseless children into the world. She chose to earn a clean, honest living and make a way to provide a home for her brothers. She had decided that long ago and nothing was going to get in her way.

If fate had thrown a curve at her with this broken arm, she'd just have to make the best of it and turn it into something she could use to her advantage. And that was exactly what she was doing.

Dr. Chaney was paying her more than she'd made at the Arcade. And the work was infinitely easier and her sleeping area private.

Ellie could put up with a lot to earn these wages and make some progress toward her goal.

What she couldn't do was allow herself to do anything reckless or impulsive, like trust this caring man or accidentally answer any of his innocent questions about her past. It would be easy to become comfortable here, to allow a seed of hope to bloom in her heart. Her only hope lay in keeping her secrets and guarding her carefully tended barriers.

Her future, and that of her brothers, depended on it.

Chapter Four

Ellie woke with a start. Sunlight streamed through the crack in the rose-patterned curtains and warmed the mattress where she lay. She leaped from the bed, glanced at the chair still beneath the doorknob and awkwardly washed with the tepid water in the basin. She had to face her employer this morning…after seeing him in his bath the night before.

She dressed in a plain navy skirt and white shirtwaist, and pulled on her serviceable black boots. She concentrated on admiring the smooth, well-polished leather. They were the first pair of shoes she'd ever worn that hadn't belonged to someone else first, and she never got dressed in the morning without being thankful for her job at the Arcade. The pay afforded her personal effects she'd never before owned.

She'd worn a threadbare gray union suit beneath her clothing until she was thirteen, when it had become too small. After Ellie had gone without for a week, her mother had begrudgingly released an old pair of drawers and a chemise.

Sometimes the church ladies had given her and her brothers cast-off clothing and occasionally someone anonymously left a bag at their door. Nobody seemed to think of stockings, however, and she'd worn men's socks most of her life.

She'd had a new dress once, but she couldn't even think about that dress without the nightmares returning.

Ellie struggled one-handedly with her bootlaces, finally tucking the loose ties into themselves, and scolded herself for wallowing in bleak memories when she'd already slept too late.

She wrapped her hair into a knot and secured it in the less than tidy fashion she'd made do with since her accident. The mirror reflected a young woman she barely knew. The new Ellie.

A phony.

The real Ellie was still in there. Still as frightened and alone as ever. But she was no longer weak, and she would never be weak again.

She removed the chair and hurried out the door and down the stairs. The smell of coffee wrapped her in its welcoming morning cloak, and Ellie hurried to the kitchen.

He was seated at the table, a cup of coffee and an empty plate before him. "Morning, Ellie."

Nate was secured in the high chair, and she observed the streak of syrup that had crusted in the front of his hair. "Morning."

"We've already eaten," he said unnecessarily. "There are buckwheat cakes in the oven."

That was surprising considering the amount on Nate and the floor.

Dr. Chaney raised a brow at her expression and, after glancing at his son, grinned and brushed at the sticky syrup. "He grabs at every bite."

Warmth crept up her cheeks. Their conversation seemed so normal. Was it possible he didn't realize she'd seen him in the tub? She took a few cakes and found a fork. "I know. I give him something to hold while I feed him."

"That's very clever," the doctor said appreciatively.

She shrugged and took a seat at the other end of the table, stealing a glance at him in his fresh white shirt and string tie. She could forget. She was good at that.

A lovely resonating chime sounded, startling Ellie into dropping her spoon.

Caleb glanced at her and stood. "I'll get it."

Get what? She watched him leave the room and hurry toward the front of the house.

Voices accompanied his when he returned a minute later.

A tall, brown-haired man and an elegantly dressed matronly woman preceded him into the kitchen.

Ellie folded her hands in her lap.

The couple studied her curiously. She knew her clothes were nice, and she had taken care with her hair. There was no reason for the sense of inadequacy and shame that flooded her, but the feelings were strong and never far from the surface.

"Ellie, these are my parents. Mother and Father, this is Ellie Parrish. She's Nate's new caretaker."

"Pleased to meet you," Ellie said, standing and feeling out of place.

"You've found someone to stay with Nate?" the woman asked, looking Ellie over. "You haven't been out to the ranch all week."

"I was taking care of my patient, Mother. Remember the woman who was burned?"

"Yes, we heard she'd died," the gentleman said, and then to his credit, he cast his son a sympathetic look.

The woman moved over to Nate's high chair. "Hello, sweetheart. Have you missed Grandmama? Goodness, whatever is on this child's head?"

"Just a little syrup," Caleb replied.

Ellie hurried for a rag to wash the baby, and the woman reached to take it from her. "I'll do it."

Ellie stepped back and watched. The woman obviously thought Ellie was incapable of caring properly for her grandchild.

"Miss Parrish, you haven't touched your breakfast," Caleb said, addressing her more formally in front of his parents. "Please sit and eat."

Keeping her gaze lowered, she returned to her chair and picked up the fork.

The doctor poured coffee for his parents. Some stilted conversation about Nate and the weather followed.

"Where are you from, Miss Parrish?" Caleb's mother asked finally.

"I worked at the Arcade Hotel until I broke my arm," she replied and took a bite.

"I see," the woman said, though her tone revealed she didn't. "Do your parents live nearby?"

The pancake tasted like paste. She swallowed. "No. My parents are gone."

Could be true for all she knew. Her mother was dead, for a fact. Her father might as well have been, if he wasn't. She'd never known him. If he'd been anything like Ben's and Flynn's fathers or any of her mother's other nighttime callers, she wouldn't have wanted to, either.

"Oh. I'm sorry," Mrs. Chaney said politely, her curiosity obviously unsatisfied. She was too polite to pry any further, however, for which Ellie was exceedingly grateful.

The woman turned her attention to Nate while Caleb started a conversation with his father.

When she was sure her observation wouldn't be noticed, Ellie studied the couple. Mrs. Chaney laughed at something her husband said, touching his arm in a familiar gesture.

He gave her a warm look Ellie couldn't quite interpret.

She had noticed couples in the Arcade's dining hall who interacted with each other in this manner. And she'd wondered if it was superficial…if, in the privacy of their homes, they cursed and fought. When he scowled at something she said, Caleb's mother didn't appear afraid of her husband. She laughed and poked a finger in his broad chest. He was a big man. As tall and broad-shouldered as his son. As capable of overpowering or hurting a woman.

The air caught in Ellie's throat.

She forced herself to breathe evenly.

Caleb's father didn't look the least bit angry. In fact, the look in his blue eyes when he took his wife's hand was tender, reaching a vulnerable spot inside Ellie.

She looked back at her plate and ordered her thoughts back into line. She made it a habit to keep her feelings neutral.

"Will you come for dinner tonight?" Mrs. Chaney asked her son. "Miss Parrish may join us."

Ellie raised her gaze to the woman's questioning face. "Oh, oh, no, I—"

"We really need to get Miss Parrish settled in her room at the boardinghouse," Caleb said, coming to her rescue.

"Sunday then," Mrs. Chaney said. "You have no excuse for not coming to Sunday dinner."

"Of course," he replied. "What would I do on a Sunday if I didn't come out to the ranch? You can ride with us," Caleb said, turning to Ellie. "You'll enjoy it. Mother has a wonderful cook."

Goodness, the woman employed a cook?

"It's settled," Caleb said with finality. "We'll be there."

"See you then, darling," Mrs. Chaney said to Nate and kissed his head.

Mr. Chaney nodded politely at Ellie, and she gave him a hesitant smile. Caleb walked his parents to the door.

Whatever would she do? She didn't know the least thing about how to behave at dinner in someone's home. Would one of her work skirts be appropriate?

"You two have an enjoyable day," Caleb said, returning from seeing his parents off and kissing his son. "I'll see you around five, unless I have an emergency."

Ellie nodded mutely and watched him leave.

Nate was due for a bath, so she warmed water and washed him in the enamel basin. He loved it, kicking and waving his arms until she was soaked. The entire time she dressed him and cleaned up the mess, she considered the upcoming dinner. As she laid Nate down for his nap, she remembered the cookbooks she'd leafed through, especially the one by the Methodist Episcopal Church ladies that had a page on table manners.

She'd set tables at the Arcade, but had never eaten in the dining room. Would the Chaneys use the same table settings, with the elaborately folded napkins?

She found the book and sat at the kitchen table, thumbing through to the chapter.

Nothing is more to be deplored than ignorance of the conventionalities of the table.

Yes, and surely they would all recognize her confusion. Oh, she didn't want to do this!

An unwritten law covers every detail, and those accustomed to good society are themselves probably unaware of conformity to any special standard, but imitate unconsciously those with whom they habitually associate.

She could do that. She could imitate those around her.

The table is the touchstone of manners, and there a blunder is a crime. At a dinner to which guests are bidden, the gentlemen assist in seating the ladies before taking their own places.

She'd seen the men at the Arcade assist their wives in this manner.

When seated, the body should be about a foot from the table.

Ellie adjusted herself in the chair and gauged the distance between her waist and the wooden edge.

The napkin is next unfolded to the half of its amplitude, and laid across the lap. No elegance of attire can be an excuse for tucking it about the person in any way.

She read on, memorizing, practicing, getting out a table setting and a napkin and going through the motions of a pretend meal. It would be good for her to learn this. She could teach Benjamin and Flynn when they finally got to live together.

All day Ellie spent her free time reading the pages in the cookbooks that referred to manners. She scoured Caleb's library for a book on etiquette, but found nothing and laughed at herself. Why would the doctor need a book like that? Perhaps she could take Nate for a walk to the library the following day.

Caleb arrived home when he said he would. Ellie had used the cookbook to prepare him a meal of canned chicken and dressing. He looked at the table she'd set.

"I didn't hire you to cook for me, too. I don't expect a meal ready every day when I get home."

"I'm here. The food's here. I might as well do it."

"Do you enjoy cooking?"

She'd never thought about it. She'd scraped and scrambled for every bite that she and her brothers ever placed in their mouths. Preparing food had only been something a person did to make it edible. It was part of survival.

Here cooking was…enjoyable. "Yes. I do."

"Lucky for me. And even luckier that you're good at it."

Ellie blushed and filled his plate.

He stood beside his chair, noting the single place setting. "Aren't you eating with us?"

"I ate before you got here," she replied. And she had. She had been delighted to taste the savory meal she'd been able to prepare with the wealth of ingredients in his kitchen and the well-stocked pantry.

"You know, you don't have to eat alone like you're a servant." He seated himself.

"I am a servant."

"But there are just the two of us. We might as well take our supper together."

"If that's what you want."

"I do."

She nodded. "If you'll excuse me now, I'm going to get my things ready."

"Take them to the porch. I set some crates there for you, and I've arranged for the Jenkins boy to bring a wagon and carry them to the boardinghouse."

She had made a couple of trips back to the Arcade for

more of her belongings, so it would have taken her more than one trip by herself. "That's very thoughtful of you. Thank you."

"Nate and I will ride along to get you settled."

"You don't have to do that."

"Don't you want us to?"

She didn't know how to behave around him. She didn't know where to look or what to say. His presence made her uncomfortable, but she couldn't admit that openly. It wasn't that she minded his company...it was just that he set her on edge so and she feared saying the wrong thing or giving herself away. "No. Yes," she said, not wanting to insult the man who'd been so kind to her. "That will be fine."

He forked a bite of dressing into his mouth. "Mmm. This is good."

She scurried from the room.

She had her belongings packed and waiting on the porch when a young man arrived with a horse and wagon.

"This all of it?" he asked.

"I have a few more things at the Arcade's dormitory."

Caleb exited the house with Nate on one arm. "We'll drop by the hotel on our way to Mrs. Ned's." He pulled the door closed, handed Nate to Ellie and helped the boy load a few bags and crates.

At the dormitory, Ellie left Caleb and J. J. Jenkins in the courting room with Nate and went upstairs to pack the rest of her meager possessions. Goldie greeted her with a hug.

Ellie endured the embrace, then gave her a heartfelt smile.

"I've missed you, Ellie. How are you doing with the doctor's baby?"

"We get along just fine. He's a pleasure to care for."

"How is your arm?"

She moved to the chest that held the last of her clothing.

"It's a complete nuisance, that's what. It doesn't hurt much anymore, but I want to rip this cast off so I can do more. And in the heat of the kitchen, it itches something fierce."

"Where are you taking your things?"

"The doctor got me a room at Mrs. Ned's boarding-house."

"My cousin stayed there for a few months. It's clean and quiet. You'll like it. Let me help you with those." Goldie gathered the clothes Ellie had piled on the bed and carried them downstairs.

A bevy of young women had gathered around the doctor, all pretending to talk to the baby. J.J. stood in the throng of females, his narrow face scarlet. He grabbed the stack from Goldie and shot out the door.

It took Caleb a few more minutes to politely disentangle himself and his son and follow Ellie outside.

Mrs. Ned's was as clean as her friend had predicted. Ellie used the key Caleb had given her and opened the door to her room on the third floor.

The space was rectangular, with the bed and bureau at one end and a scarred desk at the other. The ceiling was slanted all along the outside wall, so that a person couldn't stand to their full height except where the window had been set into a dormer. A cushioned bench offered enough room to sit and space beneath for storage. Braided rugs and a faded quilt made the room seem comfortable and homey.

Caleb set her belongings inside the door. "Will this be all right?"

A bed with clean linens and all this space just to herself. What wouldn't be all right? "It's nice," she replied.

"It's not too far for you to walk over in the morning," he said, while J.J. made a stack of the crates. "That's one of the reasons I chose this location."

"I'll enjoy the walk," she replied to assure him.

J.J. went back to the wagon to wait for Caleb.

The doctor glanced around. "If you need anything..."

"I don't need anything."

Caleb studied her wide violet eyes for confirmation of that statement. The girl's behavior was odd, to say the least. Her words were meant to give the impression of confidence and independence, but her expressions and the sorrowful look in her eyes implied differently. On the one hand he wished he understood the pain behind her careful control and brave demeanor, but on the other, he worried that it might be something he couldn't help her resolve.

He felt as though he was deserting her by leaving her here alone. He wouldn't have wanted his sister or his wife to stay alone in a boardinghouse, no matter how reputable. But he couldn't have Ellie staying in his home, and there hadn't been time to make arrangements with a family in town. She would be perfectly safe here. There was no choice.

But it took all his discipline to take Nate from her arms and walk back to the door. "Don't use that arm now."

"I won't."

At least she'd had female companionship at the dormitory, he thought, worrying now about the wisdom of leaving her here. "Mrs. Ned is on the main floor should you have any problems or questions."

"I'll be just fine. I'll see you in the morning."

"Yes." He left, closing the door behind him. He looked down at Nate, who blinked up at him. "You having trouble with this too, son?" On his way down the hall he glanced at the other doors, wondering who stayed behind them. There'd been only women in her previous quarters. Here there were men, and Ellie had no one to protect her.

He had known Mrs. Ned for years, he assured himself.

Her boarders would all be respectable citizens. He had no grounds to worry.

It was just that Ellie seemed so vulnerable and so alone in the world. Seeing all of her possessions in only a few bags and crates had emphasized her fragility. Material belongings were no indication of a person's worth, he reminded himself, and her lack of personal items reduced their importance even more. She'd been doing just fine on her own until she'd broken her arm.

Her quiet strength and determination impressed Caleb. But the sadness that seemed to come from deep within her disturbed him. Why was someone so young so incredibly sad? He sensed the very edge of a darkness so bleak he couldn't imagine its source.

He'd seen her smile only once and that had been at Nate. She intrigued him, that was certain, and he was drawn to her in a way he didn't understand. Perhaps it was just his doctor's instinct to comfort and heal.

But he had a feeling that the comfort and healing Ellie needed was something he'd had no training for.

Ellie filled the drawers and tidied the room in which she would be staying. She would have to spend part of her earnings on having her laundry sent out now. At the dormitory, the girls all sent their clothing to the hotel laundry, and it was returned clean and pressed.

She needed to wash up before bed, so she took the heavy pitcher and carried it down the stairs, searching out the kitchen. An enormous kettle of warm water stood on the back of the stove. She scooped the pitcher full and made her way through the strange rooms and back to her new sanctuary. There was no straight-backed chair to wedge beneath the knob, but she locked the door and tested it.

After donning a nightgown, she blew out the lamp,

opened the window and lay down on the bed. Sounds drifted through the walls, voices and doors closing. The roof creaked overhead.

Moonlight streaming through the window reflected a rectangle on the ceiling. She would get used to this place, just as she had the dormitory, and here she was blessedly alone.

This was going to work out fine. The doctor was paying her a handsome wage for tasks she could easily handle. She didn't have to deal with customers, and she had only one employer who seemed more than generous.

Ellie fought down the discomfort that thought brought. This job was too good to be true.

But she was not the same person she had been. She was not young or helpless. She was making decisions about her life and choosing her future. Her independence and control over her own life meant everything.

But Dr. Chaney was a man, that irritating little voice in her head taunted. *What would he want in return?*

Chapter Five

A clap of thunder yanked Ellie from the bed. Her first chaotic thought was to check the door. She stumbled forward and tested the lock. Secure. She was safe. She composed herself and her heart rate settled back to normal.

The overcast sky made it difficult to tell the hour, but she guessed it wasn't too early to get up and start the day. Lighting a lamp, she washed and dressed.

At the bottom of the stairs, a smiling white-haired woman greeted her. "Miss Parrish. How lovely to meet you. I'm Mrs. Ned."

Ellie smiled hesitantly and said, "Hi."

"Is your room all right? I assured the young doctor you would be comfortable here."

"Yes. The room is nice."

"Good. Well, come have some breakfast and meet the other boarders."

In Ellie's mind, the wisdom of walking into a room full of strangers rated right up there with knocking down a beehive with a stick or rolling naked in poison oak. She never knew what to say or do in front of people, and she always feared someone would know her from her life in Florence.

Ellie drew a breath. She had bolstered her courage to work in the hotel dining room, and she could do this, too.

Mrs. Ned led her into a room where half a dozen people sat around a table. Each one turned their head to see her. The four men stood, and Ellie wished they hadn't.

Her landlady introduced the gathering in seating order. "This is Mr. Hershey, Mr. Davis, Miss Shaw, Mr. Cassidy, Mr. Montgomery and Mrs. Henderson. Ladies and gentlemen, this is our new boarder, Miss Parrish. Have a seat over here, dear."

Wishing she'd been able to slip out without being embarrassingly displayed, Ellie took the proffered chair and the men once again sat. Having them at eye level eased her dismay marginally. Now the questions would start. She braced herself.

"It seems you've had an accident," commented Mr. Davis, a short fellow with a ruddy complexion.

"Yes, I took a fall at the depot," she replied.

Mrs. Henderson, a petite woman with a streak of white through her black hair, clucked sympathetically. "How dreadful."

"Have you been in Newton long?" Miss Shaw asked.

Ellie fielded their questions and ate a few bites of the breakfast she would never remember afterward, then hurriedly excused herself to get to work.

"Where's your umbrella, dear?" Mrs. Ned called after her.

Ellie paused in the hallway momentarily. "I lost it."

"Take mine," the woman said with a nonchalant swish of her hand. "It's in the stand there by the door."

Ellie escaped out onto the porch without stopping for the umbrella. Lightning zigzagged across the dismal sky, eerily illuminating the morning, and the following thunder spooked a horse in the street.

The quavering voice that calmed the animal sounded familiar, and Ellie stared through the downpour to see the young man who'd helped her move the day before waiting in a buggy.

"Wait, Miss Parrish!" J.J. called. "The doc sent me to fetch you." He ran toward her with an umbrella and held it above her head.

She plucked the hem of her skirt above the mud and darted to the waiting buggy, climbing up into the dry safety of the leather seat before replying. "He did?"

"Yes'm," he said, coming around to the other side. "I been waitin' here for nigh half an hour 'cause he wanted to be sure I didn't miss you. 'Don't let her walk in the rain,' he said. When it rains I always go get the doc and take 'im to his office. Good thing he just told me yesterday that from here on I was to come get you first."

Nothing like this had ever happened to her before, and Ellie didn't quite know what to make of Caleb's arrangements. That he should be concerned over her walking in the rain touched her unexplainably. Mrs. Ned appeared in the doorway to wave her off as the horse pulled the buggy away from the boardinghouse and down the puddled street. Ellie gave a self-conscious wave.

The humid air wasn't what brought a new and never before experienced warmth to her chest. She felt like a princess riding in an elegant carriage. Ellie racked her memory for a time someone had done something thoughtful for her. Something just to make her life easier. Something nice.

There had been one instance. The time Mrs. Conner had sewn her the blue dress. She tamped that thought down firmly and savored every second of the ride.

J.J. reined in before Caleb's house. "Take this," he said, handing her the umbrella.

Ellie knew she wouldn't melt if she got a little wet, but she accepted it and looked it over.

"Here." He moved a lever and the contraption sprang out, sending raindrops flying.

Ellie held it over her head, thanked him and hurried up to the house and into the foyer, then wondered what to do with the dripping thing. She placed it open and upside down on the braided rug.

Just then Caleb galloped down the open stairway, his shiny boots loud on the polished wood. Bouncing on his arm, Nate laughed out loud and, at the sound, Caleb laughed, too.

"Did you hear that, Ellie?" he asked.

She nodded.

So swift that he surprised her, Caleb turned and ran back up the stairs. "Here we go again," he said, and once again thundered down the stairs.

Nate giggled appreciatively and Caleb laughed. Ellie watched in fascination. With emotion welling inside, she couldn't help wondering if another little baby she remembered had ever known someone who loved her as Caleb loved this child. She hoped with all her might it was so.

"We could play that game all day, but I have to go to work," he said, interrupting her thoughts and handing over Nate. "He's had his breakfast."

He picked up the wet umbrella and collapsed it.

"Dr. Chaney?"

He turned back slowly. "Yes?"

Now that she had his attention, discomfort rattled her. He was unlike any man she'd ever known. "Thank you for sending J.J. for me."

"You're welcome. And I thought you were going to call me Caleb."

She looked away, uncertain how to respond.

"If it makes you uncomfortable, then call me Dr. Chaney," he said impatiently, and stepped toward the door.

She followed. He turned back and leaned toward her.

She sucked in a quick breath and froze.

He kissed Nate's head, the warm scent of bay rum and starch stirring Ellie's senses. For a moment, her head swam dizzily. He moved away, picking up his jacket, and she watched his broad back with suspenders crisscrossing the white shirt as he crossed the porch, opened the umbrella and climbed onto the seat of the waiting buggy.

Ellie stared after it, her mind in a state of confusion. He created such mixed feelings within her. As a man, he was everything she'd learned to fear and loathe. As an employer, he'd proved considerate and generous. And as a father, he was more than she'd imagined a man could be. He truly loved this baby.

Against her midriff, Nate was warm and solid. She looked down into his luminous blue eyes. In her mind, a loving parent had been only a concept until now. But now she'd seen it.

And the reality shook her previous understanding of the world. Caleb's goodness intensified the sordidness of her own life and enhanced each of her many inadequacies. Knowing he existed was painful and wonderful, and made not feeling anything difficult.

He made her feel things. Deep, disturbing, inexpressible things.

Thunder clapped across the heavens. Nate's eyes widened in curiosity. Ellie peered at the overcast sky and the pouring rain. So much for her trip to the library. She'd have to scan Caleb's books once again and reread the Episcopal ladies' cookbook. Only one more day remained until Sunday and dinner with Caleb's family.

* * *

Ellie enjoyed that day as well as the one that followed. Both days she prepared a supper for the doctor from the recipes in the cookbook and, still too uncomfortable to sit at the table with him, ate before he arrived home. Once she'd set his meal before him she then hurried to the boardinghouse.

She had more time for herself with this arrangement, not like at the hotel where she'd worked until after dark every evening. With Caleb's permission, she borrowed some of his books and read them by oil lamp in her room until her eyes got tired and the hour grew late.

On Sunday morning, the church bells tolled, and she watched from her window as other boarders walked to morning services. Ellie had never been to church in her life and she couldn't imagine herself among respectable citizens in a house of worship. The only church people she'd had much experience with were either condescending or pitying, and neither trait attracted her to their kind.

She spent the morning in Mrs. Ned's deserted kitchen, pressing her skirts and blouses.

As she waited for the doctor to arrive, her heart hammered and she paced the wide front porch nervously.

"Going for a ride?"

Ellie turned to see Miss Shaw moving to sit in one of the wicker chairs. She placed a bag at her feet and took out a small wooden hoop that held partially embroidered fabric. "I'm having dinner with Dr. Chaney's family," she replied.

"He do that to your arm?"

The question confused, and then startled her. What did she mean? Did she think Caleb had hurt her? She frowned, but then sensibility returned. "Oh, you mean did he fix it! Yes, Dr. Chaney set my arm."

"Don't be surprised if people wonder how well it will heal. He doesn't have many supporters in Newton."

Ellie recognized the rush of anger that swept through her. "Well, that's ridiculous. He's completely capable and competent and thinking otherwise is foolish."

"Unfortunately, too many people in this town are foolish. And his wife's dying in childbirth didn't help. Three people he treated died of influenza over the winter, and then, recently, that Bowman woman."

"Joanna Bowman died because of a fire, not because of her treatment."

Miss Shaw was probably in her thirties, a slim dark-haired woman with a pleasant face. She raised a hand. "You and I know that. I just wonder if the rest of this town will figure it out."

She poked her needle through the fabric and stretched the thread taut.

Ellie studied her and wondered what she did and why she lived in the boardinghouse. But Ellie wasn't one to ask questions. She respected privacy. "What are you making?"

"A pillow."

Ellie stepped closer and noted the pair of cardinals the woman had so deftly created with her needle and thread. The birds seemed to be merely resting on a slender limb before returning to flight. "I've never seen anything so pretty," Ellie said with heartfelt admiration.

Miss Shaw inserted the needle and plucked it back out a few times. "They're just simple stitches."

"Well, it's beautiful."

She looked up at Ellie. "I certainly don't need another pillow. My room is full of pillows and wall samplers. But it passes the time." She bent her head over her work again.

Ellie sensed her loneliness. Single women were scarce in Kansas. Why hadn't Miss Shaw married?

The sound of hooves and harness rings made Ellie turn. Caleb halted the buggy at the foot of the stairs.

"Afternoon, Miss Shaw," he said politely, touching the brim of his hat as he rounded in front of the horses. He'd hitched two to the buggy this day.

"Dr. Chaney," she replied. "Lovely day for a ride."

"Yes, it is." He assisted Ellie onto the seat. She turned to find Nate asleep in a padded basket on the wide bench in the back. Caleb climbed back up and slapped the reins over the horses' rumps.

Ellie gave Miss Shaw a hesitant wave. "Is she one of your patients?"

"She's come to see me a time or two," he replied. "Why do you ask?"

"I just wondered. Will there be many people at the ranch for dinner?" she asked after they'd left the streets of the town behind.

"Hard to say," he replied with a grin. "My sister and her family. Quite often the preacher is there."

Ellie observed the surrounding ranch country, noting the direction and the road she'd never traveled before. The day was warm, but Caleb hadn't rolled back his shirtsleeves. She plucked at the front of her blouse. She'd never ridden in such a fine vehicle before J.J. had picked her up in this one. She realized it was the same buggy.

"This is your buggy?" she asked.

He nodded.

"Do you call on patients during the week?"

"A few. I'm still working on building up my practice."

"I think you're a very good doctor."

He turned his gaze to her. "I wish a few more people thought that."

"They will."

He grinned.

She smiled shyly and looked away.

"This is all Chaney land," he said several miles later.

Ellie gazed in awe at the grazing cattle on the far horizon. "All this?"

"Yep. My father wanted me work the ranch with him. Take over one day. I disappointed him by becoming a doctor."

"You didn't want to ranch?"

"Ranching's all right. But ever since I can remember I wanted to help people. I wanted to know how to heal them. I placed my share of the Arabians and a bull up for sale so I could afford my schooling. My father wasn't very happy about it, but once he found out I was serious, he bought the stock from me. Since I wasn't there, he had to hire a foreman and that cut into his profits."

Ellie listened and thought about what he was telling her.

"The thing is, I understand his feelings. He's getting older. He wants someone to take over the ranch he worked his whole life to build. I'm his only son."

Ellie glanced up and caught his handsome profile against the cloudless sky.

"Sometimes I wonder if I did the right thing," he said. "Maybe I should have listened to him and saved myself the expense and the trouble."

"But look how many people you've helped," she said in surprise.

"Not that many."

"You helped me."

He gave her a sidelong glance. "Just about any ranch hand can set a broken arm, Ellie."

She was taken aback. Where was the confidence he'd always projected? How could he even think for a minute that his work wasn't valuable?

"There's the house," he said before she could pull any more thoughts together.

To the east of impressive whitewashed stables sat a two-story house. The yard—if an expanse the size of a field could be called that—was bordered by a pine pole fence and dotted with shade trees and evergreens. The long drive was free of ruts and weeds, and the horse pulled them to a stop beneath the shade of a towering oak behind the house.

"Mother will give me a tongue-lashing for bringing you in through the kitchen." He reached for Nate, who was starting to fuss.

"Maybe we shouldn't then."

"Nah. It wouldn't be near as much fun."

Ellie followed him up the porch stairs. He held the door open and she stopped uncertainly.

"Go ahead."

Her heart hammered at the prospect of entering his family's home, and she fought the urge to turn back and run. She stepped inside.

The kitchen was enormous and mouth-watering aromas emanated from it.

"Caleb! You should have brought Miss Parrish to the front door," his mother said, rushing forward. "You'd think this boy was raised in a barn. I apologize for my son's lack of manners, Miss Parrish."

"I—I don't mind."

Caleb cast her a grin.

"Let's see Nathaniel!" another woman said, moving up to touch the baby.

"Ellie, this is Mildred," he said, kissing the woman on the cheek. "She's my other mother."

The woman with faded red hair and vibrant dark eyes patted Caleb's shoulder fondly. "I work for Mrs. Chaney," she said to Ellie. "I'm pleased to meet you."

"I'm pleased to meet you," Ellie said, using her words. They must have been appropriate, because Mildred smiled.

Caleb's mother caught sight of something through the window that brought a broad smile to her face. She hurried to the doorway.

A fair-haired girl of about five ran up the stairs and into her waiting arms. "Don't you look beautiful today, Lucy!"

"Mama made this dress for me an' I wore it to church an' then I wore it all the way here to show you." She spun in a circle, the frilly dotted Swiss pinafore billowing.

"Unca Caleb!" she cried, spotting her uncle and running toward him.

"Lucy, Lucy," her mother chided from the doorway. "A lady moves slowly and gracefully."

Caleb handed Nate to Ellie and quickly bent at the knees to pick up the little girl, who immediately wrapped her legs around his waist and grabbed his neck. He hugged her soundly and she placed a kiss on his tanned cheek. "Best kiss I had all week," he said with a wink.

She giggled.

"Lucy, Patricia, Denzil, this is Miss Ellie Parrish, Nate's new nursemaid. Ellie, this is my sister, Patricia, her husband, Denzil, and my pretty niece, Lucy."

"I'm pleased to meet you," Ellie said again.

"Delighted," Caleb's fair-skinned sister replied. She wore a fashionable pin-striped green dress with a white bodice. She pulled the pin from a matching hat.

"Miss Parrish," the tall gentleman said with a nod. He was dressed as nicely as Caleb, in dark trousers and a white shirt and tie.

"Lucy, what do you say to Miss Parrish?" her mother asked quietly.

"How do you do, Miss Parrish," she said, around the finger she'd stuck in her mouth.

Lucy's lesson in manners placed Ellie in an embarrassing position. She had no inkling of the appropriate response. She felt her cheeks grow warm.

"You have eyes just like your uncle," she said without thinking.

That must have pleased her, because the finger popped out of her mouth. She grinned and gazed at Caleb adoringly. "I do?"

He kissed her cheek and set her back on the floor. "Where's that grandfather of yours?"

"He's probably sneaked back to the stables to stare at his Welsh cob," Caleb's mother said wryly. "I don't think he paid this much attention when *I* gave birth. Lucy, why don't you go tell Grandpapa that dinner's almost ready?"

Lucy clambered out the door, and her mother rolled her eyes.

Denzil followed at a more sedate pace. Patricia removed her hat to reveal upswept fair hair, held in place by pearl-studded combs. She carried her hat and bag to a cabinet where she stored them, then immediately opened a drawer and pulled out an apron. Obviously at ease and in familiar surroundings, she tied it around her narrow waist. Ellie could taste her discomfort at being out of place.

Mildred took Nate from her arms and tied him upright in a well-worn high chair. Immediately Ellie missed the security of hiding behind him.

"May I help, too?" she asked uneasily.

"You're company," Caleb's mother said quickly, discouraging the idea. "And besides, your arm is in a cast."

Ellie's face flamed at the rejection. She'd blundered already.

"Ellie's obviously not helpless," Caleb said, "since she takes care of Nate every day. And she fixes my meals without help."

Patricia glanced from her brother to Ellie, and a look of understanding passed across her features. Once again she opened the cabinet and withdrew a folded apron.

Caleb took it from her with a grin and shook it open. "Here, Ellie. Let me help. Hold your arm out."

Ellie did as instructed and he reached both arms around her to catch the apron ties. She experienced a moment's panic at the restricting closeness, but the next second he was behind her tying the sash, and the feeling passed.

"What can I do?" she asked.

"Why don't you help set the table?" Caleb's mother suggested.

She had read the section on table settings. She'd practiced with Caleb's dishes and silverware. She moved stiffly to the trestle table. "Where are the plates?"

"Not this table," Patricia said kindly, coming to her side and leading her out of the room and into another. "This one."

"Oh my…" Ellie caught her breath. The room in which they stood was elegantly furnished with a glossy walnut table that stretched eight feet or more and stood surrounded by cushioned straight-backed chairs. An enormous glass-paned cabinet on one wall held gold-rimmed dishes.

"The silver is in this drawer," Patricia explained, "the tablecloths and napkins in here. We usually set for about ten. If there are extra settings when we get seated, that's fine."

Ellie stared at the table, at the intimidating size and decor of the room. Her knees trembled. What if she dropped one of those plates? What if she spilled while she was eating?

"What happened to your arm?" Patricia asked.

She took out a pressed white linen cloth and shook it out above the table. The fabric floated down a little to one side, with only a few wrinkles that needed straightening. "I fell off the platform at the train depot."

"How awful! Are you from around here?"

Ellie smoothed out wrinkles, hoping her hands were clean. She should have washed them in the kitchen. "No. I'm from up by Florence."

"Really? That's where we live. I've lived there since I married Denzil—about six years now. Whereabouts did you live?"

"Um. Outside town really."

"Parrish. Hmm. I can't place the name."

Ellie closed her eyes and stood in the overwhelming silence that followed. What if Patricia went back home and asked about her? No worry, she reminded herself. No one knew her as Parrish. She'd made that name up. Besides, there were many families who lived outside of town and came in only occasionally for supplies, and Ellie had never attended school regularly. As outcasts, she and her brothers stayed to themselves. She opened her eyes and discovered the young woman was simply going about her tasks.

Patricia opened the china cabinet and took out a stack of plates. She started placing them at intervals around the table and Ellie followed her lead.

She opened the drawer Patricia had indicated and counted out ten pressed and folded napkins. She handed half to Patricia and waited for her to place one at the left of a plate, and then added hers.

She did the same with the silver, counting forks and knives and spoons, handing her half, then mimicking how she placed them. Patricia did it just as the Episcopal ladies had instructed, and Ellie followed her example without a hitch.

Ellie's first experience with seeing huge quantities of elegantly prepared food had been at the Arcade Hotel, but it never ceased to astound her that people went to so much work and expense. She'd spent too many years scraping for enough to keep herself and her brothers alive.

As the family gathered around the table, the women carried in a platter of curried lamb and bowls of steaming savory-smelling yams and other vegetables.

Ellie studied the food in the gold-edged china dishes and thought of the simple fare she'd taken such pleasure and pride in preparing and serving to Caleb. What must he think of her pathetic attempts? Her humiliation knew no bounds.

"Afternoon, Miss Parrish," Caleb's father said, arriving and standing behind his chair at the head of the table.

She'd been standing back, waiting to see where the others sat. Her heart tripped a little faster at his recognition. "Hello."

Caleb carried Nate, high chair and all, into the room and situated him near his own chair. He gestured for her to move beside him. She stood behind the chair he'd indicated the same way the men were standing.

"Ellie, this is Reverend Beecher," Caleb's father said.

"How do you do?" the gentleman said with a polite nod.

Ellie nodded back.

"This is our ranch foreman, Hayden, and his brother, Soapy."

Ellie nodded again.

Soapy was the only one who seemed as uncomfortable as Ellie. He said something in his brother's ear and Hayden said, "Soapy says he's pleased to meetcha."

Caleb grinned and touched Ellie's arm, urging her forward. She thought of nothing but his fingers through her sleeve until he slid out the chair and urged her to sit.

Recalling the table-manners section of the cookbook, she sat at the same time he slid the chair in closer. Caleb's father did the same for his mother and Denzil assisted his wife and daughter. Ellie measured the distance between her midriff and the table edge with a nervous glance.

Lucy was seated directly across from Caleb and Ellie, and she gave her uncle a broad grin. "I saw a frog last night, Unca Caleb," she said. "It was jumping by my steps."

"Did it scare you?"

She shook her head importantly. "No. It was just a baby frog. It was looking for its mama, I think."

"I'll bet you're right."

"Mama, do I have to eat yams?"

"Just a small portion, Lucy, to be polite." Her mother placed a small dab of the orange glazed vegetable on her plate and reprimanded her pout with a raised brow. "Lucille…"

The child wore a disgusted expression and frowned as her plate was filled.

Having to encourage a child to eat was beyond Ellie's experience. She'd only known hungry children who gobbled up whatever scrap was placed in front of them.

"I'm five," the child reported, holding up all the fingers on one hand to demonstrate.

Ellie gave her a smile, noting the girl's obvious comfort within the circle of her family and in their elegant home. The child showed no signs of neglect or fear or abuse. She was the apple of this family's eye.

Years ago Ellie had stumbled through the night to find a home for a baby girl. So many times she had wondered how the child had fared. So many times she'd wished she could see for herself if she'd done the right thing. But she'd never allowed herself to check.

The reasons for cutting herself off were complicated. And painful.

She had to believe that the child had a home and a family

like Lucy's, that she was secure and pampered in the midst of people who loved her and saw to her well-being. Anything else was unthinkable.

Caleb's mother raised a brow at Ellie. "Are you finding the food to your satisfaction, Miss Parrish?"

"Oh, yes." Ellie glanced down to see she hadn't touched anything on her plate. Her fingers trembled as she reached for her fork.

"Caleb, you oaf," Patricia said from beside Ellie. "You haven't cut Ellie's meat for her. How can she be expected to do it with one arm?" She reached over and sliced the lamb on Ellie's plate into dainty bites.

"I guess I'm just used to Ellie managing everything with one arm," Caleb replied with a grin. "Sorry, El. Poke me in the ribs next time."

Patricia slid Ellie's plate back in place, and Ellie speared a bite.

"Hayden and Soapy are going to get ice later, so we can make ice cream," Caleb's father said.

Lucy squealed and bounced up and down in her chair. "I love ice cream!"

"Mind your manners, Lucy," Patricia said quietly. "Eat your yam or you won't get any ice cream."

Lucy stilled on her chair and looked around with a frown.

Patricia involved herself in a conversation with Denzil and her mother.

Mildred brought hot rolls and served them to each person.

"Mildred doesn't eat with your family?" Ellie whispered to Caleb.

"No. She works for Mother."

Ellie blinked. "I work for you, but I'm eating at the table."

Caleb glanced past Ellie's shoulder. Reaching across the

table, he speared the yam on Lucy's plate and popped it into his mouth, chewed and swallowed. "You're not kitchen help."

"Hayden and Soapy are eating with the family," she said, and then realized she was showing her ignorance again.

"Ranch foremen always eat in the big house. Soapy just kind of fell into it because he never leaves Hayden's side."

Ellie observed the conspiratorial look between Caleb and Lucy. The child took a bite of her buttery roll, her blue eyes twinkling. "My yam's gone, Mama," she said. "Now I get ice cream."

"That's a good girl, Lucy," Patricia replied.

Ellie covered her amused grin with her napkin.

Somehow she made it through the meal without spilling or making a spectacle. And she actually enjoyed the savory dishes the women had prepared so attractively. She wasn't allowed to help with the cleanup, so she washed Nate and gave him a bottle.

"We'll let our meal settle," Mrs. Chaney said a few minutes later, leading the way through the house.

Ellie glimpsed the elegantly furnished rooms they passed and wished she could peek into each one. The women all gathered on the wide front porch while Mildred cleared the table and washed dishes. Ellie was used to waiting tables at the hotel and she felt guilty for not helping, but the Chaney women were obviously comfortable with this arrangement.

"Thank you for inviting me, Mrs. Chaney," Ellie said. She sat and adjusted Nate on her lap.

"Do call me Laura," the woman replied. "And I'm pleased you could come. I haven't seen you at our church. Which one do you attend?"

"I haven't been to church since I've come to Newton."

It was the truth. She'd never been to church before she'd moved to Newton either, but she wasn't going to admit that. These women assumed everyone attended church. "Are you an Episcopal lady?" she asked.

"Oh, no, dear. Our family has always been Presbyterian."

"Oh."

She turned to discover Patricia studying her. Had she said something dreadful?

"I suppose you're the answer to Caleb's problems," Patricia said.

"What do you mean?"

"I've been pestering him to let me take Nate." She studied the boy with obvious affection and tears welled in her luminous eyes. She blinked them away. "As my own, I mean. I thought it would have been best for him to come live with us, where he would have two parents. Especially a mother to care for him."

"Caleb loves his son very much," Ellie said.

"Yes, I know. Part of the pressure I placed on him came from selfishness on my part."

Her honesty surprised Ellie. She obviously wanted this baby very much. Ellie glanced at Lucy, who sat on the stairs playing with the prettiest doll Ellie had ever seen. Patricia's child was five years old and she hadn't had another. Even Ellie knew that was unusual for a young married woman.

She glanced across the yard at Caleb. Tall and broad shouldered, he stood beside his father, his weight on one leg and his hand on his hip while he listened to something the older man said. She also knew how difficult it was to give up a child, and she was glad Caleb had the resources to keep his son. She was grateful that for now she was able to help him do that.

But what about after her arm healed? What would happen after she went back to her job at the hotel?

Against her breast, full and content, Nate slept soundly. What if she didn't go back to the hotel? What if she could keep this job? Oh, she shouldn't even let herself imagine that.

Ellie chastised herself. She thought of Mildred in the kitchen doing all the dishes while the Chaney women sat on the shaded porch. That was Mildred's job. And caring for Nate was Ellie's job.

But somehow, right now, it didn't seem like enough.

Besides, she had to have a place of her own where she could bring Benjamin and Flynn once she'd made enough money.

Ellie glanced around, studied the rich green land and the fat grazing cattle as far as she could see, and couldn't even fathom how much money it took to buy or maintain a place like this.

Right now her dream seemed an impossibility. She hadn't saved even enough to pay for the food she'd seen consumed today. How would she ever pay for a place of her own and provide food and clothing for her brothers?

The hopelessness of her situation made her eyes smart and her mouth dry. Maybe it was never meant to be. Maybe she was only fooling herself to think she could get her brothers away from the Heaths' farm and give them the life they deserved.

If that were the truth, she didn't know how she could go on.

What was she doing? Here she was letting herself fall for another child whom she would have to let go.

Her heart had already been broken and stomped on. Another kick and it would stop beating. She would have to toughen her hide and resist falling for Nate. Either that or find a way to make this situation permanent.

Chapter Six

When Nate woke, Laura asked to hold him, so Ellie used the opportunity to stretch her legs. Lucy followed her, picking clover, asking a myriad of questions.

She and Ellie sat beneath the shade of a maple and Ellie tied the clover stems into a chain for Lucy to wear around her neck. Loose tendrils of hair had fallen from her neat braids and lay in curls against her ivory cheek. She had a sprinkling of freckles across her nose and sweet smooth rosy lips that puckered when she thought.

Ellie's heart swelled with an aching kinship and the pain of loss. She'd had a child like this one. Her little girl probably had dark hair like hers…but it had been hard to tell that night. Ellie had been so young, so afraid, so alone…her only thought had been to save the baby from a life like hers, from a life like her brothers', where hunger and hurt and want were all they'd ever known.

So she'd used her last ounce of strength to creep through the night and leave the baby with a young couple who had recently lost their own child to illness.

Ellie had never been sorry. She'd done the right thing.

But she'd never stopped hurting or wondering. She was a master at burying pain. But seeing this enchanting child brought it all out again, as fresh and as agonizing as when it had first happened.

Her child would be a year or so older than this one. All those years…all the times she'd never allowed herself to go see—to discover if she'd done the right thing. She had to believe she had.

The welling thickness in her chest made every breath burn like fire. Lucy smiled up at her and tears smarted behind Ellie's eyes.

"Are you sad, Ellie?" the child asked, her expression turning to concern, her exquisite pale brows drawing together.

"No. The sun is just bright is all."

Lucy squinted up at the sunlight filtering down through the leaves. She had a smudge of dirt on her chin that her mother would want to wipe away, but Ellie thought it was endearing. "I wonder where the sun goes at night."

"I guess you'll learn that at school."

"I'll be smart then, won't I?"

Ellie agreed with a smile.

"This rock looks like a wolf tooth, doesn't it?"

Ellie inspected the chip of stone, wondering if she'd ever had a youthful imagination. They made another chain before Patricia called them to come watch the ice cream being made.

Caleb and Soapy took turns turning the crank on the wooden bucket. Caleb's father added salt and cream, and before long the mixture turned white and smooth.

Every once in a while Soapy whispered something to Hayden, and his brother would convey the message.

"Doesn't Soapy talk?" she wondered aloud.

"Never have heard the man talk and he's worked the ranch for seven years," Laura said with a shrug. "Maybe he speaks when there are no women present, I don't know.''

Ellie observed the gathering with interest, her attention moving time and again to Caleb's stern-looking father, Matthew, interacting with his family. Though he and Caleb apparently held opposing views on Caleb's career, Matthew treated his son kindly. He held Nate gingerly, but engulfed the child's head in his enormous hand and touched his nose to the baby's hair more than once. He obviously doted on his granddaughter, too, pulling her into his lap so she could reach the plank table to eat.

Ellie accepted a bowl of ice cream from Patricia and tasted the creamy vanilla flavor. The surprising cold almost hurt her tongue and made her teeth ache, but she swallowed and let another spoonful melt in her mouth.

"Like it?" Caleb asked.

"It's wonderful! I didn't know it would taste so cold."

"Well, it's *ice cream*."

She blushed. "I know."

"Haven't you ever tasted ice cream before?"

She shook her head.

"Next time I'll have Mildred bake you an apple pie to go under it. Now that's a treat!"

Next time. Ellie gave him a hesitant smile. Could she ever again expose herself to the empty ache that being near Lucy carved in her heart? Could she watch Matthew and Laura with their children and grandchildren and hurt once again for what had never been hers?

Yes, she could. If he asked her, she would gladly come. It must be a sickness, this need to torture herself with the reminder of her sorely lacking life.

But she felt alive here—more alive than ever before. More accepted. More like the people whose lives she'd only observed and imagined. And if it hurt to feel this alive...then she would bear it.

But in the back of her mind, in her subconscious, she experienced a twinge of guilt. Should she be here eating ice cream while Benjamin and Flynn were being worked like slaves?

Ellie corrected her thinking. She was doing everything she possibly could toward the day when she would be able to save her brothers from that life. She was making more money working for Caleb than she'd been earning at the hotel, so she was doing something important.

Yes, she had moments of doubt that it would never be enough, but she couldn't give in to that weakness.

Caleb's hand rested on her arm, snagging her thoughts back to the moment. Her heart jumped and she looked at his long, hair-dusted fingers against her white sleeve, resisting the impulse to pull away.

"I'll take your bowl," he said, and she knew from his inflection that he'd offered before.

"Oh, sorry."

"Are you tired, or shall we stay awhile longer? Reverend Beecher usually reads something aloud when he's here. He has a way of reading a story that keeps us hanging on every word. Sometime Patty plays the piano."

"I'd like to stay."

"Is your arm hurting?"

"No."

"Okay, come on."

She followed him in through the kitchen, and he led the way to a room filled with overstuffed chairs and sofas, potted ferns and a piano.

Ellie took in all the furnishings and studied the framed daguerreotypes. "Who are these people?"

"That's my father with his family. This is Patty and me

when we were babies. And this," he said, picking up one of the frames, "is my parents' wedding portrait."

"Oh." Ellie leaned closer to study his parents' youthful faces and serene expressions. They'd married long ago and had lived all these years as a pair, raising children and running a ranch. Thinking of them being together for so long, imagining the solidarity of such a life, made Ellie's own shaky upbringing all the more wretched in comparison. "How amazing to see them so long ago."

She straightened and looked at the likeness of Caleb and his sister. "And Nate will know what you looked like as a baby. You looked a lot like he does."

"You don't have any family portraits?"

Immediately, Ellie realized her mistake and backed away to take a seat on a sofa. "No."

Caleb didn't ask any further questions.

How nice that you know who your father is, she intoned silently, the scorn in the thought meant for herself.

The reverend read from a story by Charles Dickens, one Ellie had read only a few weeks before. She enjoyed the story much more with the man's inflections and interpretation, and the added pleasure of watching the others' faces.

Ellie's reactions fascinated Caleb. The smallest thing was like something grand and new to her, and he wondered how anyone could be so obviously naive about so many things. She attempted to keep her curiosity and her awe hidden, but he'd been around her for weeks now, and had seen through her act on many occasions.

The look on her face as she listened to Reverend Beecher read matched Lucy's youthful fascination. Ellie studied the faces of the others as they listened, too, and a wistful expression softened her delicate features as her gaze touched each one.

Her eyes met his, and Caleb smiled. She gave a shy smile

in return and lowered her gaze, embarrassment tingeing her cheeks with a rosy hue Caleb found becoming.

Nate fussed in Laura's lap, and Ellie quickly went to take him. She located the small flannel blanket he seemed to prefer, tucked it into his chubby hands and, sitting back down on the sofa beside Lucy, snuggled him close to her breast.

Comforted, the infant quieted immediately; his eyelids grew heavy. He reached a tiny hand upward and Ellie took his fingers and kissed them, all the while gently rocking.

An ache blossomed in Caleb's chest at the stirring sight. He tried to picture his wife in Ellie's place, cuddling and comforting their child, but the image wouldn't come. Leila had been miserable throughout her entire pregnancy, appalled at her misshapen body and disgusted over the unfashionable clothing she was forced to wear to accommodate her growth. She had cried to move to the coast where she'd made friends while visiting Caleb at the university.

Leila had loved the parties and the theater and the whole social whirl. She'd pleaded with him to go into practice with one of the surgeons who'd offered him a position out East. But Caleb had missed his family, missed the serenity and familiarity of the stark, windy land where he'd been raised. The hardworking farmers and ranchers and their families were the ones he desired to help. There were plenty of doctors in the big cities. His skill was precious out here in Kansas, and he planned to make the citizens recognize that. He'd never made Leila understand.

Her displeasure with their Kansas home and her inconvenient pregnancy had disappointed him. He'd married a beautiful, happy young woman and he'd loved her. He'd had such hopes for their future. Perhaps if he'd given in and taken a position in Massachusetts or Pennsylvania it would have prevented her misery and ultimately her death.

Guilt tore at his insides, just as it did with every memory of his dead wife. The fact that he was happy here in Newton seemed wrong. He should have more regrets about moving here. He should resent this place that took his wife. But he didn't.

Reverend Beecher finished the story. Laura and Patricia served coffee and cookies, and Lucy skipped off to play.

Denzil and Matthew set up a checkerboard and launched a game.

Caleb took the seat Lucy had vacated beside Ellie and offered his lap for the sleeping baby so she could rest her arm.

She lowered Nate and the back of her hand rubbed along his arm where he'd rolled up his sleeve. She drew her hand away and sat back stiffly. Her skittishness puzzled him. Was she overly aware of him as a man—perhaps attracted to him?

It was an appealing concept. Caleb nibbled the oatmeal cookies he'd snatched off the tray on his way over. "Do you know how to make oatmeal cookies?"

"I could do it if I had the recipe."

"Ever made 'em?"

"No."

"Ever had curried lamb before today?"

"I've served it at the Arcade."

"But you'd never eaten it?"

"No." She glanced over at him and away. "I guess the meals I fixed you weren't what you were used to, were they?"

"I enjoy the meals you prepare, Ellie. You don't have to cook for me, but you do. I appreciate that after a long day."

"You're used to having things fancier, though."

"Just because something's fancy doesn't mean it's better," he said. "I think your cooking is excellent."

"You do?" It sounded like the excited way Lucy would have responded.

He nodded and smiled.

Patricia took a seat at the piano and began to play. Laura seated herself and nodded in time to the music. The reverend listened with his eyes closed.

Caleb threaded his fingers through Nate's silky blond hair, caressing the strands as the notes eased his earlier unpleasant thoughts.

A few songs later, he glanced over to see Ellie watching his fingers stroke Nate's hair. His hand stilled.

Her gaze moved up to his and their eyes met briefly.

Ellie blushed and looked away.

What had she been thinking that had brought on that becoming rosiness? Caleb studied his innocent son, glanced at his own hands, one in Nate's hair, the other on his gently rising and falling tummy.

Ellie was overly sensitive regarding him. Was there something there? A magnetic attraction between them?

Everything about Ellie appealed to him. Her gentleness, her delicate beauty, her quiet strength, her obvious pride. Seeing her with Nate touched him deeply. She was a loving and tender caregiver for his son. She fit into his family.

A stab of unease rose in his chest. What was he thinking?

He glanced at her arm in the cast he'd molded. She was young and healthy and had obediently followed his instructions; her arm would be perfectly healed in a few more weeks.

She would want to go back to her job at the hotel.

Suddenly, with ethereal music filling the room and his family seated comfortably nearby, he knew he couldn't let that happen. Ellie was the best thing that had come into his life in a long time.

He could offer her a permanent position as Nate's nurse-maid.

Caleb thought of Mildred, whom he'd grown to love over the years but who was still regarded as an employee. That wasn't the family he envisioned for Nate—or for himself.

His other option was to marry Ellie.

The thought brought a nervous thump to his heart. But why not? Marriages were made for far less logical reasons. And there was *something* there.

He realized this thought had been in the back of his mind for days. Marriage was the perfect idea. What could he say to convince her? His practice wasn't exactly thriving. He had a long way to go before he'd earn the trust of the citizens of Newton. But he had a decent house and because of some wise investments he had the means to provide for her. Her life would be easier.

Patricia finished playing, and Nate woke. Ellie prepared him a bottle and Caleb fed him, wondering how to approach her with the idea. The hour grew late and they prepared to leave. His mother hugged him and Lucy begged one last piggyback ride.

Reverend Beecher didn't have his own rig, so he rode back to town with Caleb as he had many times before. But this time, Ellie sat on the bench in the rear with Nate. Caleb stopped at the parsonage first, wished the reverend a goodnight, and then prodded the horses toward Mrs. Ned's.

He pulled up in front and Ellie gathered her skirts and prepared to get down. He stopped her with a hand on her arm.

She stared at it and froze.

Caleb released her and she settled back on the seat.

Nate fussed in the back.

This was hardly a perfect situation in which to propose marriage. But then he didn't think a perfect situation would reveal itself anytime soon.

"Ellie, I've been thinking about something."

"What's that?"

"I'd like you to think about marrying me."

Her eyes opened wide and she faced him with a look of pure shock on her face.

"Nate needs a mother," he said, and then realized how awful that sounded. "I need a wife. I know this sounds selfish. I make an adequate living right now and I am sure it will get better. I have a home to offer you." What more did he really have to offer her? "You wouldn't have to work at the hotel and you'd have more leisure time to pursue your own interests. Perhaps needlepoint or..."

A strong breeze blew a loose strand of hair across her cheek and she pushed it away distractedly. Her gaze had turned to the street, but he knew she wasn't really seeing anything. He'd probably shocked her and he hadn't really offered enough to be convincing. "I'll be able to afford a housekeeper eventually."

She turned to look at him finally.

"Just think about it," he said, disgusted with himself. He'd bungled the whole thing. "Will you do that?"

She nodded mutely.

He got down and came around to assist her from the buggy and she immediately drew away from his touch and stood aside.

"I'll see you in the morning then."

She nodded and he got back into the buggy, then watched her climb the stairs and enter the boardinghouse.

Well, he'd lost nothing by asking. She would either say yes or no. He drove the team to the livery, lamenting what he'd do if she said no. For some curious reason it had suddenly become imperative that she not turn him down. His proposal hadn't been the least bit convincing, however. What more could he have said? How could he have sweetened the pot?

Ellie seemed a practical sort; his suggestions had all been practical. Or perhaps he'd missed the mark entirely by being so practical. Maybe she would have responded better to romance. He could start over again and court her.

Caleb spent the rest of the evening second-guessing himself and wondering how he could go back and earn a chance to convince her.

Ellie's head, which had already been filled with all the new sights and experiences of the day, was now in a whirl. Her mind replayed Caleb's astounding words. *I'd like you to think about marrying me.* She'd think of nothing else for the rest of her life. The rest of her sorry, stinking, miserable life.

Caleb Chaney, a respectable man who'd been raised in a respectable family and had graduated from a respectable university…now a *doctor*…had asked her to marry him.

If she lived to be a hundred she would remember his voice saying the words. *I'd like you to think about marrying me.*

Of course she couldn't do it.

He wouldn't have asked if he knew who she was, who her mother had been, and where she'd been raised. He wouldn't even allow her around his son if he knew her secret shame.

Ellie greeted Miss Shaw and Mr. Davis on the wide front porch and hurried up to her room for her pitcher and bowl so she could retrieve warm water from the well on the stove.

She carried the water back to her room, removed her skirt

and blouse, her petticoats and chemise, brushed out her hair and washed the day's dust from her face and body.

In the golden glow of the oil lamp, she caught her reflection from the waist up in the grainy mirror attached to the bureau. For once, she allowed herself to look. Her dark hair was thick and wavy and shone in the lamplight. Her features wouldn't curdle milk by any means, and she had full, solid breasts and a narrow waist. *Is this why he wants to marry me?* Had she done something to encourage him in that way?

Being attractive to a man was a detriment, not an asset. She dried quickly. Ellie wasn't so blind or ignorant that she didn't know what she'd lost. She would have made a good wife and mother.

But her mother had ruined all that. Her mother had ruined her life and hadn't cared. No man would ever want her now if they knew. She could barely stand to look at herself.

She pulled her white cotton nightgown over her head and laced the ribbons that held the neck closed.

Ellie ran the brush through her hair again and unwillingly met her own gaze. The stroking of the hairbrush fell still.

She'd lived with the secret this long. No one could tell by looking at her. Caleb didn't know. His family didn't know. No one in the entire town of Newton was any the wiser.

What if she accepted Caleb's offer? What if she married him? She could glimpse the first shred of security she'd ever known. She could have a home. Her brothers could have a home.

Her chest ached and her fingers tightened on the brush. They could live together in that beautiful house with all the books and the full pantry.

Ellie placed the brush on the bureau and blew out the

lamp. She moved to the window, raised the shade and lifted the pane as high as it would go. Leaning out the open portal, she peered into the darkness, identified a few lights and buildings and squinted, knowing full well she couldn't see all the way to the doctor's house from here, but imagining she could.

The warm summer breeze flitted across her face, lifted her hair and blew her nightgown against her damp skin. She closed her eyes and smelled the moonstruck air.

What about sacrificing the freedom she valued? Right now she was in control of her own life.

Some life, she thought with self-derision.

She would never allow herself to be vulnerable again, however. And the physical aspects of marriage were simply an impossibility for her.

But what about Flynn and Benjamin? Her whole purpose for the past year had been to somehow make a home for them.

Caleb Chaney needed a mother for his son. She needed a home for her brothers. Could they strike a bargain?

She hadn't seen the boys for weeks and she ached to know if they were well and fed, if not happy. It would take a miracle and a lot of time ever to see them happy.

Ellie opened her eyes and studied the silent heavens for a sign. Maybe, just maybe, an arrangement could be made that would accommodate everyone.

She left the shade and the window open and climbed into bed.

Before he left for work that morning didn't seem like the appropriate time to discuss a marriage arrangement with him, so Ellie saw Caleb off and went about the routine she'd established.

Everything had changed, however. She looked at the

house and the furnishings with new eyes. This could be a home for her family if Caleb still wanted to marry her after he heard her conditions.

Before it grew hot, she took Nate outside and wandered in the yard, imagining a garden with towering beanpoles and fresh, leafy lettuce. She pictured flower beds with bright nasturtiums, asters and snapdragons. Remembering a book she'd seen in Caleb's study, she carried Nate back in and pulled the volume, *How to Plant and Plan Your Dooryard and Kitchen Garden,* from the shelf. She placed a blanket in the shade of the side yard, propped herself beside him and began to read.

Ellie's eyes grew heavy and she turned over, rested the book on her stomach and looked up into the whispering leaves. Nate slept soundly beside her. The scent of roses drifted across the yard. She'd never had a more perfect or restful afternoon. Her thoughts drifted to Benjamin and Flynn and she wondered what they were doing that day. She missed them terribly.

After Nate's nap, she began work on dinner, making fresh rolls to go with the hen she was roasting and the creamed carrots Caleb had a fondness for. She stirred a pan of rice pudding and left it in the oven.

Caleb arrived home a little later than usual. "Sorry I'm late," he said, coming into the kitchen. "I was called over to Mabel Connely's only an hour ago and spent some time reassuring her she's not having heart failure."

"She's ill?"

"She's fat. And she won't take my word for it that she needs to take off some pounds so she can move about more easily. Her heart will go one of these days if she doesn't do as I—" He stopped short and studied the table. "You're staying to eat?"

A flush warmed her all the way from her toes to her ears. "If that's okay with you. I thought we could talk."

"About?"

This wasn't how she'd planned to discuss it. "About what you asked me to think about."

"You're not making a decision this quickly, are you? Maybe you should take some time to think about it before you turn me down. I know we don't know each other very well, but—"

"Why don't you sit? I'm almost finished here."

Caleb moved to the small wooden table and folded his long body onto a chair. Ellie didn't turn while she took rolls from the oven and spooned the carrots into a bowl, but she heard him talking to Nate.

Once all the food was on the table, she stood beside her chair.

Caleb jumped up and pulled the chair out for her. She sat.

He filled his plate, mashed a few bites for his baby and blew on them before giving him a taste. "I love these carrots."

She knew.

He took a few bites and then laid his fork down.

Ellie looked up. "Is it all right?"

"It's fine. It's great. Just tell me your decision."

She'd only taken a few bites herself, because her stomach fluttered as though a thousand butterflies had taken up residence. She touched the napkin to her lips and laid her fork on her plate. "I thought about what you asked me to think about."

"About getting married."

She nodded.

Nate slapped his palm on his wooden tray and Caleb gave him a bite of mashed carrot.

"Nate needs a mother, you said."

"That wasn't a very romantic proposal."

"This is a hard land and neither of our situations are easy. Survival isn't very romantic."

He studied her, waiting.

"There's something I need, too."

A line formed between his brows. "What's that?"

"I need a home for my brothers," she blurted. "I can give you my word that I would be a good mother to Nate." She hadn't wanted children of her own; she'd had enough responsibility and hardship taking care of her brothers, but if her compromise would meet their needs and ease their sadly lacking young lives, she'd do it gladly.

"He would be like my own child," she said, her voice trembling with the solemn promise. "And in return, my brothers would have a home here with us."

He seemed to turn the idea over in his mind a few times, his gaze moving from her to Nate and back. She was the answer to his being able to keep both his son and his practice. He was the answer to her dreams of a home for her family.

"They're not young children, is that right?"

"Flynn is nine and Benjamin is fifteen. They're doing farm work for no pay right now. They could work, but they have to go to school. That's all I've ever wanted for them."

Caleb fed Nate another bite and took a few for himself. "I believe I can agree to that, Ellie."

She was so encouraged she almost laughed, but then she remembered to add, "You will have to promise me that you won't ever hit them."

His expression was stricken. "I've never hit a child in my life. Nate might need a whipping or two when he's old enough, but I do not beat children."

She'd had to say it. She'd had to be sure. She nodded. "There's one more thing."

He raised a brow and studied her.

"We will not share a bedroom." Quickly, she lowered her gaze to her plate. Her face burned, but she hardened her resolve. Better if he knew ahead that it could never be.

Nate made happy-baby noises. A dog barked somewhere outside. Caleb said nothing.

Finally she chanced an upward glance.

He was studying his fork, his brows drawn together in thought. She knew what he was thinking. He was a man, and men wanted to perform those repulsive acts with women. He was probably wondering how many others were available if his wife wasn't. Ellie knew about that kind of woman only too well.

"What about more children?" he asked.

A little crack opened near her heart. She'd already borne one, but he would never know that. She could never have another. He didn't deserve the anger and resentment burning on the inside of her. But that didn't change things. "I don't want more children."

"You might change your mind someday."

And she might walk out that door and find a tree growing money, too. "I wouldn't set any store by it if I was you."

His jaw tensed as if her words had made him mad. But he looked at Nate and the muscles relaxed. He raised his chin a notch. "Anything else?"

"That's it."

He picked up his fork with a smile. "All right. I'll make arrangements with Reverend Beecher. Do you want to plan a wedding?"

She didn't have the first idea how. "I just want to go get my brothers."

He gave a nod and ate. ''We'll do that first thing Saturday.''

''It has to be legal.''

''I'll see an attorney and have adoption papers drawn up. For both of us.''

She would adopt Nate? She looked at his sweet face with carrots smashed on his chin and prayed she was doing the right thing. For all of them.

Chapter Seven

The following day Caleb dropped his instruments into the water he'd boiled on the tiny stove in his office for the purpose of sterilizing them and thought for the millionth time about what he was preparing to do. *She might change her mind.*

He'd thought that part at least a hundred times. Surely she'd change her mind. He'd already been married to a woman who liked the idea of children, but not the reality. Leila hadn't been entirely wild about the intimacy part, but she hadn't refused.

If Ellie truly did not want children for whatever reasons, he could certainly take care of that. He was a doctor, for heaven's sake. He could explain methods to prevent her from becoming pregnant. He would have liked more children, of course, but right now his concern was the child he did have and the best way to care for him.

At this moment he couldn't see past keeping Nate with him and not having to let Patty and Denzil take him. He could make this arrangement work. If Ellie was willing to make a go of it, he could, too. He had Nate. And her brothers would be with them. Maybe someday Ellie would change her mind. After all, she didn't really know Caleb or what kind of a husband and father he would make. And he would have the opportunity to erase the loneliness that accompanied her like a dark shadow.

He visited the reverend over the noon hour, taking a pie he bought at Hintz's Bakery on the way. Reverend Beecher had a penchant for peaches, and his face lit up when he saw the sugary crust with golden juices glistening through the slits in the pastry.

"You sure about this, son?" he asked when Caleb told him their intent.

"Sure as I'm going to be," he replied. "Ellie is the answer to my prayers."

"God works in mysterious ways," the reverend said with a nod. "Perhaps she is at that."

They made plans for an informal ceremony on Saturday afternoon. Caleb would post a handwritten, open invitation at the post office and at the grocer's. He shook hands with Reverend Beecher. On his way back to the office he stopped by Isaac's Restaurant and made arrangements for food to be prepared and delivered to his house, then remembered to return to Hintz's Bakery and order a cake.

His parents took it well when he told them that evening. He knew because his mother didn't faint or cry, and his father didn't try to talk him out of it. They both just looked at him with such sad eyes and pitying expressions that he knew they were thinking he was doing this out of desperation.

The fact that they were right lodged in his craw like a fishbone. But this was the only acceptable option. They were just going to have to live with it. Not every marriage was made in heaven like theirs. Their own picture-perfect lives had skewed their sense of reality.

Saturday delivered a hot, sultry Kansas morning. Caleb bathed Nate and shaved himself before he dressed. With their hair parted and slicked back from their foreheads beneath their hats, father and son traveled the distance to the livery and Caleb harnessed both his horses to the buggy.

Ellie, dressed in her plain white shirtwaist and navy skirt, a bonnet shading her eyes, was waiting on the porch when he arrived at the boardinghouse. She picked up a small battered satchel and hurried forward eagerly, not even waiting for him to assist her up onto the seat.

"Morning, Ellie," he said.

"Morning." She placed her bag on the rear floor.

They glanced at each other, and she looked away.

"We'll move your things to the house tomorrow, if that's all right."

"That's fine. I only brought a change and a few personal things."

Not exactly packed for a honeymoon, he thought wryly.

She plucked Nate from his basket and seated him upon her lap so he could see the scenery and feel the breeze.

"You two will burn in this sun." Caleb had never known a lady to travel without a parasol. Ellie was a most unconventional gal, and sometimes he felt as though she'd just arrived from a foreign country. Then she'd speak, sounding just like everyone else in Kansas, and confound him further.

She looked up at him with new worry creasing her lovely brow.

"Here." He reached beneath the seat and handed her his black umbrella.

She expanded it and shaded herself and the baby. Caleb pulled his hat brim down over his eyes.

Perhaps she was just excited over being able to bring her brothers home. But the closer they got to Florence, the more nervous Ellie appeared. "You'll have to show me the farm," he said, and she nodded and shifted on the leather seat.

A few miles south of the town, she directed him along a rutted road toward a farmhouse. The morning was hot. Sweat trickled down Caleb's spine and pooled at the waistband of his trousers. A youth stood in the blazing sun, hammering at a wooden trough, but he straightened at the sight of the buggy.

Ellie's face broke into a brilliant smile, and she rose off the seat with Nate in her grasp.

The rear wheel hit a rut and Caleb grabbed her by the waist to keep her from plummeting off the side of the buggy.

She plunked back down on the seat and pulled away, glancing from him back to the lanky boy. "It's him! It's Benjamin," she said, excitement lacing her tone. "Benjamin!" she called.

The boy dropped the tool he held and limped toward the road. He wore threadbare overalls without a shirt beneath. His thin shoulders, though deeply tanned, had blistered and peeled to an uneven, dirty brown color. A battered straw hat shielded his face, and Caleb couldn't tell until the lad got close that his eyes were a vivid blue. "Ellie?" he questioned in a voice that cracked on the last syllable in that age-old way of growing males.

Caleb had halted the team.

Ellie fairly shoved Nate into Caleb's arms so she could leap from the buggy and embrace her brother awkwardly with one arm. His long, slender arms wrapped her waist and back, and his hat tipped and fell. Shaggy sandy hair, thick and damp with sweat, fell forward. He pulled away self-consciously and, while glaring at Caleb, asked his sister, "What happened to your arm?"

"I fell. This is Dr. Chaney. He set it for me."

He frowned when he looked back at her. "You gonna be all right?"

"I'm fine. This will be off in another week or two. Ben, I've come to get you. For good. Dr. Chaney and I are getting married, and you and Flynn are coming to live with us."

He cocked a scornful glance up at Caleb. "That so?"

"That's so. Your sister has her mind set on it."

"He's not makin' ya do this, is he?"

"No, Dr. Chaney is a very nice man. You'll see."

"I bet I will."

She touched his arm. "Where's your brother?"

"Shuckin' corn last I saw him. Over by the barn there."

"Let's go tell him!"

Benjamin picked up his hat and, favoring one foot, hurried after Ellie, who'd set out at a run.

Caleb urged the horses forward.

A woman stood on what couldn't really be called the porch of the square, unpainted house. The yard was neat, the steps were swept, and the woman wore a clean calico dress.

Two girls sat in the shade beside the house, a blanket spread beneath them and cloth dolls on their laps. Placing the dolls on the blanket, they stood and moved up beside their mother. They wore cotton dresses, white aprons and polished brown shoes. Their hair had been braided and the ends tied with ribbons.

There wasn't any shade except near the barn, so Caleb led the horses on, let them drink from a trough. He left them standing hitched to the buggy.

By the time he was finished, Ellie had found her youngest brother and the three of them were walking toward him. Ellie's hand rested protectively on the boy's bare brown shoulder. He, too, was shirtless, and Caleb frowned at the foolishness of not wearing protective clothing against the glaring prairie sun.

This boy's hair was dark, as dark as Nate's was light, and his eyes were a rich warm umber. The skin on his nose and cheeks was pink and peeling like that of his shoulders. Like Benjamin's shoulders. "This the doctor?" he queried in his little-boy gruff voice.

"This is him. Caleb, this is Flynn."

Caleb shifted Nate to one shoulder and stretched out a hand.

The child backed up an inch and moved closer to his sister.

"He wants to shake your hand," she said coaxingly. "It's something polite men do when they're introduced."

Caleb thought it a little odd that she'd thought she needed to explain something so elementary to him.

Flynn looked from his sister to Caleb and stepped forward, hesitantly putting his hand out awkwardly. Caleb shook it.

"And you saw Benjamin," she said, nodding at the taller boy.

Caleb extended his hand.

Benjamin gauged Caleb with those icy blue eyes and ignored his hand.

The three of them stared at Caleb and he stared back, noting finally that they looked nothing alike. There was some resemblance in facial structure between Benjamin and Ellie perhaps, but one would never know they were siblings.

"What's goin' on?" A man's voice echoed from the other side of the barn, and a stocky man rounded the corner and hurried toward them.

Flynn turned toward Ellie, and when he did so, Caleb caught sight of dark blotches on his ribs. The boy was so tanned and so dusty that at first Caleb didn't realize what he was looking at. But he was a doctor. When the realization struck him, it numbed his thinking for a moment.

The boy had been injured. "Flynn, what happened to your side?" Caleb asked.

Flynn turned so that his back was against Ellie. "Nothin'."

"You've been hurt. Let me see." Caleb moved closer to inspect. The child flinched and grabbed for his sister. Caleb slid the denim strap from his shoulder and exposed his scrawny back. Bruises marred skin that blended into untanned white, and there, where the sun hadn't reached, the purple and green shone vividly. Another area revealed yellowish, almost healed bruising.

He knew immediately that someone had done this to the child. This was not from a fall. Some of the bruises were newer than others. "Who did this to you?"

Flynn's expression was shuttered, and he looked down at his scuffed and torn shoes.

Caleb met Ellie's eyes where tears pooled. A single tear ran down her snowy cheek and she swiped it away quickly. He saw anger and resolution in her eyes, as well as something he hated: fear.

He jerked his gaze to Benjamin, who glared at him with a muscle jumping in his fuzzy cheek. Benjamin turned his stare to the man who had reached them, and hatred flared in eyes too old and too jaded for someone so young. His belligerent behavior immediately became clear.

"What're you doin' here?" the man asked Ellie. "You're not supposed to visit for a couple more weeks."

"I've come to take my brothers, Mr. Heath." Her voice trembled, but she kept her liquid gaze squarely locked with the man's.

"Like hell you are. The county gave me these boys and they ain't said they were takin' 'em away."

"We've had legal papers drawn up." Her voice gained strength and she tightened her hold around Flynn's shoulders. "I'm marrying this man and he's going to adopt my brothers."

"You got proof? You got a judge in that fancy buggy?"

"We have proof that you're not fit guardians," Caleb said angrily, unable to keep out of the discussion any longer. Gently he turned Flynn so that his ribs and back were visible to the farmer. "This is no way to treat children."

"He's clumsy. He fell."

"He did not fall."

"Did you fall, boy?" Heath asked, jerking his whiskered chin at Flynn.

Flynn still looked at his shoes, but he nodded.

Caleb pulled Flynn's strap back up over his shoulder and turned to Benjamin. "Why are you limping?"

The youth cast him a surly look. "I musta stepped on somethin'."

"Let me see."

"Go to hell."

"Benjamin," Ellie said with authority. "Take off your shoes right this minute."

Benjamin looked from the Heath man to his sister, and after a moment, sat on the ground to comply. He wore no stockings inside the worn-out old work boots.

Caleb handed Nate to Ellie and knelt to examine Ben's dirty feet. His soles were blistered and callused, and he had red, infected sores on his heels as well as on several of his toes.

Fury, like nothing he'd ever known, welled up inside Caleb, and he saw nothing but a red haze for a full thirty seconds. When it cleared, he looked up at Benjamin, but the boy's jaw was set and he'd cast his belligerent gaze aside.

Slowly, Caleb rose to his feet and deliberately looked at the sturdy pair of boots on the Heath man's feet before looking him in the eye. In all his life before he'd never wanted to strike a human being or an animal, but the desire to pummel this man standing before him beyond recognition was a living, breathing beast inside of him.

He could probably do it, too. He was bigger, younger... His fingers flexed and formed fists with the consuming need to make this man suffer, but that was exactly what he couldn't allow himself to do.

These boys had seen their share of violence, and had obviously been on the receiving end more than once. Behaving the same way that this man did was not the way to show them a wiser choice. Nor would it assure them that Caleb was any better, and he suddenly wanted their trust badly.

He silently counted to ten...then to twenty.... Sweat trickled down his temple. He took a breath and relaxed his stance and his hands. Then he allowed himself to look at Ellie.

Stark terror had blanched the color from her face. That did it.

"It's obvious that these children have been treated cruelly," he began in the calmest voice he could manage. "Flynn has bruises in various stages of healing. They're not the result of a one-time incident—or an accident. Benjamin's feet are in need of medical attention. He has blisters from poorly fitting shoes, and they have become infected and gone untreated far too long."

Because he didn't want to frighten the boy he didn't

mention that it would take skill and probably prayer to save a couple of those toes.

"Both of them have been exposed to heat and sun without proper clothing. I'd bet my horses that they've had very little nourishing food in their stomachs for months. Both are underweight and appear to suffer from exhaustion. Your animals don't look like they've been treated as badly as these boys."

"What do you think you are, a doctor?" the man asked with a snarl.

"As a matter of fact that's exactly what I am. I'm taking these boys with me, and I'm reporting their condition to county welfare."

"You don't have any right!" the man blustered. "Get the hell off my land."

"Even if the papers for their adoption weren't already filed, I'd have enough legal rights to take them away from here. You'll never do this to another child, Heath. Your days of starving and smacking foster children are over."

Caleb walked toward the two girls huddled against their mother's skirts and observed their clean, healthy appearance and well-nourished complexions. They were obviously this woman's own children—probably Heath's daughters, but not farmhand material.

Though assured that they weren't treated like the foster children the Heaths had taken in, the comparison sickened him, and he imagined the mental anguish of those two boys, seeing these girls being fed and pampered while they were mistreated.

He looked into Mrs. Heath's eyes, where a deep and abiding shame was reflected. She dropped her gaze. He took a brief inventory of her face and hands, wondering if she'd received any of the abuse her husband dealt so freely. He couldn't even think of anything to say to her.

Caleb turned and walked back to Ellie, who stood trembling. Nate looked perplexed and hot in her grasp. Caleb took his baby from her one good arm, freeing her to guide her brothers toward the buggy.

"If you have anything you want, go get it," Caleb said. "I'll see that Heath stays right here while you do."

Benjamin spoke up. "I want the clothes Ellie bought me."

"No, Ben, let's just get," Flynn said with a tremor in his voice.

"I want them clothes," his brother insisted.

"Go get them." Caleb stood between Heath and the barn while Benjamin limped barefoot toward the barn.

"You're not gonna get away with this!" Heath bellowed his anger at losing two unpaid farmhands.

Caleb ignored him, knowing the weasel wasn't man enough to attack someone his own size.

Benjamin returned a few minutes later and bent to retrieve his boots.

"Leave them," Caleb ordered.

Benjamin straightened. He studied the dilapidated boots only a moment before carrying the bag and tossing it up into the buggy. He assisted Flynn up into the vehicle, then helped Ellie. He finally climbed into the back where he moved Nate's basket and Ellie's satchel to make room for his own long legs, then he gingerly sat.

Caleb climbed up, handed Nate over to Ellie and flicked the reins over the horses' backs. The team pulled them away from the Heath farm.

Ellie's heart finally settled down to a normal beat. For a while there she'd been afraid it would burst from her chest. Caleb had been furious. She'd barely breathed, waiting for something dreadful to happen, for him to yell and hit that man. What would she have done if he'd been seriously hurt?

His reaction had caught her completely off guard, and his calm and deliberate words and the meaning behind them had diffused the explosive situation.

Guilt and pain tore through Ellie's chest, and she bit her lip to keep from crying. If only she'd known what had been happening on that farm. Why hadn't her brothers told her? What could she have done if they had? She'd have had to take the boys and run from the county authorities, because she'd already tried to get them legally and had been denied.

Those bruises on Flynn's skinny ribs were like arrows stabbed into her heart. He'd endured so much in his short, painful life—both her brothers had. And the thought of them hungry and hurt and without someone to love them twisted her insides into a knot of racking torture. It was so unfair...so unfair....

Nate had fallen asleep and her arm ached from holding him. "Flynn, can you help me lay Nate in his basket between you two?"

"Where'd you get this baby, Ellie?" the boy inquired as he moved the basket and clumsily helped her place the baby.

"This is Nate," she said. "He's Dr. Chaney's little boy."

"Dr. Chaney's really gonna 'dopt us?"

"Yes," Caleb replied, turning his head so he could glance at Flynn. "And you're to call me Caleb."

"If we're 'dopted, then does that make Nate our brother?"

"I guess it does," Caleb replied.

Flynn grinned, and his frank pleasure brought more tears to Ellie's eyes. She blinked them away.

Benjamin sat with his hat brim over his eyes, looking out across the fields.

"Where we goin' anyhow?" Flynn asked.

"Caleb has a beautiful house in Newton," Ellie supplied. "You'll be able to go to school—he promised."

"School's for babies," Benjamin snapped.

Ellie glanced at Caleb, but he said nothing, just faced forward as though the horses held his attention.

"I wanna go to school." A note of wistfulness tinged Flynn's voice.

"You will," she promised.

They entered Newton, and the boys studied their surroundings. Caleb pulled the buggy up in front of Gerson's Clothing Store. "We're all going in," he said, reaching into the back for Nate's basket.

They followed him without question. In a state of numbness, Ellie watched Caleb speak to the store owner, who obliged him by measuring the boys and selecting items from his shelves. With a stack of clothing and shoes already piled on the counter, the balding, spectacled little man approached Ellie and looked her over.

"I think I have a few dresses that will fit."

"Oh, I don't need a dress—"

"Choose something for today, Ellie," Caleb said gently from beside her. Flynn was inspecting his surroundings with awe and Benjamin was trying to act uninterested. Apparently Caleb wanted her to have a nice dress for the ceremony.

She nodded mutely.

Joseph Gerson led her to a display of ready-made dresses. The man's perusal of her height and size made her want to run out of the store, but he turned aside, all businesslike, and gestured. "These three should fit you without alterations."

"I'd need to take out the seam in the sleeve for this cast."

"My wife will do that for you. It'll only take a minute."

She selected one of rose fabric with a white insert bodice and a full pleated skirt. "I like this one."

"She'll take all three," Caleb said. "And a pair of opera slippers, something stylish. Kid if you have it."

Mr. Gerson's face lit up. "I have just the pair! French kid with a bow across the arch. Let's test the fit."

Self-consciously, Ellie took the two pairs he handed her and sat on a stool to remove her plain black boots. They were good boots and she'd been proud to purchase them with her first pay from the hotel. The first pair of soft leather slippers fit perfectly. She tied the black bow and admired the dainty shoe.

"We'll take them," Caleb said. "Send me the bill."

All that clothing had to cost a fortune! With a sick feeling in her stomach, Ellie clutched Nate and said softly to Caleb, "I—I can't pay you back for all that."

He cast her a gentle smile. "You're my family now. That's my responsibility."

"But—"

"Money's not a problem," he assured her. "I lease my share of the ranch, and receive a comfortable sum each month. I also own a few horses that my father breeds for me."

Dazed, Ellie returned to the buggy, not even noticing the heat as Caleb drove the team and pulled up in front of his house.

"This it?" Flynn asked, jumping down and eyeing the two-story structure. It must have looked like a castle. Ellie remembered her reaction the first time she'd seen it.

Caleb looked at his pocket watch. "We have time for baths—Ellie, will you help me heat water?"

She'd bathed the night before and could have managed quite well with a pitcher and bowl, but she caught his drift. The boys needed baths and their heads washed.

''One can eat while the other is bathing,'' he said when they were alone for a moment in the kitchen. ''Just don't let them eat too much at a time just yet, and nothing too rich or spicy. Their stomachs will need to get used to ad-equate amounts slowly.''

Hearing their undernourished condition referred to in such a way angered Ellie all over again. She nodded her understanding.

Nate had awakened and was crying with an empty tummy. She and Caleb pumped water, then Caleb stoked the stove while Ellie fed the baby and prepared small portions of bread and fruit for the boys. Flynn ate, then explored the house and yard, returning often to express his delight.

Benjamin, however, sat on the back step as though unimpressed.

''Who's first?'' Caleb asked.

Flynn volunteered, and they left him alone to scrub. In spite of his protests, Ellie returned to make sure he did a good job washing his hair and behind his ears and under his nails.

Eventually both boys sat on kitchen chairs wearing spanking new knee-length union suits, the tops of which hung at their waists, while Caleb donned his gold-rimmed spectacles, then cleansed and treated their shoulders, necks, ears and faces with unguent.

''I want you to drink this,'' Caleb said to Benjamin.

Benjamin looked at the cup. ''I don't have to take nothin' from you if I don't want to.''

''No, you don't. But as a doctor I think you should drink it so it doesn't hurt quite as bad while I work on your feet.''

The lad's expression faltered, but he caught himself. "What is it?"

"Laudanum. A small dose. If I were going to poison you, I wouldn't have traveled all the way to Florence in the heat to bring you here, now would I?"

Benjamin drank the liquid reluctantly and grimaced. Caleb waited for the medicine to take effect before starting to work. Benjamin held his expression in stoic reserve while Caleb disinfected the sores on his toes and feet, applied salve and bandaged them.

Ellie and Flynn watched his sure gentle movements. It was apparent that he took great care not to hurt Benjamin any more than he had to, and when Ben flinched, regret crossed Caleb's features.

Ellie remembered the concern and care he'd given the Bowman woman, and wondered how his father could have missed the rightness of this occupation for his son. Caleb truly cared for the patients he treated, and that concern was evident in his every touch and glance. She remembered how much better she'd felt knowing he was tending to her arm, and drew comfort that her brothers were receiving that same special care. Surely his confidence and manner gave them ease, too.

"I'd really prefer you didn't walk for several days," he said, studying his handiwork through his lenses. "But I wouldn't want you to miss your sister's wedding, so you're free to walk until we get back here afterward. Then I want you off your feet, except for a few minutes at a time."

"He kin go to the outhouse, right?" Flynn asked.

That was what Caleb had meant, but Flynn spelled it out as plainly as only a child could. Caleb smiled, noting the boy's neatly parted wet and wavy dark hair. "Right."

Ellie studied her brothers' clean hair and freshly scrubbed skin as they buttoned up their union suits. Flynn had begun to unfold his new trousers and shirt. Overwhelming gratefulness rushed over her and she locked gazes with Caleb. She wanted to thank him. She could never repay this debt. The clothes and shoes were material, but a chance for a new life was invaluable. And that was what he'd given them. All of them. The words stuck in her heart.

"Before this afternoon," Caleb said, wiping his hands on a towel, "I want to let you know that you will be able to eat as much and as often as you want in this home. But right now, for these first days, we need to go slow so you don't get sick."

He looked at each of the boys. "Understand?"

Flynn nodded and Ben ignored him.

"We'd better change clothing now ourselves," he said to Ellie, closing his leather bag.

She gathered her satchel and the packages and hurried up to the room she'd used before. Caleb had thoughtfully placed a walnut-framed cheval mirror in the corner.

Flynn brought her water. "I'm a'sposed to help ya if ya need anything."

"I'll call if I need anything."

He seated himself on the floor outside her room and she grinned, closing the door. She washed her hands and face with the fresh water and dressed her hair, all the while replying to his muffled questions. Brushing a few wrinkles from the rose-colored dress, she slipped it on. It had a row of buttons up the back.

"Now I need help," she said.

Flynn burst into the room, and she turned her back, indicating the fasteners.

He buttoned her dress clumsily, and she checked in the mirror to make sure he'd gotten them all.

"This is sorta like a fairy tale, isn't it?" he said, sitting on the edge of the bed.

"What is?"

"Gettin' to live in this fancy house and you marryin' the doctor an' all. I looked in the pantry room and the kitchen shelves and there's food to last a winter!"

Ellie pulled him against her, mindful of his bruised ribs and back, and hugged him as tightly as she dared. Cupping his beloved face, she looked down into the dark, dark eyes of this boy she'd raised on her own with no means to do it and rubbed her thumbs over his freckled cheekbones. The salve Caleb had daubed on his peeled and burned nose glistened. "Nobody will ever hurt you again, sweet boy. I promise you. You're going to eat my cooking until you pop and then eat some more."

"Do I get ta sleep in one o' these rooms up here? There ain't no barn."

"You and Ben get a room to share, but a bed all your own. Caleb had two beds sent over from the furniture store. I haven't fixed the room up yet, but we'll have plenty of time to do that."

"I always wanted a feather pilla, Ellie. 'Member you had one once, but somethin' happened to it. You shared it with me sometimes."

Their mother had thrown it out into the yard in a drunken fit, and a dog had torn it open and scattered the feathers to the November wind. "You'll have one all your own," she promised.

She was making a lot of promises, placing a lot of hope in the doctor and their agreement. Keeping all those promises depended on Caleb Chaney. Once more Ellie felt completely vulnerable, something she had never wanted to feel again.

Chapter Eight

Ben came out dressed in the clothes Ellie had purchased for him, rather than those Caleb had selected. She started to object, but Caleb silenced her by saying, "What handsome brothers you have, Ellie."

Benjamin's disdain for Caleb was apparent in his silent glare, but Caleb took it in stride and delivered them to the church.

Ellie had never been to a wedding, so she didn't know what to expect. She certainly hadn't anticipated so many people, all dressed in fine clothes and fashionable hats, to fill the pews and murmur things she didn't want to imagine. She'd never been inside a church before either, and the varnished pine walls, hanging tapestries and brass candelabras fascinated her.

At least Reverend Beecher's face was familiar, if not the black robe and white stole with gold embroidered crosses that he wore. Facing him wasn't nearly as frightening as facing Mr. Heath had been that same morning.

Caleb's attire was unfamiliar as well, and obviously not ready-made. The black suit and tie and white shirt had been tailored to his tall frame and broad shoulders, and emphasized his masculinity. The cut and fabric were a subtle reminder of his prosperity, and for a brief moment Ellie resented her reasons for doing this. That first day when she'd walked beside this man, she'd imagined being his friend, pretended she was someone with whom he'd be proud to be seen.

And here she was using a made-up name to wed herself to him so she could have a measure of stability for the first time in her life. He was still as respectable and as kind and as honorable as she'd first thought—more so now that she'd really seen his nature. If she'd had any doubts before, they'd been erased this morning when he'd controlled his temper and handled the situation at the Heath farm calmly and firmly.

She had made the right decision for her brothers.

As she stood beside him and the crowd hushed, she smiled at Benjamin and Flynn in their new clothing and shoes and her heart welled with newfound joy.

The reverend spoke and she turned her attention to his words. In a matter of minutes, she'd repeated the vows he read from a slim volume, and Caleb did the same. Reverend Beecher took her hand and gave it to Caleb, and Ellie gaped at the gold ring set with an emerald surrounded by diamond chips that Caleb slid on her finger. And just like that they were pronounced man and wife.

Caleb placed his hands on her upper arms, and the unexpected touch startled her. He leaned forward and she stared at him.

He touched his cheek to hers only briefly, then released her and offered his jacket-clad arm. Feeling foolish, Ellie placed her hand on his sleeve and he led them away from the altar amidst a smattering of applause.

A sea of people appeared to greet and congratulate them, and the names and faces became a blur. She recognized Caleb's parents—his mother with tears in her eyes—and

Caleb's sister and her family, as well as a few of the store owners she'd met while shopping with Nate. Goldie Krenshaw had turned out to see Ellie's marriage, and Ellie couldn't have been more surprised.

"I'm so happy for you," she said, and took her hand.

Ellie smiled her thanks. "How are things at the dormitory?"

"Same as always. 'Cept your wedding made for a bit more exciting news this week."

"How did you know to come today?"

"Read one of the notices posted around town. Said everyone was welcome, so I thought I'd come over since I had the afternoon free."

"I'm glad you did," Ellie said as Caleb took her elbow. "Real glad."

Caleb ushered her down the church stairs and into his buggy waiting on the street. "The boys," she said, thinking of Nate as well as her brothers.

"My parents will bring them home."

Home. They had a home. At long last. The concept constricted her throat, and she brought her fists to her heart. Could her wish really be coming true?

"Are you all right?" he asked, slowing the team in front of the house. Concern creased his forehead, and the afternoon sun glinted off his hair.

Words failing her because of this unexpected good fortune, she nodded.

He came around, and reached up for her.

Ellie placed her hand in his and used the step to descend. "There's someone in the house!" she said, catching sight of a figure moving behind the window, and noting that the door stood open.

"Yes." He led her up the walk.

She glanced at him in confusion, then back at the house, hesitant to go any farther.

"It's okay," he said with a smile. "It's a surprise."

Puzzled, she walked ahead of him into the house and the savory smell of food got her attention. He gestured into the room he called a parlor. She stepped to the doorway. Two tables had been set up and draped with white linen. One held an assortment of meat and potato dishes, relishes and rolls. On the other stood a three-layered cake with fluffy white frosting, and an enormous bowl filled with what looked like lemonade. A silver ladle was propped against the rim and glass cups were stacked nearby.

"What is all this?" she asked.

"It's customary to celebrate a wedding," he said with the lift of one brow. The grin quickly turned to a look of concern. "You don't like it?"

"Yes." She admired the tables of food more closely. "I like it a lot. I just didn't know...."

"Well, that's why it was a surprise." He looked at her as though she'd said something foolish and she probably had. None of the surprises in Ellie's previous life had been pleasant.

Her mind raced and silently she cursed the Episcopal ladies for not mentioning wedding etiquette in their obviously incomplete book of manners. Thanks were always appropriate. "Thank you."

"You're a puzzle, Ellie."

Guests started arriving then and Caleb's friends and neighbors and relatives monopolized their attention. Mrs. Ned arrived and gave the women arranging the tables helpful suggestions.

Even Miss Shaw and Mrs. Henderson arrived and congratulated the newlyweds. A wedding in Newton was obviously a big event. Everyone seemed to know what to do with themselves, filling plates and cups and eating standing up or sitting on the furniture or even carrying their feast outdoors and standing in the yard in clusters.

"That's such a pretty dress," Patricia said. "How are you managing your clothing with that dreadful cast?"

"I've taken the seams out of the left sleeve of all my shirtwaists. Caleb just bought this dress for me this morning, and the shop owner's wife took out the stitches carefully so I could repair it as good as new when the cast comes off."

"It's a beautiful ring, too."

The piece of jewelry felt heavy and foreign on her finger, and with her arm held across her breast in the sling, it seemed as though everyone commented on the winking gems.

"Your brothers are certainly handsome young men, though so terribly shy. I haven't heard either one say a word."

"Where did you see them last?"

"Outside. Lucy is taken with your younger brother. The girl is so forward."

Ellie thought Lucy was delightful and would have loved to see Ben and Flynn show some of her confidence. Maybe she'd be good for them.

"I think I'll find them. They don't know anyone here."

Ellie spotted the children beneath the shadow of a willow tree in the side yard. The boys had removed their shoes and rolled back their sleeves. Lucy was in the process of unbuttoning her tiny leather boots and slipping them off.

"Look, Ellie," she said with an impish grin. "We're coolin' our feet."

Benjamin stared off toward the street as though he were bored.

"Lucy said you're her aunt now." Flynn systematically

peeled leaves and twigs from a willow branch he'd broken from the tree.

"I guess I am." Ellie settled herself on the grass beside Benjamin.

"You're still our sister an' that's better."

Lucy had peeled her white stockings down and they lay strewn in the grass. She wiggled her toes and giggled. "This feels funny."

Her feet were as white and delicate as Nate's, her tiny toes pink and cute. They'd probably never had sun or grass touch them before. Benjamin met Ellie's eyes, and she knew the comparison he was making. He'd kept his new stockings on over his ravaged and bandaged feet and was resting them just as Caleb had instructed. Even wearing a new pair of shoes that were large enough must have been torture these past few hours.

She laid her hand on his tanned, bare arm. "You all right?"

He nodded.

"Did you eat?"

He shook his head.

"I did," Flynn piped up. "Caleb helped me choose stuff. But Ben didn't wanna go in there with all them people."

"I'll go get you food." Ellie hurried into the house and returned with carefully selected portions on a plate. "I couldn't carry a drink too, Flynn. Go get your brother some lemonade."

Flynn scurried off to obey.

Ben accepted the plate and fork and dug into the savory dishes.

"Those two times I ate with you at the farm, and Mrs. Heath cooked a meal and we all sat in the kitchen, that wasn't how it usually was…was it?"

"Nope. We ate on the back step and we mostly got salt

pork or corn dodgers or bean porridge. Sometimes the girls brought us cookies or hunks of fresh bread. Once one of them snuck us a custard pie. I think Mrs. Heath knew, but she was scared o' him.''

She spoke around the ache in her throat. ''Why didn't you tell me?''

''It only woulda made you feel bad. I didn't want you to worry about us. You had your own problems. And there wasn't anything you coulda done.''

This was the first time in months he'd spoken more than half a dozen surly words to her. ''Things are going to be a whole lot better from here on,'' she assured him. ''You have to go to school, Ben. You have to know how to read and figure to get by.''

''I haven't been to school since fourth grade,'' he said. ''I'd be the only big dummy there. I can't go.''

''You can go. And you can make up what you've missed. I'll help you.''

He shook his head.

Lucy interrupted. ''I'm going to school pretty soon. You can sit by me.''

Ben's skin turned red beneath his deep tan. He didn't look at the little girl or acknowledge she'd spoken.

''He don't like me.'' Lucy had leaned to whisper in Ellie's ear. She'd pressed her weight against the cast, but it didn't hurt anything except where it pushed the plaster of paris into her ribs.

''He likes you just fine,'' Ellie said softly. ''It just takes him a while to warm up to people.''

Benjamin set down the empty plate just as Flynn returned with lemonade sloshing over the brims of two glass cups. ''I got one for Lucy, too, since she's so little an' all. It's kinda hard for her to carry stuff without spillin' it.''

''Thank you.'' Lucy's polite words and shy smile would

have pleased her mother, even if the bare feet and grass-stained dress would soon give her a conniption. She took the cup and sipped daintily as she'd obviously been coached.

"Flynn likes me though," she said in a stage whisper.

Ellie chuckled and sat listening to Lucy and Flynn's childish conversation while she watched the party milling on the lawn. She'd been everywhere but with her new husband—the word lodged uncomfortably in her mind—and the guests were starting to cast her odd looks.

"I'd better get back," she said finally, picking up Ben's plate and fork and the two cups.

"Whoa, you're not supposed to be doing this on your wedding day," a pretty fair-haired woman said, taking the dishes from Ellie. She smiled, showing nice teeth and attractive smile lines in her glowing cheeks. "I'm Eva Kirkpatrick."

"The dressmaker under Caleb's office?"

"That's me. But I make more than dresses. I made all of the doctor's baby's flannels. Sewed all of his little clothes, too."

"They're beautiful!"

"Thank you. I have a full-time job making dresses and aprons and the like for Mrs. Connely, though," she said with a grin. "The woman has grown a dress size every year since I've been in business. And you don't find her size in the Montgomery Ward catalog."

Ellie recalled the robust woman who'd flown past her leaving Caleb's office once. Caleb had spoken of his concern for her health.

"I didn't bring a wedding gift," Miss Kirkpatrick said. "I'd like you to stop by and let me measure you for something special. We can select a color and a pattern that will compliment your hair and eyes. That will be my gift to you.''

Ellie didn't know how to respond. She'd only had a dress sewn for her once in her entire life and now she already had so many nice clothes. She gave the woman a hesitant smile. ''All right.''

''Wonderful. Stop by whenever you have a free hour. I'll make tea.'' She hurried off toward the house with the dishes.

In the parlor Ellie dipped a cup of lemonade and looked around for Nate, finally finding him sleeping on his grandmother's lap. Laura Chaney sat in Caleb's overstuffed chair, fanning herself with a tasseled fan. She motioned for Ellie to draw closer.

''I know it's warm in here, but sit for a moment.''

Ellie perched on the clawfoot ottoman and sipped the sweet refreshment.

''Caleb says your brothers are your only family.''

''That's right.''

''Your parents are dead.''

Ellie nodded.

Laura glanced around, noting no one was paying any attention to them. Most everyone had gone outside to catch the breeze. ''I know it's late for a mother-daughter chat, but I wondered if perhaps you needed someone older to talk to.''

Ellie blinked.

''You're young. Caleb's been married once before. It would be only natural to have some qualms about your relationship.''

''Well.'' Ellie didn't know what to say, especially to Caleb's mother. Surely she knew this was an arrangement of convenience on both their parts. After all, they'd only known each other a few weeks. "I think we've both made the right choice."

"Caleb wouldn't have made the commitment if he didn't believe it was the right choice." The fan fluttered the silver hair at her temples. "There's no way to say this but to be blunt. Have you any questions or concerns about what's to happen in your marriage bed? I remember I was a tangle of nerves, not knowing what to expect on my wedding night. I almost fainted on poor Matthew when the guests departed and we were left alone. You must be assured that it's not as ghastly as you've probably been led to believe, in fact, the physical relationship can sustain a marriage through many other problems that can arise. Why I recall…"

Her words continued but Ellie shut them out and stared hard at Nate's cherubic face and damp hair. She couldn't be talking about the same thing Ellie assumed.

Not as ghastly as she'd been led to believe? The woman had no idea what she was talking about. Ellie had learned about sex as a part of growing up. Her mother had allowed men into her bed at all hours of the day or night, not caring which of her children were present. Ellie had awakened to the sounds. She'd walked in on the disgusting act. Once she'd beaten a naked drunk man over the head with a chair leg, then dragged him down by the creek where he could sleep it off.

She'd cleaned up her mother after brutal attacks and she had delivered Flynn as well as a baby sister into this miserable world with no more than a bucket of stale water with which to wash them and old rags in which to wrap them. She'd buried that starved and sick baby girl herself.

Oh, she knew what happened. And it was more ghastly than this genteel woman could even imagine. And she wanted no part of it. Ever. She didn't know what Caleb's mother was referring to, but it wasn't the same thing Ellie had had experience with.

"Well, thank you," she said, finally meeting the well-meaning woman's eyes.

A commotion outside caught her attention and she stood and moved to the window, pushing aside the curtain to see what was happening. A tall, well-dressed man stood on the lawn and the wedding guests had cleared an opening around where he stood.

A few of the women whispered among themselves and several of the men listened and nodded. Caleb appeared in the shade of the porch and stood with one hand in his pocket, the other holding a cup of lemonade. Ellie set down her empty cup, made her way to the front door and slipped out to see what was going on.

Heads turned at her arrival and she moved self-consciously closer to Caleb.

"Well, well, is this the new Mrs. Chaney?" The man walked closer to the house, shading his eyes with his hand. "*Another* wife for you, Caleb? Are you going to kill her, too?"

A murmur rolled through the crowd. Caleb's body tensed.

The man's words had shocked Ellie. "Who is he, Caleb?"

"My former father-in-law," he replied in a regretful tone.

"She's a pretty one. Young, too." The man had reached the bottom of the wooden stairs.

Caleb strode to the top step and looked down at him. "I hardly think this is the place or the time for you to voice your doubts about my medical abilities."

"Don't want your new bride to get worried?" he asked, squinting up through the bright sunlight. "Don't worry," he called to her. "You're safe as long as you don't get sick or try to have a baby. If you do, take my advice and seek a physician elsewhere. He let his last wife die."

His mocking voice was hauntingly familiar, and threaded a frisson of dread along Ellie's spine. She took a few more steps closer to Caleb and looked down at the face of the man who had accused Caleb of such a despicable act.

The late afternoon sun beat down unmercifully. A few guests spoke in hushed voices and someone's crinoline skirts rustled. The porch floor seemed to shift beneath Ellie's feet and the sweet lemonade she'd enjoyed only moments before turned sour in her stomach. She tasted bile.

She recognized him a second before he recognized her. He looked a little older, though his hair was still dark, and anyone who didn't know him would consider him attractive.

"Now if this isn't a pleasant surprise," he said, shaking his head and grinning dangerously. "Look at little Ellie all grown up and dressed like a virtuous woman."

A loud buzz sounded in her ears and she watched his lips move, but the words didn't follow until a few seconds later. "Your taste in women has gone downhill, Chaney."

Caleb gave her an apologetic glance. "You two know each other?"

"Oh, Ellie and I go back a long way, don't we, darlin'?"

Ellie wished the searing heat in her stomach would just burst into a fireball and turn her to ashes on the spot.

"I used to run into her when I had business in Florence."

Caleb studied Ellie with a frown, and she knew her face must have paled. All her fear and self-loathing and hatred were reawakened and intensified, and she struggled to grasp a clear thought.

She'd never feared anyone as she feared this man. She'd never hated anyone as she did him. She'd never again wanted to set eyes on him—the man who had raped her.

Chapter Nine

If there was a God, and Ellie doubted that possibility more today than she ever had, then He was out there somewhere in the Great Beyond rolling dice to see what awful thing happened to torture her next.

Caleb descended the stairs. "If you'd like to eat, Winston, there's food laid out in the house. There's cake and coffee and you're welcome to join our gathering. But I must insist that you not spoil our wedding day by standing out here spouting your inexhaustibly poor opinion of my character and my skill."

"I don't think I'll risk the food."

One of the ladies sputtered at that. Ellie couldn't believe her ears. Did they think Caleb would poison them, for goodness' sake?

"But I would like to kiss the bride." Winston placed his foot on the lowest step.

"No!" Ellie had finally found her voice. "No," she said again firmly, and turned and fled into the house.

Her heart hammered painfully. Her head swam with every unspeakable thought and memory she'd ever banished. She ran through the house, out the kitchen door to the outhouse and, finding it occupied, threw up in the tall grass behind.

Head throbbing, she retched until her stomach was empty and her torso muscles ached. Shaking uncontrollably, she wobbled back to the house and kept her head down and her face away from the two women in the kitchen who were stacking clean dishes. She dipped water into a pitcher and carried it upstairs, trembling so fiercely that the liquid sloshed as she went.

In her room, she propped the chair beneath the knob before washing her face and shaking hands and rinsing her mouth.

Winston Parker. Even thinking the name was vile.

She'd never told anyone what he'd done. There'd been no one to tell, no one who cared. The person who should have cared already knew. She'd tried to forget. But there was no erasing his cruelty. The scars were on her heart, in her soul.

Even if she told someone now, they'd never believe her. It was her word against his. A whore's kid or a respectable banker—whom they would believe wasn't much of ques- tion. How could she stay here now? How could she live in this town, sleep at night, wake up in the morning, knowing he was here? She couldn't live with herself if Caleb or his family found out.

A rap on the door startled her, and she stifled a shriek. "Ellie?"

Caleb's voice. The voice of reason and sanity. She placed a hand on her chest and willed her racing heart to still. "Yes?"

"Are you all right?"

She looked at herself in the mirror, a stricken, hollow- eyed girl, and ludicrously straightened her hair and her dress before going to the door, removing the chair as quietly as she could, and opening the barrier.

"Are you sick?" A characteristic look of concern graced his features.

"I think it's the heat." She stepped back and he entered.

He reached for her wrist and pressed it gently between his thumb and fingers. "Perhaps that and all the excitement," he agreed after a minute. "You should probably get some rest. People are starting to leave."

Ellie had to keep up appearances for his sake. "What should we do?"

"I can see them out if you'd like to rest."

"Is he gone?"

He nodded.

"We'll see them off together, and then I'll lie down," she suggested. To her own ears she sounded so calm.

Caleb didn't make a move to leave. "I'm sorry about Winston."

Her heart lurched and she was grateful he hadn't been checking her pulse just then. She rationalized his words and realized he meant the incident just now on the porch. "Don't apologize for him."

"I wanted this day to be perfect." His deep soft voice held regret.

She met his earnest gaze.

"For you."

She'd never known anyone like Caleb in her life. She hadn't known anyone like him existed in this foul world. She would never be able to face him again if he found out. "It *was* perfect. Thank you."

His posture relaxed. "And the ring? Do you like it? If not I can exchange it."

"Oh, no—I mean yes, I like it very much. But I didn't expect something so—so..." She lifted her cast and looked at the sparkling ring on her hand. She'd never dreamed she'd have anything so beautiful.

"Symbolic?"

"No."

"Permanent?"

"No, well, yes it's that, but...I meant so grand!"

"Just so you like it."

"I like it."

"Good. Let's go say goodbye."

He guided her down the hallway and she descended the stairs ahead of him. Still shaky, but with a smile plastered on her face, she thanked each person who had come and accepted their good wishes.

She was a phony, but she was getting pretty good at it. It took a lot of evasive tricks to keep from losing one's mind, but she'd learned to hide and block out and pretend so well that it took a day like today to bring it all sharply back into focus.

She spoke harshly to herself, remembering the rare gift of opportunity that she'd been given so recently. Was she going to let that man scare her into losing all she'd gained for her family?

Winston Parker couldn't hurt her here. He was her past, and as long as she kept him there she was safe. She was safe in Caleb's house and as his wife. This was her refuge, and she meant to hang on to it.

He can tell Caleb who you are. He can tell Caleb's friends and family what kind of person he really married.

She wanted to clamp her hands over her ears, but the warning voice was in her head. She never wanted to bring shame on Caleb and his family. She couldn't bear the thought of the citizens of Newton learning that Caleb had aligned himself with Florence's trash family, with a whore's daughter.

He already had enough troubles getting people to trust him and come to him for medical attention. As it was, they liked and respected him as a person, if not as a doctor. If they knew the truth about her, he would lose that esteem, too. She wouldn't let that happen. Somehow she'd keep the secret.

All the guests were gone, and the women from the restaurant finished cleaning up and packing their wares and left, too. Ellie gave Benjamin a spoonful of the powdered laudanum mixed in water and got him settled in the bedroom he and Flynn were to share.

"It's been a big day," she said. "Get some rest now."

Benjamin looked at her with weary eyes and a grave expression only someone much older should wear. She didn't know how much he knew or remembered about Winston Parker, and she'd never asked him. If he didn't know—and she fervently hoped he didn't—then she didn't want to plant any questions in his mind. And if he did know, nothing either of them said would change what had happened.

He'd been aware of the baby growing in her belly—that wasn't something easily hidden and he'd been old enough to understand her condition. But he'd never asked her about the child, about what had happened to it, if it had survived the birth or died. And she hadn't told him because she'd feared her mother finding out where the baby was or, worse, Winston learning. The less Benjamin knew, the better off he was, the more he could protect himself and Flynn.

She didn't see any hope in his eyes and that frightened her. She might have been jaded and pragmatic from a young age, but Ellie had always harbored a twinkle of hope that their situation could get better—that if she did all the right things and worked hard, someday, some way, she and the boys would have the life they deserved.

Ben's bleak attitude showed he didn't share her same vision. At least not yet. "Life is going to be good here," she assured him. "I hate how you had to grow up, how we all grew up. It wasn't normal, Ben. Other people don't live like that. Other people live like this." She gestured to the bed beneath him, the papered walls and the curtains at the window. "And now we live like this, too."

"You sold yourself for all this, Ellie."

Her ears rang. Her heart constricted, but she bristled and denied that hurtful accusation. "I did not sell myself! I am going to be Nate's mother. That's it."

"He's a man, Ellie. You know what men want."

Why had he spoiled everything and said that? Her own fears had touched on that, but she'd stashed them and believed in Caleb's sincerity. "He's not like that. He's *not.*"

Benjamin's icy blue gaze rankled her further. She stood. "Rest now. I'll bring you some milk or tea later—which do you want?"

"Don't care."

"All right then." She turned and left the room.

Caleb poured water from a tub that had held ice into the azalea bushes behind the house.

"You sure have a lot of friends," Flynn said from behind him. He'd changed into a cotton shirt and a stiff new pair of denim pants that had to be rolled at his ankles, and he tagged alongside Caleb as he carried the tub through the deepening twilight to the back porch.

"Yeah, I guess I do. Acquaintances anyway."

"What's acquaintances?"

"Those are people you know, but who are not necessarily your friends. I know a good many people. Few of them have proved to truly be friends."

"How can ya tell the diff'rence?"

Caleb sat on the back steps and pondered that question. "Friends forgive you when you make a mistake. They believe the best of you and trust you. They listen if you have something you want to talk about." He glanced at the boy when he said that, and Flynn seated himself with one foot on the second step and the other on a lower one, just like Caleb.

"And they don't judge you," he finished. He'd left the conversation open for Flynn to talk if he wanted to.

"Kinda sounds like Ellie, don't it?" the boy observed.

He'd been speaking in generalities and trying to offer friendship, but now that Flynn mentioned it, yes, it did sound like Ellie. He smiled. "It does."

In the fading light, Flynn appeared as young and innocent as all boys his age should be.

"We'd better put some salve on that nose before you go to bed." And he needed to check Benjamin's feet. He stood and they entered the back door. Caleb located his black bag, and dotted the unguent on the boy's nose.

"Can I sit on the steps for a while longer?" he asked. "I seen a cat slinkin' out there by the woodpile, and maybe it'll come back."

"All right. But don't try to get too close to an animal you're not familiar with."

"Oh, I won't. I just wanna see it."

Caleb climbed the stairs and tapped on the boys' closed door.

"What."

He opened it and stepped in. "I came to check your feet before you go to sleep."

"I sleep real light."

"Do you now?" Caleb pulled his spectacles from his pocket and slipped them on the bridge of his nose. He spread a sheet beneath Benjamin's feet and unwrapped the bandages.

"If you hurt her, I'll kill you."

The vehemence in the lad's young voice and the glower on his narrow face startled Caleb. He stared. "Why on earth would I hurt your sister?"

"Because you're a man and that's what men do."

Caleb rolled that one over in his mind. Had it taken only one angry man to give this boy such a damning opinion? Did he think all men beat women and children because of his experience over the past year or so? He could understand him hating the one man for his deeds. What he couldn't comprehend was his assumption that all men were like that one.

His and Flynn's reactions were so different, and Caleb thanked God that Flynn didn't have this same hatred roiling inside him.

"Some men do. I can't deny that. But not all. And certainly not me. I will never hurt your sister. Or you or Flynn. You have my word. You're my family now. Ellie's my wife and soon you'll be my sons. Legally."

Benjamin's bitter expression showed that those words didn't mean much to him. He snorted. "You think people don't beat their own kids?"

"Did your father hit you?"

Ben clamped his mouth shut and looked at the wall.

"You're almost a man. Do you hit women?"

"Ellie's my sister!" he shouted, glaring at Caleb.

"You just said it makes no difference. Other women then—you gonna hit your wife?"

"Ain't gonna have one."

"Lucy, then. You plan to sock her sometime soon?"

"You just shut your yap," Benjamin said bitterly. "You think you're so goddamn smart 'cause you're rich and you can boss people around with your money. Well, you can't tell me what to do, and you can't boss Ellie around neither. And if you hurt her, you'll be the only one I ever sock. I'll get a gun and I'll blow your puffed-up brains to kingdom come!''

At that moment Caleb could believe he would do it, too. The boy had so much hatred festering inside that it frightened him.

But then Ben's scrawny throat bobbed and his nostrils flared and he looked away, and Caleb knew those volatile feelings frightened Ben, too.

Caleb knew how to treat and heal Ben's feet. He knew now after seeing the improvement that just this one day had made that he could save his toes. The diagnosis was plain; the treatment within his capability.

But he didn't know how to treat and heal the boy's spirit. The diagnosis was a mere guess. Abuse. Abandonment. The symptoms of his misery had infected his young mind and heart and Caleb had read no book or received any knowledge on how to treat a malady of the mind or soul—emotional wounds.

He'd had similar thoughts about Ellie when he'd first met her. How was it that all three of them could be so wounded? What had happened that had traumatized this entire family?

''Your toes look a lot better tonight,'' he said after several minutes had passed, and Ben once again turned his face to the wall. ''You're a fast healer.''

''Have to be.''

Caleb's hands paused only briefly before he competently wrapped Ben's feet back up, gathered his supplies and stood.

''Good night, Benjamin. I'll send Flynn up now.''

He expected no reply and he received none. He left the room, closing the door behind him. He hated the feeling of helplessness that engulfed him. All he knew to do was earn the boy's trust. And that would take time.

He called Flynn inside, locked up the house and climbed the stairs. Ellie was just coming from his room.

"Nate's been asleep for nearly an hour." She paused in the hallway and glanced toward Caleb's room, which held Nate's cradle.

"Night, Caleb," Flynn said.

"Good night, son," he replied.

"You gonna tuck me in, Ellie?"

"I wouldn't miss it," she replied. Caleb gave her a kind smile and she followed her brother into his room.

She'd already told Ben good-night, and now he lay beneath the sheet, his eyes closed.

Flynn stripped down to his union suit, and Ellie folded his clothes and placed them on one of the shelves in the small wardrobe.

"Caleb's gonna let me ride one of his horses. And he said we could go fishin' sometimes. He knows a real good spot."

Ellie perched on the side of the bed and brushed the near-black hair back from his forehead. "Won't that be something?"

He nodded and yawned.

She'd protected him her whole life until he'd been torn from her and sent to the Heaths'. She'd let him down. But the experience hadn't soured him on people, and for that she was thankful. He trusted Caleb and he liked Caleb's family. He was still dear and innocent and she had years to make it up to him.

Ellie placed her head gently on his chest and treasured having him close while he drifted to sleep. Benjamin, on the other hand, had seen and experienced more—so much more than Flynn. His heart had been hardened and he wore belligerence like armor. But his spirit wasn't broken, not if the fire in his eyes was any indication.

He was a fighter. He had survived the only way he knew how.

Flynn breathed slowly and evenly now. She kissed his cheek, blew out the lamp and left, pulling the door closed behind her.

Caleb stood waiting in the hall.

Apprehension crept through her limbs. They had an arrangement.

"Thank you, Caleb. For everything."

He nodded. "It's going to take some time, you know."

She looked up at him in question.

"For them to adjust to this new life. For them to trust."

"I know."

"We'll just be patient."

He was talking about Benjamin, and they both knew it. Standing there before they went to their separate rooms on their wedding night was more than a little awkward. "Thank you for not getting angry with him."

"I think he's seen enough anger for a while. At least I had the opportunity to see Heath firsthand so that I could understand a little better."

"Yes." Caleb was an understanding man, no doubt about that. But that only went so far. He'd never be able to accept the rest of it.

"Well, rest well." He moved away, toward his room, and she hated the relief she experienced.

Exhausted, Ellie slipped into her nightgown and prepared for bed. She hoped that after all she'd been through that day and all that weighed on her mind, she'd be able to sleep.

In the heat and humidity, her arm itched horribly beneath

the cast. She tried to ignore it and lay on the bed without pulling the sheet over her. Sleep came quickly.

Sounds woke her. A foot scraping. Muttered conversation. The clink of a bottle. Familiar sounds. Ellie prayed her brothers wouldn't waken.

Ellie buried her head beneath her arm and adjusted her bony hip against the inadequate padding between her and the cold floorboards.

A hand clutched her shoulder, and she jerked into alertness, turning to squint into the dimness. A light shone from behind the threadbare blanket that served as a divider between this sleeping area and her mother's. It was always a toss-up whether to use the blanket for warmth or as a pathetic veil of privacy.

Against the thin backdrop, she could see that the figure leaning over her was not her mother, but a man she knew as one of Della Foster's many disgusting nighttime callers.

"What do you want?" she whispered, shrugging his hand from her shoulder.

"Come here. Your mother has taken a fall and I need your help to get her back inside."

Ellie pulled the moth-eaten sweater she wore over her underwear around her and followed him around the blanket, tiptoeing over Ben and Flynn. She paused to see that her mother truly wasn't in the cabin, and stumbled out the door into the night in her stocking feet. "Where is she?"

"Here. Over here."

"I don't see her."

"In here."

A horse and carriage sat a hundred yards from the ramshackle shack that served as her home. In there? Where would her mother have gone with him? She rarely left with anyone. And certainly never with anyone who dressed as

*well as this man did. She wasn't the sort he'd want to be
seen with.*

*She peered into the dark interior of the carriage, a wary
feeling prickling along her spine. Was her mother dead this
time? Or was this some sort of trick? She'd have stayed in
the cabin if she hadn't been afraid he'd wake her brothers
if she refused to follow him. They'd seen and heard enough.*

"I don't see anything."

A hand closed over her neck and squeezed. "Get inside."

"No! No, I—"

"It wasn't a question." He shoved her in forcefully.

*She scrambled to get her balance, but he overpowered
her, knocking her flat on her stomach. The air whooshed
from her lungs and her knee cracked against the wood. One
hand held her fast, the other cupping her buttocks through
her baggy drawers. Panic engulfed her senses.*

*She cried out, but he clamped that hand over her mouth
until she couldn't breathe. She didn't know which was
worse. Maybe this was better. Maybe she'd die.*

*He jerked her over and she clawed at him, blindly reach-
ing for his eyes, his throat. She screamed.*

*A fist met with her jaw and she saw stars, momentarily
stunned, silenced. He tore her underwear, fabric ripping,
cutting her skin.*

*"Stop fighting. I paid good money to be the first and I'm
going to get my money's worth."*

*His hands brought more physical pain than she'd ever
known. She fought them, fought him, tasting blood, tasting
fear. She wasn't strong enough to win against his strength.
She wasn't strong enough to stop him.*

There was no one to help her. And no one who cared.

Ellie thought she managed a scream, but it was a mere
cry of anguish that caught in her constricted throat.

So much pain. So much searing, ripping pain.

A scream finally tore from her throat and the numbing blackness receded. She still had some fight left and she wasn't going to let him do this to her.

She pummeled his bare chest with her fists.

"For God's sake, Ellie, stop fighting me. I'm not going to hurt you."

Her mind snapped instantly awake, thrusting her from the nightmare into reality, and she stared at Caleb, panic still thumping in her chest.

He'd apparently carried a lantern in and placed it on the bureau, and the glow illuminated his bare chest and arms.

She pulled her fists to her own breast, realizing with horror that she'd struck him.

As though he'd been prepared to stop her continued attack, he held her upper arms firmly, but without hurting her.

"Oh, Caleb, I'm sorry," she whispered, her voice hoarse and barely discernible to her own roaring ears. The nightmare was dreadfully familiar and particularly vivid, and she'd thought she'd abandoned it years ago. Obviously seeing the man responsible had resurrected the night terror.

"What could have been so frightening?" he asked, the speculative question in his dark searching eyes. "Whatever happened to you, Ellie?"

"Uh-h-ah!" The fierce snarl came from the doorway, and Ellie caught only a glimpse of Benjamin in his union suit as he flew through the air toward Caleb, a gleaming object in his hand.

Caleb threw up his arm to deflect the blow, and the brass towel holder struck his forearm. Caleb grunted and lunged toward the boy.

"Benjamin, stop it!" Ellie shouted over the grunts and

growls as the two fought and Caleb got hold of the towel rack.

"I told you not to hurt her!" Benjamin's face was red with impotent rage. "I warned you!" He limped in a circle, holding fast to Caleb's bare torso and pounding wherever and whenever he got an opening.

Caleb threw the brass weapon down. "I didn't hurt her. Listen to me for a minute."

"Ben, he didn't hurt me." Ellie got to her knees on the bed as they fell back upon it. She clamped her good arm around her brother's forehead and tried to pull him backward.

"I told you I'd kill you, you son of a bitch!" Ben gasped, his rage making him blind and deaf to their attempts to explain.

Ellie cried in earnest.

Another howl was added to the fray. Flynn stood in the doorway, holding a screaming Nate, and when he saw what was happening, Flynn, too, burst into tears.

Benjamin pulled loose from Ellie's hold and his fists smacked Caleb's bare skin. The two rolled and tumbled off the edge of the bed with an *oof* and a curse.

Ben was crying now, too, and Ellie wanted to stop him and hold him. She crouched on the edge of the bed, her knuckles against her teeth, watching in horror. Since they'd landed, Caleb had rapidly gained the upper hand and swiftly moved so he straddled Benjamin's narrow hips. He caught Ben's fists and held them fast on either side of his head.

Ben tried to buck him off a few times, the veins in his neck straining, his face scarlet.

Ellie fell to her knees above him and cupped his sweaty face in her palms. "Oh, Ben, my sweet, you are so very brave. I love you, you know that, don't you?"

"Pardon me, but this sweet boy just tried to knock my brains loose." Caleb panted, still holding his assailant fast, his hair fallen over one eye.

"Caleb wasn't trying to hurt me," she said, ignoring him and gazing into Ben's blue eyes. "I had the nightmare and I must have screamed. You've heard me do that, so you know how alarming it can be. He came to make sure I was all right."

Benjamin panted, but his struggles to escape had ceased. His bony chest rose and fell. Tears dried on his temples.

Sobs still came from Flynn and Nate in the doorway.

"He didn't hurt me," she said again.

Warily, Ben's eyes moved to Caleb.

Caleb worked to calm his breathing and met the boy's gaze steadily. His arm throbbed from the blow with the towel rack and his knee had cracked against the floor when they'd landed. He'd had better nights.

"Let me go," Benjamin said finally.

"Please," Ellie whispered, beseeching Caleb with her eyes.

He didn't want to go another round with the wiry little wildcat, but neither did he want to humiliate him or disappoint his sister. He released Benjamin's wrists and sat up.

Ellie threw herself on her brother's chest and cried softly against his cotton underwear. His arms came up and one hand smoothed her tangled hair, the other rested on her shoulder.

Confident the worst was over, Caleb lifted away and sat on the floor. He glanced at Flynn and gestured for him to bring the wailing baby.

Flynn nearly ran to hand Nate over, then stood staring from Caleb to his sister and brother, confusion and fear warring on his youthful features.

"Thanks for getting him," Caleb said, holding Nate to his chest and calming him.

"I heard all the yellin' and I heard him cryin'. I didn't know what to do."

"You did the right thing. Why don't you go back to your bed now. Ellie will come and tuck you in."

Flynn nodded and padded out of the room with several backward glances.

I had the nightmare and I must have screamed, she'd said. *You've heard me do that, so you know how alarming it can be.* Caleb pieced all the fragments of information together trying to form an image he could understand. He'd known it was more than Heath's mistreatment that had turned Benjamin sour on people.

And Ellie's jumpiness at being touched had puzzled him several times. She'd been hurt so badly that she had a recurring nightmare about it. Someone had beaten them.

Their mother? Father? At this point he wasn't even sure that he wanted to know. Perhaps it was better that he didn't.

Nate was hot and clammy against his chest, but he'd quieted and his eyes closed. Caleb got to his feet, wincing when his knee popped, and carried the baby back to his cradle.

Nate's eyes opened. Caleb spoke softly, reassuring him, and the infant drifted back to sleep.

Caleb rinsed his face in the tepid water in the bowl on his washstand, blotted his face dry and returned to Ellie's room.

She wasn't there. The sheet lay spilled off the side of the bed, and the brass towel stand still lay on the floor. When he turned to leave, he noticed the broken chair and the door he'd broken in his panic to get to her. The implication slapped him full force. She'd had the chair back wedged beneath the doorknob. Why had she felt that was necessary?

He padded across the hall to the boys' room. The door stood ajar and he peered around it.

In the moonlight that streamed through the open window he made out Flynn's sleeping figure on his bed. On the other bed, Ellie lay behind Benjamin, her fingers threading through his hair. Her whispered words were so soft he couldn't make them out. He backed away, feeling like an outsider in his own home, and made his way down the stairs.

He poured a cold glass of buttermilk from the pitcher in the icebox and drank it on the back stairs. The cat Flynn had mentioned meowed and curled his back along the bottom step. Caleb sat and tipped the glass so the feline could lick the last ounce of milk from a puddle on the wood.

Caleb had barely fallen asleep when Ellie's scream had awakened him. He'd realized immediately that she'd been dreaming and had tried to wake her with a gentle touch on her shoulder.

Her panic and fear at that innocent touch had startled him, and he'd had all he could do to keep her from clawing his eyes out.

Ben's attack on top of that had come out of nowhere.

Caleb set the glass down and lowered his forehead to his palms, his elbows on his knees. He could pick 'em, couldn't he?

The screen creaked behind him and he raised his head to see Ellie drift through the back porch and out into the night in her white nightgown. "Are you all right?"

He moved his gaze to the cat, now licking its paws. "Yeah."

She seated herself on the top step, well away from him,

but close enough that he caught the scent of her hair. ''I am so terribly sorry,'' she said softly.

''Who was it, Ellie?'' he asked into the darkness. ''Who was it that hurt you so badly?''

Chapter Ten

"H-hurt me?" She didn't know where she found the air to speak.

"You. And Ben. Someone hurt you both, made you afraid of people."

Caleb was a compassionate man, and a smart man. It hadn't taken him long to see something very wrong with his new wife and her brothers. Did he already regret making her his wife?

In the kitchen window behind them the sultry breeze sucked the curtains against the screen and released them, a rhythmic rasping.

"Was it your father?" Perfectly logical, a perfect assumption. "Did your father beat you?"

Assuming one had a father and assuming that a father could scar a child, it sounded as good an answer as any. One he would definitely see as dreadful and yet not entirely shameful. "Yes," she replied.

"And Flynn," he said. "You protected him." It wasn't a question.

"Yes." That part was true.

"I can't pretend to know what that was like for you both."

Of course he couldn't. He had doting, well-to-do parents. He'd never had to wonder who his father was. Or where his next meal was coming from.

"Is that what the dream is about? About him hitting you?"

Lies came easier after the first couple hundred. "Yes."

"I'm sorry, Ellie."

"Nothing for you to be sorry for," she replied.

His hand found hers in her lap and he threaded his fingers with hers. She looked at his fingers twined with hers in the moonlight, so much larger, so much stronger. He'd wrestled Ben to the floor and held him fast. Her heart skipped a twittery beat.

"Nobody's going to hurt you again," he said, much as she'd promised her brothers and sounding every bit as sincere. "I understand now why you made me promise not to hit them. I wouldn't have, even if I hadn't promised. You know that, don't you?"

Somewhere inside the reasoning part of her mind she knew that. But who knew what anyone was capable of if they really got mad? Or drunk? People acted entirely different when they were drunk. Promises meant nothing.

He tugged her hand across the space to his trouser-clad knee. "Don't you, Ellie?"

"I—I think so."

He swatted a mosquito on his shoulder, the movement jerking their joined hands and reminding her that he wasn't wearing a shirt. She didn't turn her head.

He used his other hand to stroke her fingers and the sensation made her stomach flutter. Once while waiting tables at the Arcade, she'd seen a man and woman holding hands beneath the linen tablecloth. The intimacy had embarrassed her and she'd looked away.

Now, with Caleb holding her hand, his hard palm feeling

so right against hers, she realized it could be something quite pleasant. Something so gentle and fine it made her heart swell and the corners of her lips tremble.

She allowed herself to glance over at his illuminated profile, the rest of his face cast into dark shadows. He was looking at their clasped hands.

He ran his index finger over the knuckle of her thumb, up to her wrist. With the pad of that finger, he found the sensitive skin on the inside of her wrist and drew lazy circles around that pulse point with his thumb.

Though the night was sultry and her skin damp, shivers ran up Ellie's bare arm. A night owl hooted in the distance.

"You sure smell good," he said, catching her off guard.

"Just castile soap," she said hoarsely.

"I can smell your hair all the way over here."

"You can?"

"Um-hmm."

"I washed it last night."

"Bet it's soft, too."

"Oh, I don't know. It's just hair."

He looked over at her then. "Mind if I smell it up close?"

"I—" She swallowed. "I guess I don't mind."

He leaned toward her, his bare chest rubbing her shoulder because she wore her batiste nightgown without sleeves. Tilting his head, he buried his face in the hair at her neck and inhaled.

Of course that breath had to come out and when it did, the moist warmth fluttered against Ellie's ear and her neck and shoulder. Goose bumps broke out on her flesh. "Yes," he whispered, a soul-deep sound.

Ellie had turned her upper body toward him without thinking. He touched his nose to the skin beneath her ear and she stopped breathing.

He released her hand and brought both palms up to grasp her shoulders gently. The touch of his hands on her skin sent a frisson of alarm through her body, and immediately, she recoiled, bringing her forearms up and forcing his hands away.

"Ellie," he said.

She shook her head and sat stiffly, folding her good arm over the one with the cast and protectively holding them both to her midriff.

"Ellie, there are ways to prevent having a baby. We can take precautions so you wouldn't become pregnant."

Shocked at his train of thought, she scrambled to her feet.

He stood and faced her. "I respect that you don't want children," he said. "Truly I do."

She stared at him. Was that what this tenderness had been about? A plan to get her to his bed? "Then respect that I want no part of sleeping with you, either. We made a deal."

"I thought it was because of the children you didn't want."

"It was. It is. But not completely. You gave your word."

"You refuse to allow me in your bed even if I can promise you won't have a child because of it?"

"That's right. You understood that. I thought I made it clear from the first."

He raised a hand and dropped it. "It's clear."

She let her arms lower and straightened. It was the middle of the night. They'd best get back to their beds. She hurried into the house and up the stairs, noting the listing door and the chair that Caleb had smashed from beneath the knob. A good lot of protection that had been.

She was at his mercy, she realized now. Neither a closed door nor a lock could prevent him from entering this room and taking what he wished from her. Only his word prevented that—only his promise.

Ellie had never placed so much hope in a promise.

He was taking a few days off, Caleb told Ellie the following morning as she stirred oatmeal at the stove.

"Is everything all right?" she asked.

He placed Nate in his high chair. "I just think it would be good for us. As a family."

Ellie's throat got tight at the word.

"Where are the boys?"

"I think they're out back."

Caleb stepped onto the back porch and called through the screen. "You fellas comin' in to eat?"

Benjamin carried in a bucket. He didn't meet Caleb's eyes. "I milked the goat. I'll clean out his lean-to a little later."

"Thank you." Caleb took the bucket as though last night had never happened. "I guess that would be a good chore for you, lookin' after Nate's nanny." He glanced at the boys. "That was a joke. The goat provides Nate's milk and a nanny is a goat as well as someone who takes care of babies."

"Oh." Flynn stood awkwardly just inside the kitchen door behind his brother.

"Where do you want them to eat?" Ellie asked.

"Pick a chair and start in," Caleb replied.

The boys moved to the table and seated themselves, casting Caleb cautious looks.

Ellie spooned oatmeal into bowls and placed one in front of each of them.

Flynn immediately picked up his spoon and dug in, barely taking time to blow on the hot cereal.

Caleb got up and brought a small pitcher of cream from

the icebox. He poured some on his cereal and then got the sugar bowl from the cupboard and liberally sprinkled sugar on top.

The boys watched in fascination.

They'd never had cream or sugar as children. "Should I have put that in the oatmeal as I made it?" She sat.

He gave her a quizzical glance. "No. I like it this way, don't you?"

She nodded.

Caleb's spoon stopped on the way to his mouth and he looked from one sibling to the other. "Something wrong?"

They looked back at their bowls.

"Not a thing," Ellie said, picking up the pitcher, dousing her oatmeal with cream and passing it to Ben with a strong look.

Ben did the same and passed it to Flynn.

The sugar made the rounds next, and then the three of them stirred and tasted. A smile lit Flynn's face. Benjamin promptly cleaned his bowl and sat back.

Caleb finished eating and wiped his lips with his napkin.

All three of them did exactly the same.

He looked from one to the other oddly. Slowly, he stood. "I'm going to get a picnic lunch from the cook at the Side Track Saloon and we're going to go fishing."

"Hot-diggity!" Flynn said, jumping up so fast, he knocked his chair backward with a clatter. He looked at Caleb with alarm and set the chair aright.

Nobody said anything for a minute.

"Wear comfortable clothes that you don't mind getting dirty," Caleb continued, and Flynn released a pent-up breath. "I'll be back shortly. Be ready." He nodded at Benjamin. "You can take care of the lean-to when we get back."

He exited into the hallway, and they could hear the front

door open and close. Nate blinked at Ellie and she fed him the last of his breakfast.

Flynn scurried up the stairs to change.

"What did he say about last night?" Benjamin asked.

"He knows Heath beat you boys. He wanted to know if our pa hit you, too, so I just said yes."

"If we'd had a pa he'd have hit us," he agreed with a nod, obviously understanding her unwillingness to admit it had been their mother and any number of her callers who had struck and starved them.

"He can't find out, Ben," she said in earnest. "We have a home here as long as he doesn't know where we came from."

"I ain't gonna tell him."

"And Flynn?"

"I'll talk to him," Ben answered. "He won't say nothin'. He likes it here."

Ellie placed her hand over her brother's. "I like it here, too."

His blue eyes revealed his confusion. He would never admit to liking anything for fear it would be snatched away from him, but he had to see that this was by far the best situation any of them had ever been within sniffing distance of. He would never spoil it purposely.

Caleb returned as promised, his handsome team pulling a rented wagon, which provided more room for the delicious-smelling covered basket he'd purchased, as well as Nate's basket, Caleb's medical bag and three fishing poles.

The spring wagon still had two seats, so the boys perched on the high rear seat and Ellie sat beside Caleb, Nate on her lap.

Caleb took them in a southwesterly direction along a road that followed the train tracks for a time, then wound along a stream and sloped down to a flat, shady area.

The boys leaped down and Flynn ran off to discover what lay along the banks of the stream. Caleb shook out a couple of Hudson's Bay blankets and spread them on the ground. He pulled a short-handled shovel from beneath a seat just as Flynn returned.

"I'll get the worms." Flynn took the shovel importantly and headed for a shady patch of weeds.

Ellie rested on the blanket and observed them from a distance. Flynn was right there beside Caleb, talking to him, turning his face up and listening. They put their lines in the water and Flynn hunkered down next to him.

Benjamin, on the other hand, situated himself a bit downstream, which in itself wasn't unusual. He probably didn't want his exuberant brother scaring the fish away. But in conjunction with everything else, his isolation—no matter how self-imposed—disturbed Ellie.

In the distance a train clacked by, reminding her she didn't have to ride a railcar to visit her brothers any longer. She vowed she would never take this good fortune for granted. She watched them and relaxed.

Caleb rested his forearms on his knees and answered Flynn's questions. Some of them, like how did the fish get in there in the first place, and where did they sleep, and did they close their eyes when they slept, he either made up answers for or engaged the lad in a game of supposition. He laughed at Flynn's imaginative ideas and, at the boy's urging, removed his shoes and socks.

"Ain't never had nobody but Ben to fish with before," Flynn said, sliding his rear end down the bank until his toes dangled in the water. "An' he makes me be quiet. Don't my yappin' make ya tired?"

"No, but I'll let you know if I need a little quiet one of these times."

"Awright. Ain't never been to a picnic before either. Me

an' Ben ate outside a whole lot at the Heaths', but we didn't know it was a picnic.''

It probably hadn't been, Caleb thought. "It must have been hard for you when your mother died and you got sent there.''

Flynn shrugged his shoulders noncommittally.

"Did they die at the same time?'' He'd never learned what their parents had died of. "A sickness of some sort?''

"Same time as what? Who?''

"Same time as each other. Your mother and father.''

The boy bobbed his pole over the water. "She just died. Didn't have no father.''

"Everyone has a father,'' Caleb disagreed. "You probably just don't remember him if he died a long time ago.''

"Everyone?''

Caleb nodded. "That's where babies come from, a mother and a father.''

"I think it just only takes a ma sometimes,'' he said quite seriously to the Harvard Medical School graduate who sat beside him.

Caleb considered the wisdom of pursuing the subject and decided there was nothing wrong with innocence. He glanced farther downstream, to where Benjamin sat with his pole, and wondered why Flynn couldn't remember his father. Ellie had admittedly protected him from the same abuse she and Ben had received, but he didn't remember the man? Perhaps he chose not to.

"Look at that!'' Flynn cried, jumping up and pointing to the crested bird, bluish in color and flapping its wings in irregular bursts, that dived into the water headfirst and emerged with a fish in its long beak. It flew toward the stand of trees farther upstream, giving them a glimpse of its white-ringed neck and white-feathered belly.

"That was a kingfisher," Caleb told him. "A female by the looks of that reddish brown along her sides."

"Do you think she has a nest with some baby birds up there?"

"Kind of late in the year," he replied. "If she had babies, they're probably grown."

Benjamin was the only one besides the kingfisher who caught any fish. He strung four catfish and left them staked in the shallow water while they ate.

Caleb had purchased fried chicken and cabbage slaw, pickled beets and pickles along with four jars of buttermilk.

Flynn polished off his third chicken leg and rubbed his rounded belly. "'Member that chicken Ben stoled from ol' man Higgins that one time, Ellie? You said that chicken was so old and tough that—"

"Ben *bought* that chicken, Flynn," his sister said.

"No, he didn't, we—"

"Yes, he did. He bought that chicken." She gave him a deliberate glare.

Flynn glanced at Caleb and back to Ellie, then picked at the bones on his plate. "Yeah. He bought that chicken. I guess I forgot."

A silence fell over their small group. Ellie packed up the dishes and remaining food.

A horse and rider caught their attention a few minutes later. J. J. Jenkins rode up on a gray with two white stockings. He wore a hat pulled low over his forehead. "Doc!" he cried, jumping from the animal's back and running toward them.

Caleb walked barefoot to meet him.

"Saw the note on your door and rode out to find ya. The Douglases' daughter is havin' a baby an' Mrs. Douglas don't want Doc Thornton. Her and Tyrone sent me to fetch ya. She said to tell ya that Tyrone took so long to give in that their ain't much time left and her daughter's in a bad way.''

"Let's go," Caleb said, grabbing the poles and the string of fish.

Ellie placed their belongings in the wagon and gathered Nate and her brothers. J.J. rode alongside for a short time, then galloped ahead to tell the Douglases that Caleb was on his way.

"This woman isn't one of your patients?"

"No." Caleb handed her the reins while he pulled on his socks and shoes. "Her husband ran off and left her a while back and I'd heard she'd gone back to live with her folks. They have a ranch this side of my parents'. Tyrone's been pretty vocal with his opinion of doctors who got their education in a lecture hall rather than on a battlefield or as an apprentice." He finished tying his shoe and took back the reins. "His wife and daughter must have really done something to convince him to let me attend her."

Ellie remembered to open Caleb's umbrella and protect Nate from the glaring sun. He got fussy and cried, refusing to fall asleep. Flynn took him and held him until they reached the Douglas ranch. J.J. had staked his horse and sat on a stump in the yard.

Tyrone stepped off the wide porch of the low, rough-wood house and shaded his eyes. "She's in the bedroom."

"Benjamin," Caleb said, grabbing his bag. "Stay off your feet as much as you can."

Ben nodded.

"Flynn, will you keep an eye on Nate here on the porch? Maybe he'll fall asleep in his basket."

"I kin watch 'im," Flynn said. "He likes me."

Caleb turned to Ellie. "Clella might not be much help if she's worked herself into a state. I might need you."

Ellie swallowed her distress at the thought of going in there. Caleb was trusting her to help him.

She nodded and accompanied him into the house. The interior was dim, but roomy and clean. They followed the sound of women's voices to the bedroom.

Ellie didn't want to go in. The sound of the woman's distress was familiar and frightening, but Ellie bolstered her courage and stayed with her husband.

A young woman lay on the bed, her red-gold hair plastered to her forehead and neck, a thin white sheet covering her swollen body.

"Oh, Caleb," Clella Douglas gasped, seeing him and turning to draw him forward. "She's getting so tired, and the baby's not coming!"

"It takes a while to have a baby," Caleb said in his usual calm tone. "Let's have a look at her." He glanced around. "Do you have soap and water ready?"

She shook her head.

"Bring me soap and water and towels. Some more clean sheets, too."

She hurried to do as he'd requested.

"When did the pains start?" he asked the woman on the bed.

"Last night they came and went, but this morning they got worse. I don't think I can bear it." Tears streamed from her eyes.

"Rachel, this is my wife, Ellie."

"Hi," she said. She had blue eyes and a thin face, prettier, Ellie was sure, when she hadn't been crying and laboring.

"I've known Rachel since school," Caleb said, turning back to his patient. "This probably seems a little awkward, does it?"

She shook her head. "I've seen you with animals," Rachel said with a quavering smile. "And you've delivered babies before. Haven't you?"

"I have."

A pain gripped her then, and she straightened her body, grasping the sheets in her fists. Tendons on her neck stood out and sweat beaded on her forehead.

Ellie found herself holding her breath right along with her. The pain passed and Rachel panted.

Rachel's mother returned with a basin and soap, and Caleb washed and dried his hands and instructed Ellie and Clella to do the same. Then he sent Clella for more clean water.

"I'm going to check the baby now," Caleb said gently. "See where he's at. I want you to relax. Ellie, wet a cloth and wash her face and arms. Make her comfortable."

Ellie did as instructed, her fingers trembling. Rachel met her eyes and they shared an unspoken message. Ellie gave her an encouraging smile.

Caleb pulled the sheet down and Rachel's nightgown up and worked his hands over her belly. When a pain came on, he tested the contracting muscles and spoke soothingly.

Ellie held her hand and rubbed her forehead with the damp cloth.

"Now I'm going to check for his head," Caleb said, pulling the sheet back up over her belly and raising it from the bottom half of her body. He instructed her to raise her knees and look at Ellie.

Ellie gazed into her blue eyes, sharing her uncertainty and confusion. She wondered where this girl's husband had gone and how she would raise a child without him. Her parents seemed like good people—concerned and loving.

"I think he might need a little more help getting into the right position," Caleb said at last. "This will go a lot easier if we can get his face to your spine instead of the other way around. Before the next pain, Rachel, I want you to turn over and get on your hands and knees.''

''What?'' Clella cried from the doorway.

''That will give him more room to turn,'' Caleb went on as though she hadn't spoken. ''Help her, Ellie.''

Ellie did, and they got Rachel on her hands and knees before the next pain. Her arms trembled and Caleb spoke soothingly. Ellie wet the cloth and bathed her face.

''Just a few more pains should do it,'' Caleb encouraged.

''I can't,'' the girl cried. ''I'm too tired.''

''I know you're tired,'' he replied. ''And you can rest all you want after you get this baby out. You're the only one who can do this.''

''Oh, that John Allen!'' she shouted. ''If he was here I'd scratch his eyes out!'' Another pain came and went, and she bawled. ''He let me think he loved me and that we were going to have a wonderful life together. Now look at me! I'm dying and he's off somewhere doing God knows what!''

''You're not dying,'' Caleb corrected with assurance. ''But you have permission to cuss him good if it makes you feel any better.''

''John Allen's a dirty rotten weasel,'' she panted.

''Weasel's strong,'' Caleb said, feeling the shape of her belly. ''But I don't think it'll hurt his feelings.''

''He's a low-down good-for-nothing pus bag!'' she screamed.

''That's more like it. Help her out, Ellie.''

Ellie whispered a few curses in Rachel's ear and Rachel half sobbed, half laughed them out. Clella gasped and clutched her hands to her chest.

Rachel's next string of curses ended with a deep groan.

''Okay, Rachel, turn back over. Help her, Ellie.''

Ellie helped her maneuver her girth until she was once again on her back.

"Next one you're gonna hold your breath and push," he instructed.

"I can't."

"Yes, you can."

"No, I can't. I can't do this."

"You can do it," Ellie chimed in. Glad to be there for this frightened girl, she climbed onto the bed and supported Rachel's upper body with hers. Having a doctor and another woman present had to make this less frightening. "I'm gonna hold you up and you're going to push."

Rachel sobbed.

A pain gripped her and Ellie propped Rachel's head and shoulders. "Push!"

Rachel pushed until her body quivered.

"Easy now," Caleb said, his attention directed on the emerging baby. "Wait for the next one."

Rachel and Ellie's combined sweat stuck their cheeks together.

"Okay," Caleb said authoritatively. "Push!"

After two more contractions, Caleb held a slick, pink infant in his strong hands. "It's a boy."

Chapter Eleven

After checking him over, clearing his mouth and nose and cutting the cord, he handed the squalling infant to Clella. Tears streaking her face, she washed him while Caleb finished with Rachel. "Rachel, honey, he's beautiful," she said to her daughter. "He looks like you did when you were born."

Finally, Rachel got to cradle her newborn son. "Oh, he's just perfect," she said in awe.

"That he is." Caleb dried his hands on a towel, a tender expression on his face. Perhaps he was thinking of his own son's birth. Ellie couldn't even imagine how horrible it must have been for him to lose his young, beautiful wife.

This experience had dredged up memories for her, too. She stared at the baby, grief knotting her chest. Rachel could forget the difficulty of giving birth now that she had a precious son to hold and love. The milk that came to her breasts wouldn't have to pain her and dry up without a child to ever suckle. Her body would heal and she would watch her baby grow. Even without a man, she still had this baby. And the Douglases would help her care for it.

This was what it was like when a baby was loved and accepted, when a baby had a family.

Ellie didn't resent Rachel or her baby. She was sorry that John Allen was a low-down, good-for-nothing pus bag, but this family would welcome and raise this new life with love.

The sense of emptiness she'd endured her entire life had been reawakened with Winston's appearance, then, by comparing Caleb's family to her needy brothers, by meeting Lucy, and now by this emotionally draining experience. The horror of giving birth alone and in fear of what would happen if her mother got her hands on her baby had never been far from the surface.

What had become of her own child? It became clear to her, as Caleb packed his things and Tyrone came in to meet his grandson, that she would never know if the little girl she'd given away was loved and provided for. And because of that she would never have any peace.

Heart aching, she slipped from the room. J.J. and Benjamin were seated at the end of the porch and Flynn had found a long-haired collie who retrieved sticks. Flynn laughed and tugged one away, throwing it as far as he could. Ears flopping, the dog loped after it.

"Is she okay?" J.J. asked.

"She's fine. And so's the baby."

"Good." He stood. "I'd better go on home. My ma was sick with a fever this mornin'."

"Maybe Caleb should come check on her," Ellie suggested.

He looked at her as if the idea had never occurred to him. "Would he?"

"Of course he will. I'll let him know."

J.J. mounted the gray horse, waved to Benjamin and rode off.

Ben glanced up at her. "J.J. says there's lots of older

boys in school on account of all the time they miss during plantin' and hayin' and roundup.''

''Are you thinking it won't be so bad, then?'' She sat in a weathered rocker.

''Maybe.''

A few minutes later he added, ''J.J. said he'd even help me if I needed some extra studyin' to catch up.''

''I think that's a fine idea,'' she replied, not wanting to show too much excitement and scare him off the idea. He already knew how she felt about it and how badly she wanted him to go.

''Watch, Ellie!'' Flynn got her attention and ran in a circle with the collie nipping at his trouser legs. He laughed and stopped to pat the dog's head.

Ellie smiled and talked with Benjamin, but her thoughts turned back and tallied the events that had occurred over the past weeks. Those reminders renewed the uncertainty she couldn't shake. She'd always been sure she'd done the right thing regarding the child she'd brought into this world. Always.

But now her heart needed some proof of that. And that was impossible. Proving it would mean losing everything she'd gained for herself and her brothers. They were finally experiencing the first stability they'd ever known and she couldn't risk that. She wouldn't. Not now. Not ever.

Ellie told Caleb about J.J.'s mother, Kate, and after dropping off Ellie and the boys at the house, he left to pay the Jenkinses a call.

Examining the feverish woman, he found blotches on her abdomen. She coughed roughly and covered her lips with a handkerchief.

He didn't like her symptoms. They could point to any number of things, and none of them was good. But he hadn't seen enough actual cases himself to be certain. "Have you vomited?" he asked.

She nodded.

Dread wound up his spine, and he looked inside her mouth, finding her tongue rough and red. "Have you been around anyone else with these symptoms?"

"My sister's children have been sick," she replied. "Is it bad?"

He didn't want to scare her—or anyone—but he needed to make a swift diagnosis and do what he could do prevent further spread. "Who else have you been in contact with?"

"My family."

"Where have you gone?"

"The mercantile. My sister's. That's about it."

"Which mercantile?"

She told him. "What do you think it is?"

"I'm going to have Doc Thornton come see you because he has a lot more experience than I do. Meanwhile, I don't want anyone else to come into this house. I'm going to examine your son and husband and order them to stay in the barn for the time being."

She looked at him curiously, but didn't question his judgment. "All right."

"You just rest and don't worry. We will decide on a treatment and get you well just as soon as we can."

Caleb washed thoroughly before going outside. "J.J., come here." He examined the boy, finding no signs of illness. "Have you been coughing?"

"No."

"I want you to go find Doc Thornton and bring him out here. Don't get close to anyone. Stay as far away from people as you can. You might be contagious."

"I feel fine, Doc."

"I know you do. Just do as I say. It's very important."

"Okay."

"Then I want you to go to your mom's sister's. Tell her to bring her sick children over here so we can keep them all together."

"Okay, Doc." J.J. rode off.

Caleb sponged Kate's feverish brow while he waited for J.J. to locate the older doctor. He prayed the man hadn't passed out down at the Side Track and been hauled home the night before. Experience was still the best teacher, and Doc had seen and treated more people in his lifetime than Caleb had ever met. Getting his opinion might make the difference in saving lives.

Doc Thornton smelled of cigars, but he wasn't staggering or reeking of stale whiskey when he entered the Jenkins house.

He looked Kate over, checking her neck and underarms, then urged Caleb out of the bedroom. Caleb didn't like the look of dread in his bleary eyes. "Scarlet fever," he said.

A mixture of dread and relief swept through Caleb. Though many times fatal in adults, scarlet fever caused far fewer casualties than smallpox. And he knew if the complications could be prevented, they stood a much better chance of saving these patients' lives.

"We have to quarantine everyone who's been exposed," Caleb said with certainty, thinking ahead.

"This ain't diphtheria or typhoid," the old Doc said with a harrumph.

"It's contagious, all the same. And you have to wash your hands before and after every patient you touch."

"Horse dung," the huge-bellied man replied. "I've been doctoring since before you were born, and no wet-behind-the-ears college boy is going to tell me how to treat patients."

"I know you have, sir," Caleb replied. "And I have

great respect for your experience. That's why I asked you to come. But with all due respect, medical discoveries over the past decade have enlightened our profession to the spread of disease through germs. When quarantine and cleanliness are incorporated with the antitoxin, the results are far more promising.''

Doc picked his front teeth with his thumbnail and Caleb waited for him to vocalize his thoughts.

When he didn't speak, Caleb went on. ''What do we have to lose? If I'm wrong, all we can say is I was wrong. I'll concede. But if I'm right, we'll stop this from spreading and save lives.''

''There ain't no stopping this once it sweeps a town,'' Doc said fatalistically. ''I seen whole families die back in the forties.''

''We can prevent that.''

Doc waddled to the screen door.

''If I'm wrong, some of them will die anyway,'' Caleb said, hating the words and the fact. ''But if I'm right we'll save some lives. That doesn't leave me much choice.''

The man stared out across the dusty expanse of yard.

Caleb walked up behind him. ''People trust you. They don't trust me. If you tell them to do it this way, they'll listen. I'm asking for your help. Please.''

Doc turned and their eyes met. His bleary expression was tired, but quiescent. ''I passed my prime a long time ago. My relationship with the bottle ain't no secret. But you're right, some of the people still trust me. I might not trust you, and I might not like it, but you're the future of this town....'' He turned to glance across the landscape once again, then turned back. ''Unless you give up.''

''I won't give up,'' Caleb said, more certain than he'd ever been.

''Didn't figure you would. Okay.'' He walked over to

the basin of water on the kitchen table. "We'll do it your way."

His cooperation eased Caleb's mind and gave him new confidence and hope. With Doc's support, they'd be able to prevent a rampant spread of sickness. "Okay. First we figure out everyone Kate has been around and we quarantine them. We should quarantine anyone J.J. was in contact with, too, since he's been exposed. Lord, that's going to be a list." He thought of the Douglas family he'd just left and that new baby, and a sinking feeling dipped in his chest.

His own family, he realized with a start. J.J. had been with the boys all afternoon. Suddenly all he wanted to do was go to his family and assure himself they were safe. The threat of the disease was real. "The sooner we get this going, the better. I'll go out to the Douglas ranch myself—then to my family. Stay here and treat Kate's sister and her kids when they arrive. I'll be back."

Caleb hit the door at a run.

Ellie knew the situation was more serious than Caleb let on. He didn't want to frighten them, but Ellie felt his urgency all the same. They were to stay in the house. Groceries and ice would be delivered and left on the porch.

"Promise me you'll stay right here," he said, placing his hand on her arm as they stood on the front porch away from the eyes and ears of the children.

"I promise," she said. "You don't have to worry about them. I'll take care of them."

"And you won't let anyone in the house. The threat works two ways. They could make you sick, or you could make them sick."

"I won't let anyone in the house."

He took his hand away.

"I wouldn't leave you if I didn't have to." His warm brown eyes held so much regret and concern.

"Your patients need you," she said, wanting to set his mind at ease so he'd be comfortable leaving them and able to concentrate on his work. "This is why you went to the university. You can help them."

He nodded, a less than confident gesture.

Ellie surprised herself by placing her hand on his shirt-sleeve and feeling the strength of his upper arm through the warm fabric. "You're a good doctor. You have the knowledge and the ability to heal people."

"God does the healing, Ellie. I just administer the treatments."

"Then go do your job. We'll be waiting for you."

He looked into her eyes, and she knew there must have been something more she could have said or done, but she was at a loss to know what.

"Thank you, Ellie," he said softly.

She smiled, thinking how silly it was for him to thank her when she owed him everything.

He leaned down then, taking her chin on his forefinger and raising her face to his, and touched his lips to hers in a sweet, warm melding of damp flesh and unspoken feelings.

Ellie was so surprised, she didn't move, didn't breathe, didn't do anything but register the feel of his mouth on hers, the scent of his hair and his damp shirt, and the subtle movement of his biceps beneath the fingers she still rested on his arm.

Slowly he moved back, breaking the contact, his gaze touching her lips and her hair, and she realized she'd wrapped her fingers around his arm.

She released him immediately.

He smiled.

She blushed in confusion.

He descended the stairs, placed his supplies in the buggy and climbed up to take the reins.

Ellie's stomach quivered with a new and not unpleasant sensation of longing and anticipation, tempered by wariness. She placed her hand on her belly, then raised it to wave.

He drove the team down the street and away.

Long after he'd gone she remembered the gentle touch of his lips against hers and pondered the implication of that brief contact. The kiss was outside her realm of experience and understanding. It had been sweet and tender, but not comfortable like kissing one of her brothers.

If he'd meant to comfort her, he'd failed. If he'd meant to distract her, he'd succeeded. Her thoughts took a whole new direction.

She fed the three boys, read to them and allowed Benjamin and Flynn to sit on the back stairs and play with the cat who'd made himself at home under the porch.

It grew late. The boys went to bed. Ellie put away a few wedding gifts and hung the exquisitely embroidered cardinal sampler that Miss Shaw had sent. She sat at Caleb's desk and wrote a few notes of thanks, then tried to concentrate on one of Caleb's books.

Finally, looking weary, he arrived home late.

"Are you hungry?"

He shook his head. "Just tired."

She carried the water she'd kept warm for him to his room and poured it into the basin on his washstand. He'd already lit a lamp. "Is there anything I can get you?"

He shook his head and sat on the edge of the bed.

She hurried to help him remove his boots. Setting them aside, she looked up to find him studying her.

She thought of the kiss earlier that day and grew uncomfortable with his gaze. "I've taken Nate's cradle to my room for now. I hope that's all right."

"It's thoughtful of you. Is he all right? Are all of them all right?"

"They're fine." She stood and walked to the door. "Good night."

"'Night, Ellie."

She closed the door behind her and walked to her room. She gazed down at the sleeping baby, then turned and changed into her nightgown.

She slept fitfully, hearing Caleb in the hall while it was still dark outside. She dressed and hurried down the stairs.

"You're going to eat breakfast before you leave," she said. "I'll have some coffee ready in a few minutes."

He opened the back door and stepped out onto the porch, standing and peering into the early-morning darkness. Crickets chanted.

The coffee perked and Ellie poured him a cup and placed it on the table. He sat and spooned a little sugar in, stirring. "It's been touch and go with one of J.J.'s nieces," he said. "She seemed better yesterday, but then she took a turn for the worse. Doc Thornton stayed with her last night."

"I'm glad you came home to sleep," she said. "You have to take care of yourself in order to be of help to others."

"I know. But it's hard to leave them when they're so frightened."

A knock sounded on the front door. Caleb got up and entered the hall. Ellie followed.

He opened the door a crack. "It's Luke Swensen, the grocer," he said to Ellie, dread lacing his tone. He spoke through the opening between the door and the jamb. "Move back into the yard."

"I need to tell you—" the man called.

"Move back, then tell me."

Boots sounded on the wooden stairs. "My wife is sick."

"Stay in the house with her," Caleb ordered. "Don't open your store today. I should have had you close it yesterday when I knew Kate Jenkins had been there."

"I have to open my store. All my customers will go over to—"

"You've been exposed, Luke. Everyone who comes in contact with you now could catch the fever your wife has."

"I'm not sick. Are you going to come see her or not?"

"I'm coming. And you're not opening your store. Go straight home and I'll be right there."

The man moved away with a curse.

"I have to run over to my office for fresh supplies. I need to make an order at the druggist's, too."

She untied her apron. "I'm going to help."

"No, Ellie—"

"I am. I've already been around J.J.—and you."

She read the regret in his eyes. He was trying so hard. With all the people he had to help, he wanted to protect her at the same time. The knowledge did her heart good.

"You can't do everything," she went on. "J.J. normally takes care of your horses, so that's added work. You need help, and I'm the logical one to do it."

His shoulders slumped with resignation, and it seemed the most natural thing in the world to reach over and touch his arm.

"Cut this cast from my arm and then give me a list for the druggist."

"I…"

"I've worn it the length of time you ordered. My arm is fine and the cast is a nuisance."

He nodded.

"And tell me how to get to the Swensens'. I'll get the

boys up and tell them they're staying with Nate today. They'll do fine.''

"I'll take a horse and leave the buggy for you at the livery,'' he said, and covered her hand on his arm with his own. "Thank you, Ellie.''

The touches were natural for him. He touched people every day. But the episodes were foreign and disturbing for her. She wasn't used to being touched in a wholesome or pleasant manner, and she didn't know how to respond.

"Well,'' she said, "how do we do this?''

They went back to the kitchen, where he unwrapped a saw from his bag and cut the cast from her arm with care. A sharp pain stabbed through the limb as he pulled the pieces of the cast away. She winced.

"It's normal for it to hurt a minute when the bone loses that familiar support,'' he said.

She stared at the flaking white skin with distaste. It didn't even look like her own arm.

"It'll peel and grow new skin,'' he assured her. "Just use good judgment and don't lift heavy things or try to do too much too soon.'' He wrote a list, then gave her directions and hurried out into the humid early-morning air.

She watched him walk in the direction of the livery, and finally pulled herself back inside to start her day. By the time she fixed her hair and gave the boys instructions for the day, the sun was up. She hurried to the livery, where Caleb had left the horse and buggy at the ready. She placed Caleb's order at the druggist, carried the supplies and packed them in the waiting vehicle.

She found the Swensen home and drew the horse to a halt in the side yard.

Mrs. Swensen was a plump young woman, and her reddish complexion looked so natural, Ellie had to wonder whether or not the fever had caused it. The woman accepted

Caleb's treatment and advice pleasantly, however, and even calmed down her husband, who still wanted to open his store.

Caleb informed Luke how to care for his wife, admonished him to wash his hands often and he and Ellie washed and left the house.

"If only we could get more people to understand the importance of avoiding contact," he said with a shake of his head.

"What if we print flyers and distribute them?" she said, thinking aloud.

"Or buy an ad in the newspaper," Caleb replied. "You're a genius!" He tied one horse to the back of the buggy and prodded the other to pull them toward the newspaper office.

Caleb conducted his business from the doorway and asked to be billed.

He headed for the Jenkins house. "They all think I'm a quack."

She looked over at his troubled expression. "I don't."

His weary dark eyes displayed appreciation, and he gave her a smile that was worth more than words could say. "Thanks."

She tucked this tenuous new affinity away in her heart and concentrated on helping him.

Kate Jenkins showed considerable improvement and was able to sip some broth that Ellie had made while Kate's exhausted sister slept. Doc Thornton went home to grab his turn at sleep. Caleb sponged the little girl with cool water, listened to her heart and sat at her side.

She was about Lucy's age, thinner, with two brown braids that lay against the sheet. She cried in her delirium, sometimes calling for her mother, but Caleb spoke softly to her, changing the cloth on her perspiring forehead and calming her.

The child's feeble grasp on life frightened both of them, but Caleb behaved like a professional. Ellie tried to follow his example and stay calm and confident, but inside she was quaking. "What's her name?" she asked, perching on a chair beside him.

"They call her Suzanne." He lifted the girl's tiny wrist and felt her pulse.

How did he do it? Ellie wondered. He cared about these people. He'd known Kate, maybe most of them, since his childhood. But then Caleb cared as much about strangers as he did about friends. He'd used the same compassion and tenderness with her when she'd broken her arm. He was even kind to Benjamin, who'd been nothing but hostile since their first encounter.

Caleb gave so much of himself.

Ellie admired Caleb Chaney with a reverence that went beyond appreciation or respect. Watching him in this profession he'd been called to affected her deeply. Knowing she was married to him astounded her.

If only, she thought, composing her feelings and moving to heat more water.

If only she deserved to be his wife.

Or his friend.

By the time Doc Thornton returned late that afternoon, J.J. had a cough and a sore throat. Ellie put him to bed on a pile of blankets and Caleb gave him the antitoxin.

They stayed as late as they dared, but Caleb needed to rest. They arrived home late, spoke with Benjamin and Flynn and checked on Nate. They ate a cold supper, then went to their separate bedrooms. Ellie smoothed glycerin into the skin of her itching, aching arm and climbed into bed.

Some time later she awoke to the ominous sound of coughing. She leaped from her bed and paused in the hallway. The sound came again—from the boys' room. Ellie's heart filled with terror and she turned and ran down the hall. She burst into Caleb's room, the worst possible thoughts tumbling through her sleep-drugged head. Caleb sat up, his hair tousled in the moonlight shining through the window. "What's wrong?"

"One of the boys is sick!"

He stood and grabbed his trousers, tugging them on and hurrying after Ellie. She lit a lamp with trembling fingers.

It was Flynn. He lay with his covers tossed off, his head and chest burning with fever.

"Oh, God," Ellie said on a sob, helplessly wringing her hands as she stared at his flushed face.

"Go get water," Caleb instructed calmly. "You know what to do."

Benjamin sat and rubbed his eyes. "What's wrong?"

"It's going to be all right," Caleb said to him. "Do you have a sore throat or a cough, Ben?"

"No."

"I'm going to give you the antitoxin anyway, just to be safe. You too, Ellie." A concerned expression came over his sleep-lined face. "Nate will have to take it, too, but I'm not sure about the dosage. Go get the water, Ellie."

Her chest constricted with this new and urgent fear for her own family, and she bolted away to do his bidding. She would fly into a million pieces if Caleb weren't so calm and efficient. He knew what to do. He would take care of them. She had to stay calm and assist him. He was as tired as she—probably more.

After filling a basin and a kettle, she carried a bucketful of water and some cloths to Caleb.

"I don't feel good, Ellie," Flynn said. The skin around

his mouth was pale compared to the rest of his flushed face and she recognized it as the way Kate and her niece had looked.

Swallowing the panic that threatened to consume her, she brushed his hair from his forehead. "I know you don't, sweetheart. Caleb is going to take care of you and you're going to be fine."

She believed it. She did.

A wail carried down the hall. Torn between staying with Flynn and responding to the baby's cries, she assured Flynn she'd be right back and hurried to tend to Nate. "Hush now, little one. Did we wake you?"

She reached to change his wet flannel and her hand met the scorching skin of his belly. She touched his chest, placed her fingers on his head. He was burning up with fever.

A little sob escaped her throat. Not him, too!

Picking him up, she ran down the hallway and carried him into the boys' bedroom. "Caleb. Nate has the fever, too."

She couldn't hide the desperation in her voice.

He turned to her, masking his feelings behind his efficient manner. "Benjamin," he said softly, "will you please bring Nate's cradle in here? You can go sleep on my bed."

Dressed in his knee-length union suit, Ben got up and carried back the wooden cradle. "I can't sleep now. I'd rather help."

Touched, Ellie exchanged a look with Caleb. Benjamin had been exposed as directly as the rest of them. Either he'd get the disease or he wouldn't. He wanted to help and they certainly needed the extra hands. He seemed so grown-up all of a sudden. "All right," Caleb said. "You can help with the water. It's not good for Ellie to overuse that arm."

"I'll pump and carry it from now on, Ellie."

Throat tight, she nodded and placed Nate in the cradle, tearfully stripping his clothing away. His small plump body was covered in patches of a red angry rash. His hoarse cry broke her heart. The very real threat of losing one of her loved ones to this dreadful sickness tied her insides in knots.

Fevers and sicknesses like this could leave all kinds of disabilities behind, even when the patients survived. She'd heard of survivors who were deaf. Caleb certainly knew all this, too, but he worked without adding fear to her growing anxiety.

For two days they fought the fever. Caleb left only to check on Mrs. Swensen and the Jenkins family, bringing back the encouraging news that Kate had fully recovered. Suzanne had improved, but J.J. was still down with the fever.

Flynn's difficulty breathing frightened Ellie. He struggled for breath and his eyes widened with the terror of getting no air into his lungs. She could only hold him, wash his scorching hot body and pray. His rash went away, as did Nate's, but the fever and difficulty breathing remained.

Exhausted, frightened, she sat at Flynn's side. Nate had fallen asleep and seemed to be resting comfortably for the first time in days. Ellie picked up Flynn's hot, dry hand and willed healing into him with every fiber of her being.

She couldn't lose this dear, loving boy who'd never known comfort or stability, but who deserved them as much as anyone. It was unthinkable to be faced with the devastating possibility of his death, especially now when the promise of all those things was within his grasp.

She remembered then what Caleb had said about God doing the healing. She'd never had much confidence in a God doing anything to help her out, but Caleb seemed sure.

Flynn was young and innocent and deserved a chance. Surely his life wouldn't end like this when he'd only begun to see the better side of life.

"My feet are cold," Flynn said.

Ellie glanced to where his feet lay beneath the sheet.

"Gonna get some boots," he said. "A pair like was in the store window on Fifth Street. Ellie's selling lots o' cigars tonight though. She's gonna sell enough to buy me a pair o' boots."

He was delirious. Ellie glanced at Caleb where he lay dozing on Benjamin's bed. And then she offered up a silent prayer to the God Caleb set such store by. Maybe some of Caleb's favor had rubbed off on her.

She'd lived through things no one should have to. She'd survived any way she could. But she didn't think she could live through losing one of her brothers.

Dread and exhaustion clawed at Ellie's dry throat. She needed a drink of water. She filled the cup Caleb had used for coffee and drank water from the pitcher Ben kept full.

She was so tired, and the night was so hot. If she could only sleep a little, she'd feel better, but Caleb needed his rest and she had to keep Flynn and Nate cool.

She rinsed out a cloth and wet her brother's skin once again. It was possible he felt a little cooler this time.

Her head hurt terribly and she placed the rag against her own forehead for a moment, closing her eyes.

"Ellie?" Caleb spoke to her as though through a closed door. She had no idea how much time had passed or where she was. She opened her eyes and the dim light of the lantern made her head hurt. She squinted and tried to swallow, but her throat was on fire.

"Ellie," he said again, and this time his voice was so close to her ear it created shivers along her spine. Her whole body trembled. She did love his voice.

She loved those gentle words and the concern in his eyes. She loved the way he had of setting people at ease and taking control of a situation. She loved the way he looked at her with that little tilt to his lips when she said something that amused him.

She loved the way he made her feel when he stood close or when he turned those dark eyes on her. She loved the way he smelled, like freshly pressed linen and soap and man.

Yes. She loved Caleb.

Chapter Twelve

The dream came again that night...and the next...and Ellie didn't have the strength to wake herself from the feverish nightmare. The hands confused her.

The hands had always hurt. But in some of the dreams the hands were gentle. The unexpected change was confusing. One moment the voice was taunting, full of spite, and the hands tortured her body. The next moment the voice was soothing and made her want to flutter her eyes open; the hands calmed and cooled.

Ellie's head pounded with the chaos, the tumbling push-pull of the incessantly changing scenario.

She cried.

She slept.

She begged for mercy.

Caleb had thought he'd lived through the worst when Flynn and Nate took ill with the fever. All he'd wanted to do was grab up his son and hold him tightly, and he'd had to fight that panicky desire with steely determination. Flynn needed him, too, as well as so many others. He had to ignore his doubts and all the possibilities that tormented him and concentrate on doing everything in his power to help them recover.

He knew just what lengths this disease could go to. Even patients who lived could be deaf or have lung damage. Caleb had done his best to prevent its spread and save lives. He'd preached sterilization and rational thinking. Now all that fine theory and practice was being tested on his own family, and if he was wrong, he had a lot more at risk.

With little or no rest for Caleb, the days passed in a blur. When Nate and Flynn showed improvement, he thought maybe, just maybe, they'd seen light at the end of the tunnel. Nate's fever lifted first, and then Flynn's. The boys rested comfortably, breathed easily and still had their hearing.

Caleb didn't even have time to be grateful.

He should have been prepared for Ellie to fall ill. He had been prepared for more patients. He was a doctor, not a fool.

Ellie was strong. She was as afraid as anyone, but she hadn't given in to her fear. She'd been his right hand through the worst of the crisis. Now she lay helpless and suffering, and he was the only one to help her. He couldn't give in to his fear, either.

Caleb ignored the terror that welled inside him and relied on his instincts and training.

Benjamin sat in the hall outside her room, his knees pulled up to his chest, his head on his fists. He'd pumped and carried so much water, Caleb had had to make him stop. As well as caring for Flynn, he had taken over all the routine tasks where Nate was concerned, feeding the baby and changing his flannels. He'd been more help than Caleb could have hoped for from one so young.

But now that the younger ones slept and chores were

taken care of, Benjamin held a lone vigil outside Ellie's room. Caleb suspected he'd fallen asleep.

Ellie tossed her head on the pillow. Her fever had risen and her clothing was soaked. He should have had Ben help him with it, but he didn't want to frighten him any worse or embarrass the lad.

"Forgive me, Ellie." He unbuttoned her wrinkled shirt-waist and sat her forward to remove it. Her skirt and stockings followed. He'd been much more successful in bringing fevers down when he'd had the patient's upper body stripped and had bathed them often, so he apologized again and removed Ellie's chemise. She was a patient, he was a doctor. He wouldn't ogle her just because she was his wife—a wife whose body was still a mystery to him.

He soaked a cloth, rinsed it and ran it across the skin of her face and neck and arms. He bathed her shoulders and turned her on her side to wet her back and tuck a dry sheet beneath her.

"You'll be doing this often," he told himself aloud, "so get used to it." He turned her back over, lowered the sheet and ran the cloth over her upper chest, trying to see her as merely a patient. Her white skin was flushed in the lantern light, her breasts delicate and lovely.

It was silly for him to feel so guilty for noticing; he was her husband after all. He wished with all his heart that he was seeing her body for the first time under different circumstances. He gave up and filled his eyes with the exquisite sight of her, her enchanting brow and nose, the lips that he knew were sweet, the sweep of her dark lashes, down to the graceful column of her neck and her feminine collarbone and shoulders.

Her breasts rose and fell with her labored breathing, and his gaze moved to the rosy-tipped mounds. A silvery line caught his attention and he frowned, wondering. He looked more closely, though he'd told himself he wouldn't, and found a few more of the nearly invisible streaks.

Startled at what they implied, he pulled the sheet to her hips and opened the front of her drawers. Several pinkish scars lined her abdomen.

Shock numbed his thinking.

He sat on the edge of her bed in a state of weary astonishment.

Had Ellie given birth to a baby?

The question ate a ragged hole in his heart. Could his wife, this wife he'd never touched, have given birth to a child? Had some man, other than him, feasted his eyes upon her body? Had he touched her and made love to her and given her a child?

A feeling he'd never experienced clamped his insides in a knot. If so, where was this man now?

He washed her again, seeing her through different eyes, then pulled the sheet up over her and tossed her damp clothing in a pile. Anger and betrayal pressed in, though he didn't want to acknowledge them.

Why did the possibility bother him so? She hadn't lied about it—he'd never asked. He didn't even know if she'd been married before. Had she been married? Or had she simply made a mistake and allowed some scoundrel to seduce her? If she'd had a child, what had become of him?

She'd been so fervent about not wanting a baby—about not wanting to sleep with him. That refusal hurt worse than ever now. Why had she spurned him? Had she loved someone and didn't want to settle for less?

His mind reeled, trying to make sense of what he feared had happened. But when? *Flynn?* She didn't look old enough to have given birth to Flynn.

She moaned in her fever-induced sleep and Caleb smoothed her damp hair away from her forehead. When had she become so lovely to him? When had the secrets of her past taken on such importance?

It mattered because she was his wife now, and he'd married her with every intention of being faithful and spending the rest of his life with her. It mattered because the feelings he'd had for his first wife didn't compare to those he had for Ellie, and he'd begun to hope.

"It's all right, Ellie," he said softly. "Just rest."

She coughed, and he spooned a little water between her lips to soothe her throat.

"There's a pie cooling on the back porch," she said in her delirium. "Cover it so the flies don't get it."

He smoothed glycerin into her cracked lips. "I'll cover it."

"Is the door locked?"

"It's locked."

She relaxed against the pillow. "Somebody wash that oatmeal out of Nate's hair. Laura will think I'm not a fit mother."

Not a fit mother. Perhaps her baby had died. Maybe that's why she couldn't bear to have another, if she feared the same would happen. The desperate way she had looked at Rachel's newborn baby took on a whole new meaning. Caleb had been caught in the emotion of the moment, in the beauty of the miracle of life. He'd assumed Ellie had felt the same.

Had she watched that birth through the eyes of someone who'd done it herself—and lost a baby?

Through that night and the following day, Caleb bathed Ellie's skin and spooned antitoxin between her lips. Her shakes and nightmares were worse than any he'd seen. Sometimes she fought him when he tried to calm her, other times she cried brokenheartedly, pleading with him not to hurt her. Even after her rash had passed, the fever persisted.

Only in the deepest moments of fatigue did he doubt his ability to save her. Flynn and Nate had improved and Ben still showed no signs of contracting the illness. The other patients had recovered, even Suzanne, who'd had a case of fever nearly as bad as Ellie's.

His knowledge and his intuition had paid off.

In those cases, that irritating voice inside his head taunted. He'd assisted a birth, too, but no complications had arisen for him to falter over. Not like when his wife had died. He hadn't been able to save *her.*

Winston Parker had asked if Caleb planned to kill another wife. Throughout another endless day, Caleb studied Ellie's delicate profile, the fluttering pulse at the base of her throat, seeing her as a woman who'd become important to him. Damn Winston for putting those torturous thoughts in his head!

He doubled his efforts to reduce her fever.

The bell rang late in the evening, and Ben brought Doc Thornton upstairs.

"How's the wife?" the old man asked. Hearing someone else call Ellie his wife made Caleb's fears all the more real.

"Her fever's no better." He revealed her feet and showed Doc that the soles were peeling. "Did they all do this?"

Doc nodded. "All who had the fever bad. The little girl lost whole pieces of skin from her fingers."

"No one has died?"

Doc shook his head. "No one."

Caleb sighed with relief.

"And we've only had one other case. Clive Sanders's wife."

"She okay?"

"I'm going back out there now." The man rubbed his

beefy nose with his index finger. ''She was at the mercantile the day Kate Jenkins was there.''

Caleb nodded. ''We won't be in the clear until another week has passed, though. This has about a five-day incubation period.''

Doc's clothes were dirty and rumpled, but his hands were satisfactorily clean. He gave Caleb a sideways look. ''Guess you won't have to admit you were wrong. This could have been a lot worse if we hadn't done it your way.''

Caleb shrugged. He'd been right, but it wasn't as though he'd won a victory of any sort. They'd simply prevented more cases…and possibly a few deaths. That was probably the only gratification Caleb would receive, so he accepted it.

Doc shuffled over to peer down at Ellie. ''Still hard to believe there's something there so tiny that we can't see it, and yet so dangerous. Thought it was a joke the first time I heard it.''

''Some of the bacteria you can see with a microscope,'' Caleb said. ''First time I saw it was in the laboratory at the university.''

''You got a microscope?''

He rubbed his face tiredly. ''Matter of fact, I do.''

''Mind if I come over and have a look one of these days?''

''Don't mind a bit.''

Doc shuffled out and Benjamin saw him down to the door.

The night that followed was one of the longest Caleb had ever lived through. He had so many questions. So many doubts. He had done all he knew to do for Ellie. He couldn't bear to lose her. He couldn't allow himself to imagine the ramifications if she died under his care. And how he could even think that seemed so selfish that he hated himself for the thought…and the doubt.

Her life was in the balance and he was thinking of himself.

She slipped in and out of delirium while he couldn't rid his mind of the thought of another man touching her.

He told himself he was delusional from lack of sleep and he did the only thing he could do for her now, and prayed.

The next day her fever broke. Her skin cooled and she stopped tossing. Caleb dressed her in clean, dry nightclothes and tucked her into fresh sheets. She immediately fell into a deep, restful sleep.

He made himself a pallet on the floor beside her, removed his boots and socks and stretched out. Her breathing came easier. His sense of relief was palpable, but it was dimmed by this new and disturbing emotion. He shouldn't have felt the ripple of betrayal that washed over him each time he thought of her having a child. He hadn't known her until this very summer.

But the feeling was there all the same. She was his wife and he didn't know anything about her previous life because she hadn't trusted him enough to tell him. Had she ever planned to tell him? Should he have asked? Would she have told him if he'd been insistent?

Caleb drifted into sleep with those troublesome thoughts at the forefront of his mind.

Ellie woke during the night and sat up straight in the bed.

A lamp burned on the bureau.

"Caleb?"

"Ellie!" He sat and ran a hand through his hair.

"Caleb, are Flynn and Nate all right?"

"They're fine."

"J.J.'s family?"

"They've recovered. Even Suzanne. The only case right now is Clive Sanders's wife."

"The nice lady who had her husband bring me here when I broke my arm?"

He nodded.

She turned to poke one foot from beneath the sheet toward the floor. "We need to go help her."

He got up and pushed her back onto the sheets. "You need to get some rest and build up your strength. Doc Thornton is taking care of her."

"You trust him?"

"In this I do." She noticed then the dark circles beneath his eyes and the unfamiliar growth of whiskers along his jaw. She'd never seen him look so disheveled or tired.

Exhaustion claimed Ellie's mind and limbs and she closed her eyes.

Waking again late in the morning, she sat unsteadily. Caleb had been lying nearby on the floor, but he was gone now, the blankets folded and lying in a pile. The past days were a blur of scorching nightmares, cooling hands and unbearable pain in her head and throat.

Caleb had been with her through all that, she was sure. His soothing voice had been her security, her lifeline. She remembered his expression of relief and the weary look he'd worn. His sacrifice touched her deeply.

Ellie wondered how many days had passed. Her mouth felt horrible and her hair was tangled and dirty. She wore one of her batiste nightgowns. She touched the fabric, then her cheek, imagining with mortification Caleb dressing her while she was too ill to help.

"Ellie!" From the doorway, Benjamin had spotted her sitting up, and cried her name.

"Ben. You didn't get sick?"

He rushed into the room, kneeling in front of her.

She ran her fingers through his sandy hair, along his fuzzy jaw, and then rested them on his shoulder. "Flynn's all better?"

"Caleb took care of him, and of you, the whole time." His voice didn't hold the contempt she'd heard before when he referred to Caleb. He was no doubt feeling as grateful as Ellie.

She brushed back her hair with a hand, coming in contact with tangles. "I really need to bathe and wash my hair."

"I'll bring up the tub." He stood. "Flynn can help me carry water."

"Wait, where's Caleb? And who's watching Nate?"

"Caleb went to check on the Sanders woman. And Mrs. Jenkins is here looking after Nate."

Ellie digested all that information slowly. "Kate Jenkins? J.J.'s mother?"

He nodded. "She showed up this morning. J.J. is all better, too. She heard you were sick and she wanted to help, so she's here."

The woman's kindness brought tears to Ellie's eyes. She blinked them away.

The boys brought water, and Ellie was so delighted to see Flynn well and his freckled face filling out that tears trickled down her cheeks.

Concern filled his dark eyes. "You sick again?"

She hugged him tightly. "No, sweet boy. I'm just so glad to see you better."

"I'm glad to see you better, too." He pulled back. "Caleb stayed with us the whole time," he said. "I don't remember everything when I was sick, but I remember every day when you were. Me an' Ben took care of Nate an' we did a real fine job. Caleb said so. But Nate got cranky sometimes an' we didn't know what to do for him then, so he cried some. He wasn't hurt or hungry or nothin'. He just cried. Caleb said he probably missed you 'cause he's used to you an' all, an' you have a special way with him.''

''Caleb said that, too?''

He nodded.

She ruffled his hair. ''Bring another bucket for me to rinse with now and then leave me to my bath.''

''Mrs. Jenkins said to ask if you wanted her to help you.''

''Tell her I'm doing just fine, but I'll holler if I need her.''

''Okay.'' He shot out of the room.

Ten minutes later, she submerged in the warm water and tingles of pleasure washed over her skin. It felt glorious to scrub her scalp. She used the rinse water, worked the suds out and then soaked until she got chilled.

She made her way to the kitchen, freshly washed and dressed, but unsteady. Kate greeted her with a welcoming smile. ''Ellie!''

''I'm pleased to see you looking so fit,'' Ellie said to the woman.

''We all had a quite a scare there, didn't we?''

Nate pounded his palm on the tray of his chair. Ellie gave him a smile and he gurgled delightedly and emitted a squeal, raising a hand toward her. She hurried over and picked him up, hugging him against her breast. She was surprised at how heavy he seemed to her in her weakened state. She kissed the top of his head. ''I was so afraid for the children.''

''Everyone's calling Caleb a hero,'' Kate said, delight evident in her tone. ''Seems Doc Thornton told the newspaper how Caleb made him listen and go along with his treatment. There was an article in today's paper saying so.

There was a warning, too, for everyone to stay to themselves as long as they can until five days have passed without another case. 'Course the paper goes out no matter what, and the iceman's been delivering in town. He doesn't go inside, though.''

''I'll bet Luke Swensen's fit to be tied if he still can't open his store,'' Ellie said.

''Oh, he found a way around that. He left a blackboard and chalk on his boardwalk. People can leave their order and then come back later to pick it up.''

''And his wife is well?''

''Completely. I'm staying with you the rest of the day,'' Kate informed her. ''I know how weak I felt that first day, and Caleb said you had the fever longer than most. I'm caring for the baby and doing all the cooking, so you just find a place to take it easy.''

Ellie wasn't as strong as she'd hoped, so Kate's offer was a blessing. ''This is so good of you.''

''You came to my house to help,'' she replied. ''You risked getting the fever yourself to help my family. Caleb says once you get it, you can't get it again, so I'm perfectly safe. *You're* the good one.''

Ellie placed Nate on a quilt someone had laid on the floor, gave him a string of spools and sat down beside him before her shaky knees gave out. ''I think I'll stay right here for a while.''

Benjamin and J.J. clomped in the back door. ''Any of those cinnamon rolls left, Ma?'' asked J.J.

Ben spotted Ellie and grinned.

''There's a few under that napkin on the table. Leave one for Ellie.''

''Glad you're better, J.J.,'' Ellie said.

''You too, Mrs. Chaney.''

The name gave her a start. She had never actually thought of herself as Mrs. Chaney.

The boys sat at the table and Kate poured them glasses of milk. "We're going to ride on over to the creek this afternoon," J.J. said. "Maybe we'll bring back some fish for supper."

"Make sure that's all right with Ellie," his mother replied.

Ellie was so pleased to see her brother with a friend, she could only nod. Like her, he'd never been accepted in the community they came from, nor had he had the time or the opportunity to do all the things young people should do. He'd had Ellie and Flynn and that was it, until the county had separated them.

It was pleasing yet painful to see him growing and establishing a new life. She'd always dreamed of this for him—for her small family. The Jenkinses were a shining example of a real family, and Ben's spending time around them delighted her.

"Where's your brother?" she asked.

Ben set his glass down. "Out back makin' a fort out of the firewood. He's still a little kid, Ellie. Please don't say I have to take him along."

"I wasn't going to say that at all. I was just wondering where he was."

He flashed her a grateful smile. "Thanks."

The boys finished eating and ran out the back door.

"Your brothers are fine young men." Kate wiped her hands on a flour sack towel.

"Thank you. I think J.J. is quite special, too. He's certainly a big help to Caleb."

"He has a mind of his own, that one." She sat in the chair her son had vacated. "He's determined to save enough to send himself to college. His daddy and I sure don't have the money, but he works several jobs and is so determined, I can see him doing it.''

"I can, too.'' Since coming to Newton, but especially since meeting Caleb, Ellie had begun to think a person's dreams really could come true.

She had realized something frightening the night she'd fallen sick. The sudden insight had been incorporated in her fever and fatigue, but now she sorted the thoughts and recalled her discovery.

Caleb had become important to her in a way she couldn't recognize. The tortured beliefs of her childhood jaded every thought and relationship she'd ever had. Since meeting him, she'd learned that he wasn't the only good person in the world. Far from it. But he was nearly the first decent human being she'd encountered.

She felt more than appreciation.

She'd believed all along that association with him would prevent others from pitying her…even ease the sense of ridicule embedded within her. His innate goodness revealed her inadequacies, however. She felt unworthy.

Loving him pointed out the impossibility of their relationship ever developing past this tenuous and wonderful new friendship.

She was incapable, and he deserved more.

A loud meow caught her attention. She got up and found the cat sitting on the back porch, flicking his tail expectantly and gazing up at the door. She slipped out the door and scooped up the cat. His purr rumbled against her midriff as she settled on the step and petted him.

She had been foolish to think she could escape the inevitable—the physical aspect of marriage. What kind of marriage had she visualized? She'd imagined Caleb going to another woman for his pleasures, but she doubted now he'd do that. Just because other men did things didn't necessarily mean Caleb did them, too.

She still had no clue what his mother had been getting at the day of their wedding. Matthew and Laura's touches had disturbed her since she'd first seen them together. But try as she might she just couldn't conjure up a mental picture of Matthew huffing and puffing away on top of Laura, and her actually enjoying it.

Ellie didn't want to think about it.

But she needed to.

She blinked away a similar blurred image of Caleb's sister. And Kate Jenkins. Good women actually participate willingly?

Well, they must, or there wouldn't be so many children. She closed her eyes and recalled the reverent way Caleb had kissed her.

Just because Winston had forced her and hurt her, didn't mean Caleb would. He hadn't. He was good and kind and gentle.

Ellie possessed the knowledge of that fact.

Now she would have to come to understand it in her heart.

She had to if she wanted to keep this family and her dream.

By the next week it became evident that the disease had passed without a full-blown epidemic. Caleb was indeed Newton's hero. He had patients lined up on his stairs every morning when he arrived for work, and he'd hired Benjamin as his assistant.

Benjamin sterilized the instruments, cleaned the office, counted supplies and made trips to the druggist. One afternoon after everyone had gone, he finished wiping the tables while Caleb made notes in patients' files.

"It's payday." Caleb took two silver dollars from the desk drawer and handed them to his new helper. "You've earned every penny."

Benjamin's Adam's apple bobbed, and a lock of sandy hair fell over one brow.

"Once school starts, your studies will come before this work. But I believe you can do both."

"I can," Benjamin said. He turned the coins over in his palm. "Never had this much money all to myself before. I feel like I should give it to Ellie for food or somethin'." His tone sounded as though he were thinking out loud.

"It's yours. You worked for it." It wasn't uncommon for children to help out their families, but Caleb could afford to provide—and wanted to provide for them. "Ellie has everything she needs."

The boy looked up. The blue eyes Caleb had always seen as icy now seemed more open. The sister and brothers were just so damned vulnerable. Sometimes Caleb felt as if he was kicking a puppy when he spoke sternly or made a gesture that he knew was misinterpreted.

Just this afternoon, Benjamin had flinched when Caleb had reached over his head for a glass jar.

"I promised you I wouldn't hurt your sister," he said, wishing he knew what lay behind those mistrusting eyes. "I want to take care of her, too."

"There's different kinds of hurtin'," the boy said. "She's still hurtin'. It just ain't anything you did to her."

For the first time Caleb felt that a rickety bridge had been strung between the two of them. "What can I do about it?" he asked, sincere in his desire to know.

Benjamin closed his fingers over the coins momentarily, then dropped them into his pocket. "I dunno."

"If I knew what to do or say to fix things for her, I'd do it now—this minute."

Benjamin held his jaw so that a muscle flexed. He looked aside thoughtfully. "Some things can't be fixed. Not like Ellie's busted arm or those stitches you sewed into that fella's hand today. Time just knits those hurts right up, don't it?"

Caleb nodded.

"Ellie's hurt is like a bone that keeps breakin' fresh every day."

Caleb tried very hard to understand. He also kept his lips firmly clamped so he didn't scare off this first tiny offering of trust. He just nodded.

"It has to stop breakin' before it can be fixed."

He might never have a better opportunity to ask, so Caleb forced himself to plunge ahead. "Does the hurt have something to do with a baby?"

Chapter Thirteen

A look of near panic passed behind Benjamin's blue eyes. The lad worked his throat a few times, swallowed and took on a look of resignation. Didn't he believe Caleb could help her? Or maybe he thought Caleb would beat her if he found out.

"I can't talk about that with ya," Ben said finally. "Ellie trusts me."

"I understand that." The last thing Caleb wanted was to cause friction between Ellie and her brothers. But he'd become obsessed with his lack of knowledge and the wondering. "She can trust me, too."

The boy shrugged.

They'd only known Caleb a short time, of course. Ben hadn't been able to trust his own father. How could he have faith in a near…stranger? "A person has to earn trust, doesn't he?"

Ben nodded. "Don't give up."

"I don't plan to. Thanks, Ben."

Ben jingled the coins in his pocket and gave Caleb a lopsided grin.

The sight of Caleb and Benjamin walking down the street toward home warmed Ellie's heart and brought a lump to her throat. Caleb carried his bag, and Ben kicked at stones.

They spotted Ellie holding the baby on the shaded porch, and Benjamin loped ahead. He ruffled Nate's hair. "Hey," he said to her.

"How was your day?"

"I got paid." He proudly took out two coins and showed her.

"I remember what it felt like the first time I got paid at the Arcade." She smiled at the memory. "I couldn't wait to buy you and Flynn something special."

"You brought us peppermint sticks and socks the first time," he said. "And the second time you gave us each a whole set of new clothes. I still like those clothes the best."

Caleb climbed the stairs. "Your brother's the best assistant I ever had."

"He's the only assistant you've ever had."

Sharing a laugh, they moved into the house where the smells of supper permeated the hall.

Ellie's heart abounded with appreciation and hope. Her daily tasks were such a pleasure she was sure they couldn't be called work. Her surroundings were beautiful, the supplies plentiful, and her brothers ate and laughed and filled out more each day. Nate had grown every bit as precious and dear to her as Ben and Flynn, and Caleb's presence was the crowning cap of pleasure.

Each day revealed something new she admired about the man she'd married. She noticed the way he held his head and the way the corners of his eyes crinkled when he smiled, and each thing that grew dear and familiar confirmed what she'd discovered.

She loved him.

Not just out of appreciation. Yes, he was kind and generous and giving, but those qualities weren't what triggered these feelings.

Not out of admiration or respect either.

The reason was something more. Some intangible, unexplainable spark that glowed inside her when he smiled, flickered and bounced when she discovered him looking at her just so, and heated to a whole new warmth she couldn't anticipate when their hands or arms brushed.

She often thought of that kiss he'd given her, the soul-deep sweetness and rightness of it, and envisioned it happening again. As one week passed into the next and none of the other Newton citizens came down with the fever, Caleb's practice continued to flourish.

Each night he arrived home tired, but obviously satisfied, and he passed the evenings spending time with his son and Ellie and her brothers. On Sunday they attended church as a family, where Ellie accepted the praise and attention of the citizens who'd heard she'd helped Caleb during the scarlet fever outbreak.

"I didn't really do much," she said to a woman who'd stopped them after they'd shaken hands with the preacher.

"Clella Douglas says you helped birth her new grandson, and Kate Jenkins claims you tended her and her family like they was your own."

"I just wanted to help Caleb. He knew what to do and I only followed directions."

"Perhaps you'd join us for tea one morning soon," Mabel Connely said, waving a hankie that wafted the unmistakable scent of mothballs beneath her double chin.

"I...I..." Ellie was so taken aback, she didn't know how to respond. She glanced over at Nate on Caleb's arm. "I have the children to watch," she said finally.

"School will be starting in another week," Caleb said after they'd moved away from the gathering. "We could find someone to watch Nate for an hour or two while you joined the ladies for tea.''

''I wouldn't know what to wear,'' she said. It had taken her an hour to select and press a plain skirt and blouse for church this morning. When they'd arrived, she'd looked around and seen the dresses the other women had worn and had felt uncomfortably out of place. ''I wouldn't know what to say to them either.''

''With Mabel, all you have to do is listen.''

She walked beside him to the buggy, Ben and Flynn lagging a few steps behind. He drove the team away from town and Ellie relaxed, enjoying the cooler weather, but nervous about taking the boys to the Chaneys' ranch.

She'd spent two days drilling them with napkins and silverware, serving them pretend meals and drinks and making sure they were comfortable with table etiquette.

Caleb's sister and brother-in-law had reached the ranch ahead of them, and Matthew and Denzil already had a game of horseshoes under way. The two men stopped and watched them approach.

''You remember Benjamin and Flynn from our wedding,'' Caleb said to his father.

''Sure do.'' Matthew looked the boys over. Waiting for his reaction, Ellie's heart did a crazy flip in her chest. ''Heard you were a mighty sick fella,'' he said to Flynn.

Flynn nodded.

Matthew looked over at Ellie. ''You too.''

''And Nate,'' she told him.

He took the baby from Caleb's arms and held him, fondly patting his padded bottom. Ellie suspected she saw the sheen of tears in his eyes, but he blinked and it was gone. ''Good thing your daddy went to medical school and got so smart,'' he said to Nate.

Nate babbled and reached for his grandfather's nose.

Matthew grinned.

Caleb looked from his father to Ellie and then back, his warm brown eyes acknowledging his father's acceptance. As much as he'd hoped for his son to work the ranch someday, Matthew had come to terms with Caleb's desires and was even proud of him. Who wouldn't be? Matthew's admission had to please Caleb.

Ellie touched his arm without thinking, finding the flesh and muscle warm and firm through the thin fabric. She surprised herself by touching him so easily, and even more by the reaction of her senses. Touching him gave her the urge to move closer, to press against him, to inhale the scent of him. Sometimes she thought she'd just like him to hold her and not ever let go.

"You men any good at pitching horseshoes?" Matthew asked, eyeing the boys.

"Dunno," Flynn replied. "Ain't never tried it."

Matthew moved to hand Nate back to Caleb, and Ellie released Caleb reluctantly. "Well, let's check those throwin' arms and see."

Ben glanced over at Ellie uncertainly.

She gave him an encouraging nod and he followed Matthew and Flynn over to the stack of iron shoes. Flynn was already asking Denzil questions and pointing to the stakes in the ground several yards away.

"They'll be fine. Let's see what's for dinner." Caleb walked Ellie into the kitchen, where Mildred immediately whisked Nate away and Laura gave her son a hug. Ellie watched their embrace with longing welling in her chest. Caleb's mother loved him—and was free to show him. The poignant moment hung suspended.

The smell of roasting beef filled the air. Potatoes bubbled in a kettle on the stove. Patricia sliced bread on a cutting board, the knife sawing through the crust.

Mildred chanted a little song to Nate that she'd probably sung to Caleb and Patricia and her own children.

Laura released her son and he stepped toward his sister to snatch a slice of bread. Laura's eyes met Ellie's, and Ellie quickly disguised her longing.

With a swish of skirts, the woman stepped over to Ellie and took both of her hands. "Your cast is gone!"

Ellie nodded.

Laura's warm smile created fine lines at the corners of her eyes. "I was just terrified when I heard you and the children were sick." She blinked back tears.

"It was scary," Ellie agreed.

Laura enveloped her in a lavender-scented hug. Ellie had embraced her brothers, who were smaller and bonier, but she had never had a woman hold her like this. At first it felt awkward and she didn't know how to respond, but remembering how much it hurt her when Benjamin hadn't returned her embrace that time at the Heaths', she placed her arms around Laura's narrow shoulders and returned the hug.

The woman smelled powdery and feminine. Her silky silver hair brushed Ellie's cheek. At the soft, motherly squeeze, Ellie's eyes smarted and a newfound kinship and fondness blossomed.

Laura pulled away and laid her palm along Ellie's cheek. "I'm glad you're well."

Ellie realized then that Laura had lost one daughter-in-law, and that she must have been terribly afraid for Ellie as well as for her grandson. It was difficult to imagine anyone caring about her that much, but Laura was Caleb's mother after all, and Caleb had learned his warm loving nature somewhere. His parents were obviously wonderful examples.

Patricia tossed Ellie an apron. They shared a friendly

smile and Ellie found herself more at ease with the women this time.

The boys did a splendid job at the dinner table; no one would have guessed that they'd never eaten in a dining room before today. Ellie beamed at them because she knew they were enjoying themselves.

Matthew and Laura accepted Benjamin and Flynn into their family without reserve or qualm. During dessert Laura placed her hand on Benjamin's shoulder and spoke softly to him. The adoring and embarrassed joy on his face brought swift tears to Ellie's eyes.

Flynn, who'd been set on being a doctor for weeks, suddenly decided to become a rancher and asked Caleb's father endless questions about the horses and cows.

Patricia carried dishes, silverware and cups into the kitchen for Mildred. Helping, Ellie returned to the dining room to discover Matthew with his arms locked around Laura from behind. She had her hands on his forearms and smiled at something he said in her ear.

The sight embarrassed and fascinated her at the same time. She paused in the doorway, her hand on the woodwork.

Patricia came up behind her, but rather than being embarrassed, she said over Ellie's shoulder, "Are you two at it again?"

Matthew looked over at his daughter and daughter-in-law and winked. "Hayden and Soapy are saddling horses," he said. "Caleb and Denzil and I are taking Benjamin and Flynn to check on livestock. You ladies have a nice afternoon."

He released his wife and sauntered out of the dining room.

"I hope Denzil still loves me like Daddy loves you when we're grandparents," Patricia said to her mother.

"Keep those home fires burning," Laura said with a smile. "He will."

Mother and daughter laughed. Ellie followed them out into the cooling air on the porch. Had she given Patricia the same talk she'd given Ellie? Perhaps in more detail because Patricia had been willing to listen. Patricia spoke about what happened between a man and woman as though it weren't shameful. In some corner of Ellie's mind she supposed that what she'd been exposed to wasn't the way it should be. Nothing in her upbringing had shown her life the way it should be.

Nate fell asleep on Laura's lap and Patricia patiently worked on a cross-stitch sampler. Lucy brought Ellie a book and Ellie read her fairy tales.

Laura reminded Ellie of all she'd missed out on with her own mother, and Lucy reminded her of all she'd been robbed of with the child she'd given away. She longed for many more days like this, even though they pierced her with as much pain as pleasure.

She'd had a sister once, too, she thought, gazing at Patricia's serene face as she sewed, and that had been another loss.

Being around Matthew still made her somewhat uncomfortable, but she reveled in the attention he showered on the boys. He was as kind and as generous-spirited as Caleb, and the fact that Ben and Flynn would have the opportunity to grow up in the midst of the Chaneys seemed too good to be true.

She couldn't let anything happen to lose any of this precious and long-sought-after love and affection they'd suddenly become surrounded with. She had to do everything in her power to hang on to this family. Somehow she needed to secure their positions.

The glimmer of an idea had her sitting up a bit straighter.

She thought she knew how.

She studied Laura as she rocked the chair and threaded her fingers through Nate's silky hair, and she thought over her wedding day advice as well as the words she'd spoken to Patricia. Ellie had been in too much of a fog that day and hadn't wanted to listen, but Laura had said that a physical relationship could sustain a marriage.

Caleb was a healthy man with a man's carnal appetite. Ellie could pretend all she wanted. She could tell herself he wasn't like other men in that way, but she knew she wasn't fooled. She might not find the act anything but disgusting, but other people liked it and found it normal. And Caleb was one of them. Besides, she cared for him. She had admitted to herself that she loved him.

It was what she needed to do to solidify their marriage. She just hoped that carrying out the physical act wouldn't change the way she felt about him. She didn't want to lose that special feeling she had for him. She would have to keep the two things separate in her mind, give herself to him without allowing that aspect of their relationship to mar her unblemished feelings toward him.

Could she do it? Could she let him touch her in that way? She was a strong-minded woman. She could do anything she set herself to. And Caleb was a kind and gentle man. There was no comparison to her past experience.

The boys' obvious pleasure and animated conversation on the ride home only reinforced her decision. She wasn't quite sure how to go about it, but she would figure it out. It was what she had to do, and she was a survivor.

A week later she still hadn't figured anything out. The days passed pleasantly, with her brothers growing more comfortable and confident and adjusting to their new life.

Caleb worked and came home, and she watched him for

some invisible sign about what to do. He was a man of his word and he'd agreed to their arrangement. Changing it now was up to her.

On Saturday night she heated water and they took turns bathing on the back porch. She bathed Nate first and fed him and put him to bed, then made sure the boys had cleaned their nails and talked with them while they settled in. After that she took her turn in the tub.

Caleb went last so he could dump the water.

Upstairs, she blew out the lamp and sat by her open window in her nightgown for a long time, listening to the night sounds, waiting for the children to fall asleep and for Caleb to finish and come upstairs.

Finally the house fell silent.

Her hands had grown cold and clammy with nervousness, but she washed and dried them again, then padded down the hall to Caleb's room.

She must have stood in the hall for several minutes before she found the courage to knock.

She heard his feet on the floor. The door opened. "What's wrong?"

Her heart jumped. She couldn't see him in the near-black darkness. "Nothing. Were you asleep?"

"No."

She stood there, uncertain what to say. She remembered that Nate was in there sleeping and she didn't want to risk waking him with their talk. "Maybe we should talk in my room. So we don't bother Nate."

"Just a minute." The room was dark, but she heard the rustle of clothing and realized he must have pulled on his trousers. His silhouette appeared in the doorway and he closed the door softly. "Is something wrong?" he asked in a whisper.

"No." She turned toward her room.

He followed.

Her door stood open, the room dark. She hadn't lit a lamp and he would think that odd. She slipped inside, but he paused in the doorway.

"Come in." She stood a little to the side of the entrance.

He entered. In the moonlight spilling from her open window, she made out the white shirt he'd donned and left unbuttoned. She closed the door. He didn't move, but she felt his probing gaze on her.

Ellie didn't have any second thoughts about what she knew must happen. Her only doubt was how to initiate it.

"I've changed my mind," she said finally.

"About what?"

"About us sleeping together."

He didn't say anything for a moment. "What brought about this change?"

She hadn't expected him to wonder that. She hadn't actually expected him to question her. "Well, you kissed me."

"And that kiss made you change your mind?"

"I thought you would want to."

"Me wanting to was never the question. You're the one who didn't want to. I have to wonder why you've changed your mind."

"Well, it's important for a marriage. Isn't it?"

"I think so."

He still left the question hanging between them. Finally, after another stretch of silence, he asked, "Have you changed your mind about a baby, too?"

Heat rushed up her neck into her cheeks and ears. She didn't want a baby. She still didn't want a baby. "No."

Her pulse pounded so hard she thought he must hear it.

"You still don't want a baby."

"No. I don't want a baby."

"You want to make love, but you want me to take precautions."

Was that what she wanted? She was so nervous her fingers tingled and she grew light-headed. "Yes."

He took a step forward and she caught herself before she jumped away. He reached for her upper arm and his palm and fingers closed around the bare skin. Shivers ran up Ellie's shoulder. "Are you sure?"

She was sure she wanted to hang on to this home and family for her and her brothers. She was sure she'd never known anything so good or so wholesome in her life. She was sure she didn't want to see Ben or Flynn hurt and that she couldn't bear to lose this man who'd become so important and dear—to all of them. "Yes."

He flattened his palm on her arm, up near her shoulder, and rubbed it in a warm circle. "I'll be right back."

He slipped out the door and left her shivering, though her skin was warm and the air barely cool. Her knees trembled and she backed up until she sat on the mattress.

She barely had time to wonder where he'd gone and to question whether or not she should move or lie on the bed before he returned.

He closed the door and padded to where she sat.

"Do you want to lie down?" he asked in the deep-timbred voice she loved, a voice that didn't frighten her.

She scooted up on the mattress and lay back against the pillows. He removed his shirt and it dropped to the floor with a tick as the buttons hit the wood.

Ellie tried not to be disappointed at his eagerness to do this thing. His willingness was in her favor.

He sat with his hip against hers and the moonlight defined the shadows of his muscled arms and shoulders. He'd never used his strength against anyone. Even when he'd

raged with anger at that awful Heath man, he'd focused his
words and his body and had behaved with absolute control.

He'd acted in self-defense against Ben's attack in this
very room, but he'd been careful not to hurt him.

She had nothing to fear. Nothing except losing him.

She swallowed audibly.

He took her hand and stroked her fingers.

She relaxed by sheer willpower.

He placed her palm on his upper arm where she'd
touched him through his shirt a few times. His skin was
sleek and warm, the muscle beneath firm. Her fingers
moved of their own will.

He ran one finger up her arm and into the armhole of
her gown, rubbing it across her shoulder. "Do you want to
take this off?"

He referred to the fabric that kept him from reaching any
farther than her shoulder.

She didn't. She really didn't. The thought of revealing
her body made her want to curl away. But she couldn't do
that.

She unbuttoned the row of buttons at her throat with
trembling fingers. If he urged her to pull the gown off, she
would. If he didn't ask again, she'd keep it.

He leaned forward, though, catching her off guard by
pressing his lips to the skin she'd revealed at her throat.
The humid warmth of his lips moved sensuously across her
collarbone, his tongue dipped into the hollow at the base
of her throat, and his kisses continued down the open front
of her nightgown between her breasts.

He turned his face to one side and kissed the swell. Her
breath caught in her throat at the bewildering sensation.

"You are so beautiful," he said, his breath caressing her
skin. Her nipples hardened.

She pushed his name past the tightness in her throat. "Caleb?"

"Hmm?"

"Will you kiss me again?"

He raised his face to hers, which brought his trouser-clad leg against her bare one and his bare chest up to her thinly covered breast. At the tactile sensations, she caught her breath.

The purposeful contact brought pleasure and fear simultaneously. He was so strong; his limbs were so hard. With one hand he cupped her shoulder, and a trapped sensation alarmed her. She wished for a moment that she had lit the lantern so she could see his face.

He was not merely a dark, faceless shadow in the night. This was Caleb. The man she'd married. The man she wanted to please more than anything.

Quickly she brought her hand up to touch his cheek, his brow, to encourage herself with their familiarity.

"Talk to me." She needed to hear that voice again. His voice always calmed her.

"Make up your mind," he teased. "Either you want me to kiss you or you want me to talk to you."

"Do both."

"All right." His lips brushed hers gently. Warm. Tender. Lips that had spoken only kind words. Lips that kissed a baby's head each night and every morning.

She allowed herself to wallow in the sensation of his mouth against hers—satiny, hot. The pleasure of it surprised her, just as it had before.

He broke the contact. "Want me to say anything in particular?"

"Not just now." She reached up to thread her fingers into his hair and guide his lips back to hers, once again losing herself. This kiss wasn't as tentative as the last, but she found she liked it just as well. Maybe better.

His mother might have had the right idea after all.

He pressed a series of fleeting kisses against her lips, then her jaw, moved his attention up to her temple and across her brow. Sweet, so sweet.

"Caleb," she exhaled on a tremulous breath.

He pressed an unsatisfying kiss to her lips, then traveled down her chin, along her neck and up to her ear. His tongue touched her lobe, his breath creating shivers, and she grasped his arms, his shoulder, needing to hold on to something solid.

"Ellie," he whispered. He kissed her again, one hand coming to stroke her breast through her nightgown. She pressed into the sensation. He teased the hardened bud through the fabric and delight arrowed through her body.

She squeezed her legs together and pushed her body against him. She could do this! His touches melted her fears so easily. If what came next hurt, she would simply think back on this and bear it.

He ran his hand down over her hip, up beneath the fabric of her gown, and warm skin met warm skin. He stroked her hip, her belly, rolled them to their sides, pulling her close with her leg over his hip and smoothed his palm across her bottom, her back and up, cupping her breast, this time with no barrier.

Flames burst along her nerve endings, taking possession of her thoughts. The pleasure he created erased her qualms.

She returned his kisses with wild abandon. His flesh was hot and alive beneath her palms. Everywhere he touched—her arms, her legs, her shoulders, her back—sent pleasure spiraling until her entire being craved something even more delicious.

Catching one hand, he kissed her fingers, then her lips

briefly. He moved away, disentangling their limbs, and stood to remove his trousers.

The cool air touched Ellie's flesh. She took a breath, still tasting him on her lips, still feeling his skin in the tips of her fingers.

His trousers hit the floor and he loomed over her in the darkness, the mattress dipping with his weight. He pushed her nightgown up and ran his hands up her sides and back down, captured her breasts and wedged his knee between her thighs.

Ellie's breath caught in her chest. Her heart pounded.

He bracketed her hips with his hands, his thumbs brushing inward. His hair-covered thigh between hers was hard and unyielding. He moved his leg upward, forcing her to open herself to him.

Her recognition of his intent startled her. Panic washed over her. This wasn't right. This wasn't what she wanted. She wanted him to stop.

She brought her hands up in a defensive gesture and found his hard chest in the darkness. She pressed her fists against it.

He lowered himself down onto her, capturing one of her hands between their bodies.

In the darkness Ellie lost all sense of bearings. Time and place slipped away. Darkness crushed in and nightmarish memories assailed her. She was pinned beneath an over-powering weight and the fingers that probed her tender flesh were an unwanted intrusion. She cringed in horror.

She couldn't breathe, and her chest was ready to burst with the need for air.

He was hurting her.

She fought him with her free hand and then with the leg she worked loose. Oh, God, she had to get away!

Chapter Fourteen

Caleb's quickened senses rudely changed gears. The woman who'd been responsive and pliant beneath his touch only a moment ago had abruptly turned into a spitting wildcat. He didn't think he'd done anything to hurt her or scare her, but she sobbed and fought him all the same. Confused, he attempted to comfort and quiet her with a gentle touch.

Shocked, he felt her fist tighten in his hair.

Pain ricocheted across his scalp. He yelped and rolled away from her so she'd let loose.

She did, scrambling to cover herself, her breath shuddering as if she was going to burst into tears.

"Good God, woman!" He rubbed his aching head. "If you didn't like something you might have just told me."

"Oh, Caleb, I'm sorry." In the darkness her hand came toward him, but she snatched it back to the sheet at her chest. "I never meant to—I didn't mean to—I'm so sorry."

He fingered his scalp gingerly while another part of his body throbbed nearly as much. The blunt change of gears had thrown him off track, and he struggled to comprehend what had taken place. He found a semicomfortable position in which to sit and stared across the darkness at her shadowy form. "Would you mind telling me what just happened here?"

"Caleb, I'm sorry."

"We've established the fact that you're sorry. Now will you tell me what happened?"

"You're so angry." Her voice was reedy thin with something sounding uncomfortably like fear. She'd been around too many angry people in her life. She'd been hurt and he never wanted her to be afraid of the same from him. His heart melted.

"I'm not angry," he said as calmly as he could, wanting to touch her to show his sincerity, but holding back. "I was a little worked up there and I misunderstood you. I'm sorry, Ellie. Forgive me."

"No."

"What?"

"No, you shouldn't be sorry."

"Well, I am." Something had happened back there and he'd missed it. Maybe she'd been trying to tell him to slow down and it had been so long for him that he'd just pressed on like an insensitive lug. "I didn't pay attention to your needs, Ellie, and I am entirely sorry and at fault. We got off to a bad start. It's okay."

Her shoulders shook then and she cried a few silent sobs that tore at his fortitude. What a heel. He'd been so eager to bed her he'd barely questioned her change of heart. Maybe she hadn't been as ready as he'd hoped. He thought back over her words. *I've changed my mind,* she'd said and they'd straightened out that aspect. *I thought you'd want to.* Oh, he'd wanted to...but had she? *It's important for a marriage.*

She'd never said she wanted him.

She'd obviously started out with very strong reasons for not wanting to sleep with him, and he suspected that those reasons went far beyond not having a baby. She'd trusted him to prevent that.

Maybe his other suspicions were correct. Maybe she'd loved a man so deeply that Caleb's touch repelled her. "Ellie, have you loved another man?"

"What?"

"Was there someone else? Is there someone else? Some man who holds your heart and won't let you give yourself to me?"

She pushed herself to a kneeling position and the moonlight made a halo of her tousled hair. She shook her head slowly.

"No, Caleb. No." It was a mere whisper.

Should he ask her? Should he ask if his suspicions were true and if she'd had a baby? Or would that push her further away? She hadn't told him herself. If it were so, and she wanted him to know, she would have confided in him. "Why did you come to my room tonight? Why did you bring me in here?"

"You know why."

"You wanted us to have—relations." Even to his ears it sounded way too blunt.

But she nodded in the darkness.

"Not for the purpose of having a baby, though."

"No."

"Then why?"

She brushed the fingers of both hands beneath her eyes and took a breath, sitting straighter. She gave a small shake of her head. "I want to make you happy, Caleb. Truly I do."

He said nothing, thinking, absorbing her words and her actions.

"I've never known anyone like you. You're kind. And good. All the way through. You love people. You love children. You've made the boys a home and given us...so much. So very much. I can't ever repay you for that."

The first trickling comprehension of this breathless explanation threaded its way through his previously passion-jaded mind. He almost wanted to get up and leave before she could say any more, but his practical, self-torturing mind had to know. "No one ever mentioned repayment," he said. "You are Nate's mother now. That was the arrangement. *This,*" he said, gesturing to the rumpled bed and his nakedness, "was not part of the deal."

"I know." She scooped the side of her hair back nervously, then released it. "It...it didn't seem like enough on my part. You've done so much more. You've given us so much."

That *us* got to him. "So you decided you had something to give me in return," he said, his voice still soft, but taking on an edge. "For all of you."

She grew very still.

"A payment."

She gave her head a shake, but didn't speak.

"Only prostitutes pay for things with their bodies, Ellie."

He could hear her breathing. Ragged. Tortured.

"You thought you could just lie there and let me do it even though you don't feel anything for me."

A tiny sound escaped her. Not a sob really.

"You were wrong." He got up and had to walk around the end of the bed and back toward her to pick up his pants. To her credit, she didn't cower. "It didn't work out, and now you know you can't do it."

There was no dignified way to stand on one leg and pull his trousers on, so he perched at the foot of the bed, well away from her, and stuck a foot in.

"No, it's not like that at all," she denied, finally speaking in a tremulous voice and rising on her knees to lean toward him. "Please, Caleb. Please don't make it sound like that. Don't make it sound…"

He turned his face toward her, placing the other foot in a trouser leg.

She had extended a hand toward his shoulder, but she drew it back. "It's not that way, not at all."

He stood and pulled up his pants, covering his nakedness. "How is it then? Make me understand."

She covered her mouth with her open hand and sat back on her heels on the disheveled sheets. The hand moved to her knee. "We can try again."

Her voice sounded so weak he wanted to laugh. "I don't force myself on women who don't want me, Ellie. A marriage bed is not an altar to make sacrifices on. What kind of person do you think I am?"

"I think you're a wonderful person. Please don't be angry."

He cocked his head and stood grappling with his bruised feelings. She had him so mixed up right now he probably shouldn't speak. "I get angry sometimes. See, I'm not so wonderful after all. I'm mad as hell right now."

"I'm sorry."

He turned to leave before he said anything he shouldn't—before his hurt and confusion made him say things he'd regret.

"Caleb, please," she cried behind him.

He left and closed the door with a final click.

Ellie wrapped her arms around herself and ached for him. For herself. For the person she couldn't be and desperately wanted to become. She leaned forward until her forehead touched the mattress, and clamped her teeth shut against the anguished cry that threatened to burst from her throat and purge her agonized spirit.

Bitter regret and wretched sorrow turned inward, tying her heart in knots. If she could just be numb to this. If she could just guide her tormented feelings to a corner of her soul and lock them away. Would she ever be stronger? Would she ever be able to feel and give and enjoy as she craved doing? She couldn't bear to live her whole life as this bottled-up weakling who couldn't let herself feel.

If she let herself feel, she'd know that his words had cut her more deeply than any pain she'd ever endured. If she let herself feel, she'd see just how much she needed him to accept her and love her. If she let herself feel, she'd have to acknowledge that her love for him was destined to be another of her deeply buried secrets.

It was hurting him now to believe she didn't care. If she was a human with any courage at all, she'd prevent that hurt.

It angered him that she'd felt the need to repay him. People like him didn't want payment. They wanted love, and Caleb deserved love.

And she loved him, oh, she did. But loving him still wasn't enough. Just saying the words wouldn't change what had happened to her when they'd been on the verge of joining their bodies.

Ellie had no control over the panic that had seized her mind. And she could never explain it to him—not without telling him the truth. And she didn't have the courage to do that, for if she did, she'd lose him forever.

She was still alone. And she was still empty on the inside. Only now she'd hurt the man she'd only wished to please. Her foolishness had made things worse. She curled into a ball and sobbed her misery into the pillow.

* * *

Caleb behaved as though nothing had happened. She placed a cup of coffee before him the following morning.

"Thank you."

She took a platter of hot flapjacks from the oven and placed it on the table beside the bacon she'd fried, glad she'd arrived downstairs early enough to chip a slice of melting ice and hold it against her swollen eyelids.

If anyone noticed her haggard appearance they didn't say anything. The boys ate and she fed Nate. Caleb and Benjamin finished their meals and stood to leave.

"Bye, Ellie." Her brother gave her a peck on the cheek.

She returned the kiss and patted his shoulder affectionately, allowing her distressed gaze to lift to Caleb. He bent to place a kiss on Nate's head, and she remembered thinking of that daily goodbye last night when he'd kissed her.

He straightened and ruffled Flynn's hair. "You'll take care of the goat today?"

"You mean Nanny?"

"Is that her name?"

"Yup."

Caleb grinned endearingly and raised his gaze to Ellie. His smile grew stilted.

Heat rose in her cheeks. An ache swelled in her chest. She wished she could go back and change last night. Either relive the whole encounter so that she wouldn't experience that terrible suffocating panic, or go back to the point before she'd gone to his room and make a different choice.

But she couldn't do that. If she had the ability to change things that had already happened, her life wouldn't have ended up where it had.

She wanted to be someone who could walk over to him and place her arms around him, tuck her head beneath his chin and rest against him, feel the beat of his heart and the warmth of his body and his love. She wished there were words that would fix what had happened and erase the ugliness from her memories.

He and Benjamin walked from the room, and no one seemed to notice that Caleb hadn't told her goodbye. That such a trivial omission could leave this enormous cleft in her heart was amazing. She'd lived through some mighty rough times and had weathered the storms without caving in, so what made the difference?

Why did a man so gentle have the ability to hurt her in places violent people had never reached?

Ellie lived with the ache. A living, breathing wound she couldn't patch or block out. And a discovery she hadn't anticipated.

Love hurt, too.

Caleb remained unceasingly polite. Their life went on just as it had before. Only now there was a palpable undercurrent between them, an invisible boundary that kept their eyes averted and made certain there were no accidental touches.

The morning school began, Caleb arrived with the buggy and they delivered the boys to the schoolhouse together.

Caleb introduced Ellie to Mr. McCracken, a lean, balding man who wore suspenders over a poorly ironed white shirt. The collar appeared cinched at his throat by a string tie that bobbed comically beneath his Adam's apple when he spoke.

But he smiled at Benjamin and Flynn and asked them questions about their education up to this point, and when one of the boys sitting at a desk in the back in the back of the room emitted a loud belch, he merely turned his head and raised a brow, and the lad apologized.

Ellie liked Mr. McCracken immediately. She shifted Nate's pleasant weight in her arms.

Flynn had made her promise not to kiss him, so she gave him a little wave, offered Ben a smile of encouragement and followed Caleb back out the door.

Another piece of her dream was being fulfilled with the boys attending school. She couldn't enjoy it as she wished she could, because of this rift between her and Caleb— because it didn't feel as if they were sharing anything anymore. He assisted her into the buggy.

"You can drop me off on Main between Fifth and Sixth," she said. "I have some shopping to take care of."

He nodded and flicked the reins over the horses' backs in silence.

They arrived at the corner she'd indicated and Caleb helped her down. "You won't have Nate's pram, and he'll get heavy. I can go home and get it for you."

"No, I'll be fine. Everything will be delivered, and I'll only have him to carry. I'll stop and rest if I get tired."

He bent to kiss Nate's head, and Ellie's stomach quivered. She tried not to notice the familiar way he smelled or allow herself to look up at him. She balanced Nate on her hip and glanced across the street.

Caleb straightened and turned away. "I'm sure I have patients waiting."

"Goodbye."

He gave a nod, hurried over to the buggy and climbed up, driving the horses away.

She stared after him for several seconds, collecting her wits, tamping down her disappointment. There was a nip in the air that morning, making her realize Nate and the boys would need jackets. She should visit Eva Kirkpatrick and see if it would be less expensive to buy the material and have her sew them than to purchase them ready-made. Eva had promised her a dress as a wedding gift and she needed to call on her anyway.

Ellie took her time in the stores, selecting food items and placing orders. She was learning which merchants sold items for a few pennies less than others and it was a satisfying challenge to tally how much she could save. The freedom of buying food—buying anything for that matter—was still unique. She could never take money or good fortune for granted.

Later in the morning Ellie wandered through Luke Swensen's store. She had picked out a few jars of fruit for pies and stood looking over the canned goods. "My wife said next time you were in I was to send a bag of oranges and one of those new teakettles home with you," he said. "I got a shaving kit from a salesman the other day and I thought maybe Caleb would like it."

"I'm sure he would," she replied. "That's very kind of you."

"I figure we owe a debt we can never repay," the man said, coming around the counter. "Seems like just payin' a doctor bill isn't enough for savin' someone's life."

Ellie knew how he felt. She hoped Caleb wasn't as insulted at Mr. Swensen's offers of appreciation as he'd been at hers.

All the merchants Ellie had spoken with in the past weeks had praised Caleb equally. He'd proved himself and been accepted by the community he desired to help. He deserved to see his dream fulfilled.

"Will you please send them to the house with the other items? I'll be sure to tell Caleb they're gifts from you and your wife."

"You holler if you need anything else."

"I will." She had a fair walk to the dressmaker's shop and needed to start out if she wanted to make it before the noon hour. She exited the store and hurried along the boardwalk, adjusting Nate on her hip.

A prickling sensation alerted her to someone's presence, and she looked askance to see a man walking toward her from the other side of the street. He wore a dark suit and his hat was cocked to keep the sun from his eyes, but she recognized him immediately.

Winston Parker stepped up onto the boardwalk ahead of her, blocked her progress and tipped his hat in mock politeness.

She stopped in her tracks.

"Mrs. Chaney." The way he said it made it seem obscene.

A few other shoppers walked around them.

Ellie started to move past, but he stepped in front of her. Her heart thudded against her breast. She didn't want to see that face. She didn't want to acknowledge his existence. Panic welled up inside her.

Shifting Nate, she moved sideways quickly and entered through a door without reading a note tacked to the wood. Ellie glanced around. It was a tailor's shop. The bell over the door had rung, but there wasn't anyone in the semidark room. Dress forms held chalked and basted suit coats with facings exposed.

She bumped her hip against a counter.

Steps sounded behind her.

She whirled to face the man she detested and feared with all her being. She clutched Nate protectively.

"Nice of you to find somewhere for us to meet alone."

Ellie's glance shot around the deserted work space. Surely someone in the back room would step out. This man wouldn't risk doing anything to her in broad daylight and in a public place.

Nate whined, and she realized she was squeezing him too tightly. She eased her hold and pressed him to her breast protectively.

Winston's attention shifted to the baby and his expression changed subtly. "I heard he was sick."

He reached to touch Nate's head and Ellie's stomach quaked. She moved him away and took a step back.

"Come now, Ellie. I have every right to see my grandson."

Her heart pounded and she wanted to throw up. This horrible person didn't deserve any rights. Especially not to this innocent child. "You stay away from us."

He raised his brows and grinned. "I don't think so. I think we're going to be seeing a lot more of each other. In fact, I'm going to make some arrangements for us—you and I. I'll let you know when and where to meet me."

"You must be crazy if you think I'll meet you."

"Not at all. You'll meet me. You don't have any choice." He stepped closer, backing her against a dress mannequin that toppled and hit the floor with a thud. She caught her balance on a wooden counter. Nate squirmed. "I can request a meeting with you any time I please, and you won't say a word."

"I will. I'll tell Caleb what an awful person you are."

"No, you won't."

"I will!"

"Will you tell him your name is Foster and that your mother was a whore? I can always add those details for you. Then who would he believe? You—a whore? Or me— the father of the respectable woman he loved?"

She loathed him with very cell in her body. How dare he call her that vile name after what he'd done to her?

At the sound of a door opening and closing in the back of the building, he stepped away. "I'll let you know when. And you'll come to me."

He turned, replacing his hat and exiting the shop. The brass bell clanged.

A moment later a man appeared from the back room. "Hello! Can I help you?" He walked over and removed the note from the door. "You must have seen my note that I'd be right back."

Ellie collected her senses and stumbled forward. "No, no, I just needed to get out of the sun for a moment."

He studied her curiously. It wasn't a hot day compared to those they'd left behind. "Can I get you some water?"

"No. Thank you." Rushing to the door, she peered through the glass for any sign of Winston, then darted out and down the boardwalk.

He knew where she lived.

She clutched Nate and half ran until her legs got tired and she lost her breath. Finally slowing down, she glanced behind her.

She wanted to run to Caleb's office for safety, but even that wasn't an option—not with the way things were between them. He would wonder why she'd come during his working hours. Besides, he was busy.

Keeping a cautious eye on the streets behind her, she traversed the distance to the house in near hysteria.

That vile man, the grandfather of this baby she loved, had the ability to take away everything she'd worked so hard for. And his price for not doing so was one she could never pay.

He was going to rape her again. Her mind wouldn't even extend to the point of thinking that one over. He thought he could have her anytime he wanted because she wouldn't tell.

She wouldn't tell.

But neither would he have her.

What could she do?

Benjamin and Flynn were her main consideration. She

couldn't just up and run. She had promised to be Nate's mother.

The house came into view in the distance. Mrs. McKinley was sweeping her steps and waved as Ellie hurried past without acknowledgment. Ellie ran up the porch stairs, fumbled with the key in the lock and flung herself inside, shutting the door, slamming the bolt and running to check the back door.

She stood in the kitchen, panting, Nate now fussing in earnest. Collecting herself for his sake, she dropped her reticule on the table and prepared him a bottle.

She changed him upstairs, fed him and tucked him into his cradle for a nap.

The familiar scent of Caleb's room didn't comfort her. She studied his son until he fell asleep, touched the collar lying on the bureau and sat on the foot of the bed, stricken.

For an hour she sat and contemplated all the ways to tell Caleb the truth. She'd never said the words aloud. She couldn't. She was a coward.

Downstairs the chimes rang and she jumped. Moving to the window, she saw the grocer's wagon in the street and hurried down to open the door for the delivery.

Another delivery came as she was putting those items away. She finished the task and started on supper.

Nate woke and the boys came home from school, eager to share the details of their day. Ellie listened halfheartedly, hating that every moment of her life continued to be spoiled by that detestable man.

Her brothers drank milk and ate slices of bread, and Ben left to attend his duties at Caleb's office. Flynn went out back to search for the cat.

Ellie was alone with her thoughts and Nate until Caleb and Ben came home. They ate supper and conversed. Ellie fed Nate bites, but forgot to eat herself.

"Aren't you feeling well?" Caleb asked after the boys had excused themselves and gone outdoors.

"I'm fine."

He poured himself another cup of coffee and sat back down. "I was thinking we should order a table and chairs and a sideboard for the dining room. My wife died only weeks after I bought this house. I never bought furniture for just Nate and I, but it would be nice to have a set, don't you think? You could select wallpaper and a few paintings. Maybe you'd like a nice set of china."

Ellie studied her plate, wondering what difference all that made. She'd thought food and a home and school were going to change everything and make life better. Those were just physical things that couldn't fix what was wrong with her and with her life.

"Ellie," he said softly. "We have to work past this. At least we were friends before. Now...well, I don't want to lose that much. I know I'm partly to blame—"

"You're not the least bit to blame," she said fiercely. Caleb wasn't the man who had ruined her life. "Don't say that again. Don't make me crazy by saying that." She jumped up and grabbed plates from the table.

He watched her for several minutes.

Then he picked up Nate and left the room.

Ellie stared at the soapy water in the enamel pan and with every fiber of her heart and soul wished Winston Parker dead.

Chapter Fifteen

Days passed with the two of them speaking to each other in stilted sentences, only enough words to convey information and make plans. The boys had begun to look at them oddly, and Caleb tried his best to keep the atmosphere congenial.

On Saturday he took all three of the boys fishing so Ellie could have some time alone. Perhaps she'd been under too much strain lately. She'd always been quiet and reserved, but recently she'd become withdrawn and often agitated.

As a doctor, Caleb was concerned.

As a man who'd grown to love her he was worried and hated this helplessness.

Sunday, they attended church as usual. His parents were there, and Laura held Nate during the service. Ellie kept glancing over and twisting her hands in her lap.

Once, Caleb reached over and covered her hands with one of his and she tensed, rather than relaxed, so he let go.

"Why don't we send the boys to the ranch for dinner today," he suggested as they exited the building. "We can share a meal alone—at the Arcade or at Isaac's Restaurant. You won't have to cook."

The expression that crossed her features revealed that an

afternoon without the children appealed to her. Would the prospect of being alone with him tip the scales against the plan, though? She raised those luminous violet eyes and he read the doubt in their depths.

"Is that what you'd like to do?" she asked.

She was always asking what he'd like.

"Yes."

She raised her chin just a fraction of an inch and took a breath. "All right."

"I'll speak to my folks. Perhaps they'll even bring them home for us." He found his parents chatting with the Douglases.

Rachel showed him her son, wrapped in a crocheted shawl. "There's that handsome fella," Caleb said. "What is his name?"

"John Mark." Rachel beamed.

"John's a good, solid name," he said.

"Dr. Chaney?" She took him arm and guided him a few steps away from the others. "I want you to know I didn't mean all those awful things I said about his daddy. John Allen is a good man. I miss him something fierce and I keep praying he'll come back to us."

"I hope he does, too, Rachel. Why don't you go show John to Ellie? She'll be surprised at how much he's grown already."

Rachel found Ellie in the churchyard, and Ellie smiled and admired the baby.

Caleb turned and made arrangements with his parents to bring the boys home. Ben strode across the grass to where Ellie stood. "Is it all right if I go with the Chaneys?"

"Don't you want to?" she asked.

He nodded. "Yeah. I just want to make sure you're going to be all right."

His concern touched her. He'd obviously noted her distress these past days. "I'll be with Caleb," she assured him.

Ben gave her a smile and hurried off to join the Chaneys. Caleb came for Ellie.

He drove the team to the Arcade Hotel and they were seated within minutes.

Goldie spotted Ellie and stopped by their table with a friendly greeting. "You got your cast off!"

"Yes, a while ago. My arm's all better."

Goldie batted her lashes at Caleb. "That was sure a lucky fall you took that day, Ellie."

"Lucky for me," Caleb said, and gave Ellie a smile.

Goldie giggled. "I'll leave you two lovebirds alone and get back to the station before Mr. Webb demotes me back to the kitchen."

"What would you like?" Caleb asked.

She glanced over the menu. "I always wanted to try the lobster salad."

A waitress whom Ellie knew as Irma appeared to take their orders. She looked Ellie over with admiration.

"My wife will have the lobster salad," Caleb said. "I'd like the stuffed turkey and asparagus. We'll try the Roquefort cheese and water crackers while we wait. Did you want coffee, Ellie?"

She glanced up and nodded.

He handed the waitress the menus and she moved away.

Ellie admired Caleb's calm efficiency, his ability to fit in wherever he went. But then, he did fit in here. She was the one who should have been waiting tables.

He spoke to her about their fishing trip the day before, about church that morning. Their meal came and Ellie's salad was delicious. She'd never eaten anything remotely like it.

She'd never before eaten in a restaurant, except in the

kitchen of this one, and the experience was unique. She tried to respond to Caleb's conversation, wanted to make the day pleasant for him, but her mind was enveloped by the black fog of doom Winston Parker's demand had created.

He had the power to destroy her—and to destroy Caleb as well. If he revealed the secret of Ellie's family, Caleb would lose the respect he'd only recently gained in the community. Kind, generous, unsuspecting Caleb. Ellie hated the possibility that marrying her could end up being his downfall.

Nothing Ellie had worked for and gained had freed her from the horror her mother had inflicted upon her.

Caleb paid for their dinner, left a generous tip and took her for a ride across countryside that was just beginning to show the first signs of autumn. She relaxed and enjoyed the time and his concern, all the while feeling guilty for causing him extra worry. Her behavior had to seem strange, but she saw no chance of improvement in the future. Every day she waited as though she were standing on the edge of a cliff, knowing any moment it would break off and plunge her into an abyss.

They returned to the house to find a note scribbled on Caleb's blackboard. Caleb needed to call on a nearby rancher.

"I'll have to go back for a horse," he said, and turned to her with a frown creasing his forehead. "I'm sorry to leave you. I wanted us to have the evening together."

"It's your job, Caleb. Go take care of Mr. Arnold."

He checked his bag for supplies and left. Ellie stood on the porch, watching him go. She went upstairs and changed from her church clothes. Lighting a lamp, she tried to read until the Chaneys brought the boys home.

She made them coffee and they chatted for a few minutes before heading back.

"Thank you, Laura."

Caleb's mother hugged her. "You're most welcome, dear. A bride needs a little time alone with her husband now and then. Too bad he had a call."

Matthew pulled her out the door. Ellie listened to Flynn's excited chatter about their day, then sent her brothers to wash up.

She got Nate fed and ready for bed. He had just fallen asleep when the door chimes rang. Tucking him in, she hurried down the stairs.

"You Mrs. Chaney?"

She nodded.

The young boy jabbed a folded piece of paper at her and bounded off the porch. Puzzled, she accepted it and closed the door. Ellie opened the note.

Come to the spot southwest of town where the Caldwell tracks cross the creek. Ten o'clock. No later.

Her knees shook.

How could he think she'd come?

She couldn't go. She'd rather die than let that man touch her again. Ellie crumpled the paper in her fist and bent at the waist to relieve the piercing pain in her stomach. She wished she'd died the first time!

"You okay?"

She straightened and composed herself, ignoring the nervous sickness in her belly. Ben stood on the stairs.

"I'm fine."

"Who was at the door?"

"Just a boy with a note." She raised it. "I'm invited to tea." She attempted a weak smile.

"You goin'?"

"I'll have to see what the week brings."

"I wonder if Caleb needs any help with his patient."

"I'm sure he's doing fine."

"Who was sick?"

"Mr. Arnold."

"He's the man who owns the drugstore. Was it serious?"

"Stomach pain, someone wrote on the blackboard. Could be anything, I guess. You have school tomorrow. Get your sleep."

Ben shrugged, then turned back up the stairs.

Ellie rushed into the front parlor. The clock on the mantel read nine-twenty. She couldn't go. She'd be stupid to place herself in jeopardy. What could Winston do? Come and drag her out of her home?

She dropped to the edge of a chair. Minutes ticked by as slowly as hours, each beat heightening her anxiety. She got a rag and dusted the furniture.

Zeb Arnold's attack of gastritis had finally passed. Caleb left him a bottle of peppermint extract, stepped outside and peered into the darkness. Moonlight defined his saddled horse down the road. He was sure he'd tied the reins to the post. Tiredly, he carried his bag down the dirt road until he reached his mount. He strapped his bag on the back of the saddle. "What did you wander off for?"

Weeds and leaves rustled behind him. He turned toward a dark figure with an arm raised over his head. The next second pain burst through his skull and he blacked out.

Thinking she heard someone on the stairs, Ellie stepped into the foyer and glanced up. Her mind was playing tricks on her now.

The clock chimed ten o'clock and she jumped. He'd be

waiting for her. *No later.* He'd be angry. She went back into the parlor and waited until another half hour had passed.

She left a lamp burning for Caleb and went upstairs, checked on Nate, then closed herself in her room.

She removed her shoes, but left her clothing on and lay on the bed. What would he do?

Caleb's head throbbed. He opened his eyes. The moon peered down at him. What the hell had happened? He pushed to a sitting position in the weeds along the side of the road a good distance from the Arnolds' place. Blinking away dizziness, he got to his feet, climbed up to the road and whistled.

An answering whinny came from the distance and his horse galloped to where he stood.

He probed the back of his head and his hand came away sticky. There was a good-sized bump there, but he didn't seem to be bleeding profusely, so he placed his foot in the stirrup, hauled himself into the saddle and touched his heels to the animal's flanks. He'd clean up the cut at home.

Somehow Ellie had slept. At an unfamiliar sound, she woke and sat up, squinting into the blackness. Lighting a lamp, she carried it out into the hallway.

Caleb still wasn't home, she noted, peeking into his dark room. The light swept across the sleeping baby's cherubic features. Shadows danced on the walls as she carried the lamp to the boys' room and listened outside the door. All was silent.

Lifting her hem, she made her way down the stairs.

The parlor lamp had burned out.

A sound came from the back of the house.

"Caleb?" she called softly.

No reply.

Her bare feet padded soundlessly across the glossy wood floors, down the hall, into the kitchen. "Caleb?"

"He's indisposed at the moment."

The familiar and abhorred voice halted her in her tracks. She turned to run, but a match struck, lighting a lantern, and defined Benjamin's shocked face in its glow. Ellie stared.

He was seated stiffly in a kitchen chair and Winston Parker stood beside him, a gun pointed at her brother's head.

Ellie's heart stopped beating. Her vision blurred.

The scene came into focus and she zeroed in on the rope that secured Ben to the chair. She took a step forward. "What are you doing?"

"Seems you forgot our appointment. I stopped by to remind you."

"Let him go."

"I'll let him go. Just as soon as you step outside with me."

"You're crazy."

He laughed.

"Where's Caleb?"

"He had an accident along the road."

Horror coiled up her spine. "What have you done?"

"Don't worry. I wouldn't kill my grandson's father. He makes a good living. He's—shall we say—detained."

"If you hurt my sister, I'll kill you, you son of a bitch!" Benjamin shouted, his voice cracking with emotion.

"I'm *real* scared," Winston said with a smirk. "Now come on, Ellie. Out the door. I'm tired of waiting."

"Where to?" she asked.

"My carriage," he replied. "You remember my lovely carriage."

Her head swam. Her stomach lurched.

Winston looked her in the eyes and slowly pulled back the hammer of the gun until it clicked. He pressed the barrel directly against Benjamin's perspiring temple.

"All right," she said. "Put the gun away." Maybe between the house and the carriage she stood a chance to fight him off.

Ben's face contorted and he struggled with the ropes that bound him. "Don't go, Ellie!" he pleaded, a vein in his temple defined by the lamplight. "Don't go! Let him shoot me! The noise will bring someone to help."

As if she would ever let anyone harm a hair on his head. His foolish willingness to sacrifice his life told her everything she needed to know. "Move the gun away," she said calmly.

It took eight steps to reach the back door.

"No!" Benjamin howled in anguish.

Winston pulled the gun away from Benjamin's head and backhanded him across the face.

Ellie moved toward her brother, but the barrel raised to point at Benjamin's heart. She halted. Winston took a step away, the gun still aimed. "You made your choice, am I correct?"

She nodded, then walked stiffly back to the door.

Winston stepped behind her then and the minute she knew Ben was safe, she relaxed and opened the screen.

"Ellie, no!" Ben sobbed from the kitchen behind them.

The night was cool. A fog hung above the ground. The cat meowed and darted under the porch.

Winston's hand clamped onto her arm and guided her across the yard away from the house, through an alley. Rocks and sticks pierced the bottoms of her feet, but she was numb to the physical pain.

A brief memory of running through an alley years ago flitted through her consciousness. She'd been fourteen years old and desperate to hide the baby she'd given birth to. The baby this man had forced on her. Some disjointed section of her brain wondered if she'd have another baby. Maybe she would die.

She wanted to.

He'd parked his black carriage on an adjacent street. It loomed out of the enveloping darkness like a hand reaching out to squeeze the life from her.

She stopped at the door.

He opened it.

The interior yawned, ready to swallow her in its claustrophobic depths. What choice did she have? She knew his strength. She knew his power and influence.

Ben had been ready to die for her.

Her mind cleared. She hadn't made it this far just to give up, had she? As long as she had an ounce of life left in her body, she could resist him. If he shot her, someone would hear and rescue Ben. They would go get help for Caleb, wherever he was.

If she got inside the carriage, she'd never be able to fight him. She stood a better chance out here.

Before she could change her mind, she grabbed the door and jerked it. The corner hit his knee, and he grabbed her shoulder.

Her first kick caught his shin, but hurt her bare toes. She balled her hands into fists and pummeled his face. He hit her with his fist, and lights flashed behind her eyes. Her lip stung and she tasted blood.

He raised the gun to her head and shoved her back against the side of the carriage. "Get inside," he hissed.

She clamped her teeth and said through them, "Shoot me."

Nothing happened.

Caleb's reaction when she'd grabbed his hair flitted

through her mind, and in the next second, she reached up and locked her fingers against Winston's scalp and yanked for all she was worth.

He yelped and his head shot back, dislodging the gun from her temple.

At that same moment, the sound and sight of her brother barreling into Winston and both of them losing their breath and their balance bombarded Ellie's senses. Winston held fast to Ellie's arm and used her to pull himself upright.

Ben had regained his feet. He raised a piece of wood and slammed it down on Winston's head. With a grunt, Winston released her arm.

Ellie grabbed the man's hand and bashed it against the edge of the coach door. He howled and shoved her, the gun falling from his grip.

She landed on her rump, scraping her elbow, and her teeth rattled.

Benjamin struck Winston again, and he fell against Ben, rolling on top of him, arms flailing.

Ellie scrambled to her knees.

Moonlight glimmered from the barrel of the gun where it lay in the dirt. A hand closed around it.

Ellie beat at Winston's head with her fists. If he had the gun again, he wouldn't hesitate to shoot Ben.

A blast echoed in her ears.

The horses reared and whinnied; their harnesses jingled and the carriage rocked. The smell of gunpowder burned Ellie's nose. She strained to see clearly in the darkness. "Ben!"

The lump of bodies moved, and he stood, a slender figure against the foggy night sky. The bigger man at his feet didn't stir.

Ellie stared at the unmoving body. Her toes, her elbow and the bottoms of her feet throbbed.

"I didn't mean to," Ben said on a released breath.

She got to her feet slowly. A light came on in one of the nearby houses, then another.

"I swear I didn't mean to kill him!"

She moved forward. "Maybe he's not dead."

"I said I'd kill him, but I didn't mean it."

Ellie turned and wrapped her arm around Ben's narrow heaving shoulders. "I know you didn't. I've wished him dead a hundred times myself, Ben. Hush now."

She released him and knelt over Winston's prone body, almost expecting him to reach up and grab her. With a trembling hand, she pressed her fingers to his throat, then picked up a limp wrist and felt for a pulse as she'd often seen Caleb do. She couldn't detect a movement. "I think he's dead."

"Ah, hell," Ben moaned.

"Ellie!" The voice echoed from the alleyway. "Ben!" Caleb's voice! He was all right! Footsteps sounded as he ran toward them and emerged into the moonlight at the edge of the street.

"Ellie, my God, what's happened?" He knelt over the man on the ground.

"I shot him," Ellie said. "He's dead."

"Winston?" Caleb said in stunned disbelief.

Ben dangled the gun before Caleb, then tossed it inside the open carriage. "Look who has the gun. *I* shot him. I didn't mean to. He would have killed one of us. I grabbed the gun before he could get it again. It just went off. I didn't mean to kill him."

A light came on in the nearest house and a person appeared on his porch with a rifle in his arms. "What's going on out there?"

A few shadowy figures stood at the corner of a yard, carefully keeping their distance but obviously curious.

Caleb checked over the man on the ground once again, then sat crouched with one knee up and the other against the ground, staring at the two of them. "Ellie, tell me what happened."

She couldn't say anything. She couldn't feel anything.

"He sent Ellie a note telling her to meet him tonight." Ben reached into his pocket and pulled out the crumpled paper. "She didn't go."

Caleb stood and took the paper from Ben, walked over to the carriage and lit the side lamp. He held the paper aloft and read. Ellie's heart thundered.

She would have taken a hundred beatings to prevent the look of confusion and betrayal that crossed Caleb's face. "Why did he ask this? Why did he think you would meet with him in a secluded spot at night?"

Numb, she shook her head.

"Ellie?"

"He thought she would do whatever he asked," Benjamin said. "He knew she wouldn't want him to tell anyone the truth about her. About us."

"What did he know about you?"

"Ben," she warned.

"He used to come see our mother—"

"Ben!"

"He knew your parents?" Caleb asked. He lowered the note.

"Not parents," Ben denied. "The woman who gave birth to us."

"Ben." Ellie's voice rose.

"Our mother was a whore," Ben said. "He knew it. He used her himself."

"Oh, Ben." It was a cry now, a broken pleading cry. "No, please no." Ellie begged him earnestly.

"Tell him, Ellie." Ben turned to stare at her, ignoring her protests.

"Nooo," she wailed.

"Tell him, or I will."

"No, Ben. Please!"

"It's the only way, don't you see?"

"No, we'll leave. We'll go somewhere else."

"I don't want to go somewhere else. I want to stay here. Tell him."

Her feet were stuck to the ground. She couldn't move toward Ben to prevent the words from coming from his mouth.

"He raped Ellie."

The pulsating scream was entirely inside her head because the night was as still and silent as the man at their feet. Ellie's ears rang and her chest felt ready to implode.

Caleb's frantic gaze raked across her. "Oh, my God!" He moved forward. "Let's get her into the house."

"Not tonight," Ben clarified, placing a hand on Caleb's chest to stop him. "A long time ago. When she was a girl."

Caleb looked from Ben to her, his face shadowed in darkness once again. "Ellie, is this so?"

All the shame and the degradation of that night and the years that had followed were as acute and as suffocating as if the event had happened tonight. Having Caleb know was as ugly and as humiliating as the act itself. She couldn't bear for him to look at her. She couldn't bear the look she'd see on his face.

Ignoring the people now standing in clusters, watching them from a wary distance, Ellie turned and ran.

Chapter Sixteen

Everything fell into place in Caleb's mind. He'd wanted to know the depth of that sadness in her eyes and the cause of the fear that enveloped her. He wanted to know the truth and he wanted to help. But this... He should have figured it out. But she'd been good at covering up. Her skittishness, her elusive past, Flynn's mention of having no father, as well as the disaster that had resulted from their attempted lovemaking, were enough clues that he should have guessed.

The vivid realization sickened and angered him at the same time. He gazed into the dark alley where she'd disappeared, praying for the strength and the wisdom to see them through this.

"Shall we go after her?" a man called.

"No," Caleb replied. "There's been an accident here."

"That you, Dr. Chaney?"

"It's me."

"Need any help, Doc?" A few men in varying stages of undress came closer.

"Who's been shot?"

"Winston Parker. I could use some help getting the body into the carriage."

"He dead?"

Caleb looked at the body on the ground. "I'm afraid so."

"Who shot him?"

"I'd better talk to the sheriff first," Caleb replied.

Ben moved off to the side while two of the neighbors helped Caleb place Winston's body inside the carriage.

Afterward, Caleb stepped over to Ben and said gently, "Go home now."

"I didn't mean to shoot him." His young voice held fear and mistrust.

"I know you didn't." Caleb led him farther aside. "You were protecting your sister. You did what any man would have done."

"I tried to get the gun and it went off."

"I want you to go watch over your sister. Make sure she doesn't do anything foolish, like try to leave or run away. Lock her in the pantry if you have to."

Benjamin looked up at him. "I wouldn't do that."

"Just keep her there until I get back."

Ben cast Caleb a skeptical glance at the black carriage. "Where are you takin' him?"

"To the sheriff. I'll explain what happened. He'll need to talk to you. And to Ellie."

"Do you have to tell him about Ellie?"

Caleb considered Ben's question and held the same concern. "Perhaps it would be enough that he attacked her tonight. I have a feeling he's the same one who hit me over the head and left me along the road out by the Arnolds'."

Ben swiped a hand beneath his nose.

"Go to her now," Caleb said. "I'll deal with these people."

Ben turned and ran down the alley.

Ellie lay on the bed in the dark, her head throbbing, drained of every last tear and emotion. She'd tried to get up, but Ben had pressed her back on the bed, brought cool water and bathed her face, urging her to rest. "He can't hurt you ever again," he whispered in the darkness.

Didn't he know that Winston had already hurt her enough for a lifetime? "No, he can't," she agreed anyway.

"I was too little to help you that time. I heard you cryin' and I pounded on the door as hard as I could. I tried to open it."

Her lethargy lifted and she raised her hand to his face. "Oh, my boy, I'd hoped you didn't know."

"I didn't know, not for sure. Not until I was older. I went to get *her* to help, Ellie. She wouldn't help."

"I know," she said, comforting him. "He would only have hurt you. Don't blame yourself. You were just a little boy. A little boy who shouldn't have had to know about that."

She didn't know how she could possibly have a drop of moisture left in her, but tears rolled down her cheeks— tears for her beloved Benjamin. "You should have had a mother to love you and a father to bring home money for food."

"You were our mother," he answered, breaking her heart all the more. "And you found us food."

"You should have had a warm house and a bed," she added.

"I have those things now, Ellie," he said hoarsely.

She stroked his cheek. "Yes. Yes, you do."

But did they have a hope of keeping them after this night?

"Do you hate me, Ellie? 'Cause I told Caleb?"

"No. I love you."

Some of the tension left his body. "I love you, too."

"Go to bed."

"Caleb told me to take care of you."

"You did. I'm fine."

He left the room and she waited in the darkness. In some way she almost experienced a thread of relief that her secret was exposed. Carrying it had been a weighty burden, but now all her doubts and questions were brought sharply into focus. What would happen to them now? What would Caleb do, and how would he react to the knowledge? The minutes ticked away like hours.

After dropping off the body and explaining the situation to the sheriff, Caleb left Winston's buggy at the livery and hurried home. He found Ben still waiting in the kitchen, his head on his hands at the table. The chair Caleb had found broken on the floor when he'd come home from the Arnolds' now lay in pieces in the kindling bin.

Ben looked up. "Is that your blood?"

Caleb unbuttoned the shirt and shrugged out of it. "Probably. I'm glad you're up. You can look at this knot on my head for me." He poured a pan of warm water from the well on the stove.

Ben got up and Caleb sat in the chair he'd deserted.

"It seems to have stopped bleeding," Caleb said. "Can you clean it out?"

Benjamin took a rag and soap and thoroughly, but gently cleansed the egg-sized bump and the gash.

"I was comin' to see if you needed any help out there at the Arnolds'," Ben said. "I stayed up after Ellie told me to go to bed. I knew somethin' was wrong when Ellie got that note, and I snuck downstairs and found it in the pocket of Ellie's apron. I knew it was from Winston. I decided to go get you, but when I went outside, he was there. He had that gun on me the whole time and he tied me to a chair."

"I saw that chair."

"I knocked it over and busted it against the stove. Sorry about breakin' it."

"Don't be ridiculous. You were brave, Ben." Caleb turned and slid an arm around the boy's waist. Benjamin's body trembled within his easy hold. "You saved Ellie tonight, you know."

Ben's chest heaved and he broke into sobs against Caleb's hair. "I couldn't help her the last time."

Caleb stood, placed his arms around him and smoothed his hair, unable to imagine what this boy—and his sister—had been through. "How old were you?"

He sniffed. "Eight maybe."

Caleb rolled that number around in his head. Seven years ago? Ellie could only have been...fourteen? He couldn't let himself imagine it. If it was so un*think*able, what must it have been like for her to live it? And hide it? "You were too young to help her," he assured Ben. "But you did it tonight. I'm proud of you."

"She's gonna hate me 'cause I told you."

"She could never hate you. You mean everything to her. You and Flynn. You did the right thing."

"I don't want to leave here."

"It's going to be all right."

"Will they put me in jail?"

Caleb released Benjamin and lifted his chin on his thumb, noting a few cuts on his face that needed tending. "No," he said, praying he was right. "Nothing is going to happen to either of you."

Ben wiped his face and nose on his sleeve.

"Put some of this ointment on it now." He sat back down and handed Benjamin the tin he'd opened. "Then I'll take care of your cuts. Is she asleep? She didn't try to leave?"

"She wouldn't leave us," Ben replied matter-of-factly.

"I made her stay in her bed and rest. She cried. I used to hear her cry a lot. It scared me. It still scares me."

"Maybe now that the truth is out and Winston is dead, she can put those tears away," Caleb said, hoping it was true.

"I hope so."

"Me, too. Let me see to your face now."

Ben sat in the chair and Caleb disinfected his wounds. He discovered Ben's knuckles bruised and swollen and a spot on his shoulder that had begun to discolor.

"You'd better get to bed. Do you think you'll be up to going to school tomorrow?"

"I don't want to miss it."

"I'll get you there after we see the sheriff. Thank you for taking care of Ellie. And for doctoring my head. You have a gentle touch."

Obviously pleased with the compliment and relieved about the status of his involvement with Winston's death, Ben told Caleb good-night and went up stairs.

Caleb's energy seemed depleted, but now—more than ever—it was important that he talk to Ellie.

A presence in the room woke her. Somehow she had drifted into an uneasy sleep.

"Ellie?"

She opened her eyes to see Caleb standing just inside the doorway with an oil lamp. The glow revealed him dressed in a clean white shirt. She blinked and rolled to her other side to hide her face.

He set the lamp on the bureau and turned it down low, sending the room into flickering shadows.

"Will they take Ben to jail?" she asked.

"No." The bed dipped as he sat behind her. "I explained what happened to the sheriff. Seems they've had several accusations toward him over the past few years, but nothing they could prove. He denied attacking the girls in question, and it was his word against theirs, with no witnesses. This time there's Ben and me.''

Winston had done this to someone else? She'd never even considered that. ''You didn't see anything.''

''I got whacked over the head and saw stars. That was his doing, I'm convinced.''

She turned back and sat up. ''He said he'd done something to hold you up. Are you all right?''

He fingered the back of his head gingerly. ''I have a goose egg back there, but I'm fine.''

Seeing him running from that alley toward the carriage, she had experienced frightfully conflicting emotions—relief and joy at seeing him well, but dread over what he'd come upon.

He noted the tear in the sleeve of her dress. ''Can I look at that?''

She raised her elbow.

He went back for the lamp, turned it up and set it beside the bed. His sure, gentle touch only saddened her. She'd barely acknowledged her feelings for him; if only there could have been more time, if only he'd never had to know. He was treating her as kindly as he did everyone. He was looking at her as a doctor. ''You have a cut that needs cleaning,'' he said.

Ellie glanced at her dirty bare feet. ''My feet, too.''

''I'll be right back.'' He left and returned with his bag and a pitcher of water. ''I just came from cleaning up Ben.''

''Is he hurt?''

''A few scrapes and bruises. He'll be fine. How he managed to get himself out of that chair is a marvel. He's your hero.''

"He's just a boy."

"He's a very brave young man who loves you."

She nodded, aggrieved to the marrow of her bones.

"Why don't you take your clothes off and put your nightgown on. Then I can treat that elbow." He stepped out into the hall and waited until she called him back.

Ellie looked so small and so pitifully young. Her hair was a wild tangle and her eyes were red and puffy. Caleb cleaned her elbow and applied salve and a bandage. She avoided his eyes the entire time.

He placed the bowl of water on the floor beside the bed. "Might as well stick 'em in here."

She placed one foot at a time in the water and he washed the soles of her feet and dried them. Finding a pair of tweezers, he removed a piece of gravel from her heel and she winced, then he applied the salve and wrapped her feet in gauze. "Get under the covers now."

She obeyed like the lost little girl she'd once been, and he pulled the sheet up over her.

He turned the lamp wick down low because he knew it made her more comfortable and seated himself on the edge of the bed. They had to talk about it. Now that he knew, she had nothing left to hide. "It all makes sense to me now," he said.

She turned her face away. "You don't even know it all."

"Can you tell me?"

A minute passed while he wondered if she would, but then she spoke, her voice soft and faraway-sounding. "My name is Foster. Everyone in Florence knows the name."

"You made up the name Parrish to get a job?"

"No one would have hired me."

"People can be so narrow-minded," he said with a sad shake of his head.

"We lived in a shack outside of town," she went on.

"One room. There was a stove, but we never had anything to burn in it except the wood I stole from people's wood-piles. Once I burned an old wagon that had been deserted in a field. Every night I went and broke off a few more pieces until all that was left was the metal parts. I used to hunt for newspapers in the trash."

Caleb had difficulty picturing the life she'd begun to describe, but he focused on doing so. He wanted to understand.

"We didn't have food most of the time. Sometimes she was sober for a day and bought some. Usually she just bought whiskey. I stole from gardens and yards at night. When I was bigger I planted a tobacco patch as well as some vegetables. I learned to roll cigars and I sold them outside the saloons and the billiard halls in the evenings."

"You took care of the boys all by yourself?" he asked incredulously.

"Somebody had to. They were such good babies. Bright and beautiful. Not filled out like Nate. I never had enough to feed them."

As the picture became clearer, Caleb ached for her and her brothers. He almost felt guilty for his abundant childhood.

"We had a sister once," she said. "Between the boys. She died. She was never very strong. She threw up most of what I was able to get in her. We didn't have beds or covers, so we slept on the pads I made from newspapers and rags, and it was usually pretty cold.

"*She* slept by the stove. And when men came that's where they were—together—so we kept as far to the other side as we could."

Caleb wondered what kind of men visited a place like that—a place where children were starving and cold and their mother took money for whiskey. *Men like Winston Parker,* he realized with another shock.

"First time I ever slept in a bed was when I started working at the hotel and got to stay in the dormitory." She paused a moment. "We didn't go to school much. I went a few years—the years that the teachers weren't cruel. The kids were bad enough, but when the teachers were cruel, too, I couldn't bear it, and I wouldn't put the boys through it. I stole books and taught them to read and figure.

"What clothes we had people gave to us. Castoffs. I wore boys' underwear most of my life. I never had anything new until a teacher named Mrs. Conner came to the school."

Ellie had relaxed and now spoke more comfortably, though she still faced away from him.

"I thought that woman was the most wonderful person in the world," she said. "She was. She was the kindest person I'd ever met. She took time after school to help me with my lessons. She came to where we lived once, someone, one of the other kids maybe, must have told her where it was. My mother just told her to leave her the hell alone. I thought I wouldn't be allowed to go back after that, but Mrs. Conner never mentioned it.

"She treated me just the same as always. And one day she invited me to her house. I had to take the boys, of course, but she fed us and then she measured me. It was the strangest thing.

"The next week she had a box for me. In the box was the most beautiful dress I'd ever seen."

Her voice cracked and she swallowed a few times. "I've never told anyone about the dress. I've never told anyone any of this."

"It's okay," Caleb assured her. Wanting to hold her, he

merely placed his hand on her arm. She didn't object, so he gave her bare skin a comforting rub. "Go on."

"It was blue. With a sash at the waist and a scalloped white collar and cuffs. It was a beautiful dress. She meant well by it. She was a kind, kind lady.

"I only wore it to school once. The others laughed. One of them said they'd never seen trash covered in fancy wrappings before. Mrs. Conner made him sit on a stool all afternoon, but when I ran home after school, they laughed and shouted and called me fancy trash. That was what they called us—the trash family."

"Oh, Ellie." His heart ached for her.

"I never wore it to school again." She had warmed to telling him this story and she no longer hesitated. The words poured from her like floodwaters that had been dammed too long. "I hid the box and I wore the dress to town a few times when I sold my cigars. That's where *he* saw me wearing it."

"Winston?"

She nodded.

"Mrs. Conner got shot by a stray bullet when some robbers held up the bank. When I heard she died, I cried and cried and I wouldn't go back to school after that."

"I remember hearing about that bank robbery and the schoolteacher's death." Caleb's mother had written him all the latest news while he'd been away at the university.

"I was too sad to wear the dress anymore."

"What did you mean about Winston seeing you wearing it?"

"I'm getting to that. He came out to our place with that fancy carriage, and he paid my mother. Like he always did." She turned, finally, and looked at Caleb's face. Haunted distress filled her violet eyes. "This time she took the money for *me*."

Caleb absorbed her words and the incomprehensible meaning behind them. In horror, his mind grappled with the understanding.

"He tricked me into going outdoors with him. He had the black carriage waiting and once I was inside…he took his money's worth. He said I'd worn the dress to attract him—that I'd asked for it."

The facts all filtered together. Her mother had been as much the perpetrator as Winston, maybe more. She had accepted money in payment for Winston to rape her daughter. It was inconceivable. But it had happened. And Ellie had been the victim and had lived with the consequences.

"And the baby?" Caleb asked around the constricting lump in his throat.

Her eyes widened in surprise. "How—?"

"When you were sick I saw your body," he said. "I figured out that much then."

Tears filled her eyes. She attempted to turn away, but he wouldn't allow it. He cupped her face and gazed into her brimming eyes. "The shame is not yours, Ellie. You were a child. He forced you. You didn't have anyone to protect you."

The tears flowed from between her lashes and down her temple. Caleb released her face and eased himself down alongside her, fitting his body against the back of hers, with the sheet separating them. Holding her close, he stroked her hair, wanting to comfort her.

"I didn't realize at first," she said finally. "I thought I was sick. But then the baby started to grow inside me. My mother saw it and she cursed it and me. I did my best to stay away from her. She hated the boys and me, and I was afraid for what would happen to all of us. I hated her. I hated myself and my life. I had nightmares all the time."

Caleb listened and stroked her shoulder, her arm.

"I was never sure what Ben knew. He was so young, and Flynn was just a toddler then. Ben knew more than I thought. He tried to help me that night, but I didn't know it until just a little while ago. He must have figured out about the baby, too."

"How in the world did you have that baby, Ellie?"

"When the pains came I went into the woods and hid for a day and a night," she said. "I was afraid I might die, and if I did, I didn't want Ben to see it. I was more afraid of what she would do to the baby. She'd made threats."

"So you had it alone?"

"I had helped with the last two babies my mother had, so I knew what happened and about cutting the cord and all. I didn't know it was going to hurt so much."

Caleb thought of his wife dying even with his assistance and medical techniques. Ellie's accomplishment was extraordinary. If something had gone wrong, she'd have bled to death in the woods…alone.

"It was a girl."

He pictured her as a mere child, frightened and innocent, with no one to help or care. What must she have thought and felt when she brought that tiny creature into the world? He fought the urge to envelop her in his arms and hold her close. "What did you do?"

She swallowed. "I knew there was a couple in Florence—the Mastersons—who'd lost a baby to influenza not long before. I thought maybe they'd be willing to take my baby. Maybe it would even help them get over losing theirs. So I took her into town at night and I laid her on their back porch. I threw a rock at the window. They found her."

"Did they keep her?"

A tremor went through her body. "I went back a few weeks later and saw flannels hanging on the clothesline."

"And you never saw her after that?"

"No," she whispered.

"I'm so sorry," he said against her hair. "How you suffered for so long and stayed as loving and warmhearted as you are, I'll never know."

"No," she said again. She raised her clenched fists to her chest. "I have so much hate inside me, it eats up all the good parts."

"You hate her? Your mother?"

"Yes!"

"And you hate Winston?"

She didn't reply.

"They hurt you. Your mother should have protected you, provided for you. She didn't and that was wrong. He hurt you, too, in a way he had no right to do. But you don't have to carry the hurt and the secret all alone anymore."

She brought her fist to her lips and curled, bringing her knees up to her chest.

Caleb stayed wrapped around her. "You didn't do anything wrong. You didn't wear that dress to encourage him. You were fourteen years old and trying to make money to feed your brothers. He was a sick excuse for a human being. Thank God I wasn't faced with the decision to save his life. I don't know if I could have done it."

She unfolded her body enough to turn and reply. "You would have."

"I don't know, Ellie."

"You would have. I know you. You're the kindest man I've ever known."

He didn't think that was saying much, considering the caliber of people she'd known.

"Caleb, you're not just touching me like a doctor touches his patient."

"I'm touching you like a man touches his wife."

She placed her hand on his arm then. "I will understand if you don't want to be married to me anymore."

Caleb took her shoulder and urged her to turn toward him. They lay face-to-face, and he strained to take in her lovely features as well as the fear and regret in her eyes. "We had a deal, Mrs. Chaney. You are Nate's mother. I am Ben and Flynn's father. We are going through with the adoptions. Nothing has changed regarding those things. Unless you've changed your mind."

"But now that you know—"

"I know why you're so sad. I know why making a home is so important to you. I know why you can't bear the thought of a man hurting you like that again. And I know you wonder about the little girl you gave away. Those are the things I know. And they've made me understand. But they haven't made me love you any less."

Those words hung between them.

Chapter Seventeen

"You can't love me," she said finally.

"I can. And I do."

"But I can't ever love you back—not like you'd want me to."

"We can take that a little at a time." He brushed her hair away from her temple and pressed a kiss there, careful to keep his touches light and unrestrictive, while wanting nothing less than to crush her to him and absorb all her suffering and disillusionment.

She lowered her face and pressed her forehead against his chest. "How can you love me when you know all the ugliness?"

"Because you're the same person you were before I knew. I know *you*. I've watched your nurturing instincts toward the boys—Nate as well—and I've seen you take pleasure in simple things, like cooking and walking and the changing leaves. You think of others before yourself, always. Your smile lights up my world and gives me a strange but good feeling." He took her hand and pressed it over his heart. "Right here."

Ellie wept tears from a bottomless well inside her. Saying the words, revealing the truth, had purged her heart of years and years of grief and resentment, and the tears seemed to cleanse her soul. She was so empty and so tired she could barely move.

Caleb gently stroked her back and shoulders, smoothed her hair, restored her sanity and her peace of mind. He loved her. This wonderful, kind, generous man loved her. Like everything else involving Caleb, it was too good to be true.

Encircled in his arms, she drifted off to sleep.

She slept late into the morning, and when she woke, the house was still and silent. Caleb had propped a note on the kitchen table. Flynn had gone to school and Caleb had taken Benjamin to the sheriff's office so he could give his version of the shooting. He'd taken Nate to the Swensens'.

The Swensens'? Ellie dressed, drank a glass of milk and nibbled on a slice of bread. Her lip hurt where Winston had hit her, but she wasn't very hungry anyway.

Caleb returned before noon and found her taking fresh loaves of bread from the oven.

She placed them on the table and covered them with towels, then turned, seeing him in the doorway. "Caleb!"

He crossed the distance between them. His warm brown eyes darkened at the sight of her lip. She brought a finger up to the place, remembering the bruise she'd seen in the mirror.

He stood staring at her as though he wasn't sure what to do or say. She put aside the towels she'd used to take the hot pans from the oven, and faced him. She'd come out of a groggy sleep once during the night, and his arms had been around her. She wanted him to hold her within their strength and safety always.

He wasn't sure of her acceptance, she realized, and he waited for a signal. He'd said he loved her. How could she be so fortunate? She gave him a hesitant smile. "Everything all right?"

He nodded. "Benjamin answered questions for the sheriff and then I took him to school. Sheriff Fox wants to talk with you as soon as you're up to it."

She lowered her gaze to the floor where a dusting of flour had spilled. "Does he know everything?"

"Only about yesterday and last night. Ben knew you had received a note. We gave it to the sheriff. I believe Winston snuck up on me out by the Arnolds' and gave me this knot on the head."

"Is it better?"

"Hurts like the devil, but I'll be fine. Ellie, last night the sheriff told me that Winston had been accused of attacking at least four other young women. None of them could prove their stories and Winston was an important banker, so their claims got swept under the rug."

"Oh, those poor girls." Ellie immediately sympathized with them. "Sheriff Fox owes it to each one to go and tell them what has happened."

"I believe he will as soon as he's talked with you and the shooting is settled."

She removed her apron.

Their eyes met. "Nate is at the Swensens'?" she asked.

"They kept asking what they could do to repay me." He grinned. "I took them up on it and asked Mrs. Swensen to keep Nate this morning."

An awkward silence fell between them. Ellie remembered him holding her through the night. Throwing caution aside, she stepped forward. If he was going to reject her, she might as well know it now.

His eyes widened.

She moved right before him and looked up. He smelled like soap and outdoors. "Please hold me, Caleb."

He obliged her willingly, taking her against his chest and pressing his face into her hair. His chest was hard against the crush of her breasts, his thighs touching hers through her skirts. She wrapped her arms around his waist and pressed her face to the front of his shirt without restraint.

He held her the same—without reserve, as though he really did love her. His heart beat a soothing tempo against her cheek. "You'll go with me? To talk with the sheriff?"

"I will. He may want to speak with you alone, but I'll wait right there."

She raised her face to his. "Thank you. For everything."

"I don't want your thanks."

"You have them anyway." His lips were mere inches away. She wanted to feel them on hers again. She needed the assurance and the gratification. She stood on tiptoe, slid her hand against the back of his neck and their mouths met.

Sensing his hesitation, she pulled him closer, angled their noses and showed him she wanted this. He returned the kiss cautiously. Was he thinking of what had happened to her? Was he disgusted? The love she held for him was new and different and consuming. She wished she could be the wife he deserved, someone pure and worthy.

She ended the kiss and rested against his strength a moment longer, gaining courage. At last she pulled away. "All right then. Let's go."

The sheriff couldn't have been more polite or accommodating. He seemed as disconcerted as Ellie to have to discuss the situation that had occurred the night before. She told him about Winston cornering her in the tailor's shop and his eyebrows shot up. "Did anyone see you there?"

"The shopkeeper returned and asked me if I was all right. I was too embarrassed to tell him what had happened, so I just ran home."

"Which shop was it?"

"A tailor's. I didn't look at the sign. I had just left Swensen's Grocery and when...that man...approached me on the boardwalk I ran into the nearest building."

"That would be Mr. Rentchler's. I'll pay him a visit. Glad you remembered that. What did Parker say to you in the tailor's shop?"

Ellie told him Winston had asked her to meet him in a secluded spot. Of course she hadn't gone, and when she hadn't, he had shown up at their house.

"Benjamin told me what happened to him. What happened when you came downstairs and found Parker in the kitchen?"

She finished with her story, and the sheriff ushered Caleb back into the room.

"I'm sorry you had to go through this, Mrs. Chaney," the sheriff said. "From what the three of you have told me, I'd say you and your brother were just protecting yourselves. Parker had a history of complaints from females. I'll see what Mr. Rentchler has to say and we'll put this to rest."

Caleb shook his hand, then Ellie thanked the sheriff and they left his office. Relief swept over Ellie. Benjamin wasn't going to be blamed for Winston's death.

She made it a point to talk to her brother privately over the next few nights, and she had a feeling Caleb was doing the same. Late one evening, she found Benjamin sitting out on the back stairs.

Ellie seated herself beside him. "Whatcha doing?"

"Lookin' at the stars."

The night was cool and Ellie had pulled on a shawl. She gathered the fabric around her shoulders and gazed up at the sky. "There sure are a lot of them."

"Do you think there's a heaven, Ellie?"

She sighed thoughtfully. "After going to church with Caleb, and knowing him and his family, I just got around to believing there's a God. Heaven is something I'll have to think on. Why are you wondering about that?"

"'Cause I wonder where our mother is. And Winston. People like them wouldn't go up to heaven, would they?"

"I don't have to decide that. That stuff is up to God, I guess."

"I guess. That preacher man talks a lot about forgiveness, don't he?"

She nodded.

"Do you forgive me, Ellie?"

She turned toward him. "For what?"

"For not being able to help you that time. You know."

"I told you, Ben, you were a just a boy. There was nothing you could have done."

"Maybe there was something."

"There was nothing. You are not to blame for anything. You have to forget it. Put it behind you and enjoy our life now."

"Is that what you're doin', Ellie?"

The twinkling stars seemed close enough to touch, impossibly clear and bright. "Yes," she said, as though wishing on one, wanting to believe it was the truth.

"Well, if you can do it, I guess I can."

"You can."

Ben stood. "I'm gonna black my shoes for tomorrow."

She scooted aside so he could slip into the house.

Hating others wasn't healthy—a person had to forgive. That was what Reverend Beecher had said. But what about hating yourself? Ellie had lived with her self-disgust and recriminations for so long, she didn't know how to let them go. She'd been as much of a child as Ben had been, but she'd always wondered if she could have done anything differently.

She told him to let go and enjoy his life now, but she hadn't let go. How could she? How could she forget something that had shaped her life? Maybe she'd never forget.

But she could stop blaming herself. Put it behind her and live in this moment. Enjoy this new world that had been given to her like a gift.

Her gaze raked the star-studded skies. A gift from heaven?

She had a past, but she didn't have to dwell in it. She saw how important it was for Ben to believe that. It was equally important for her.

If Caleb could still love her, even though he knew, then she could certainly stop hating herself. She wasn't foolish enough to believe she could blot it all out immediately as if it had never happened. But she was going to place it in her past and move on.

Ellie steepled her fingers beneath her chin thoughtfully. One cloud remained in the nearly clear sky of her future. If this was going to be a real marriage, she had to be honest with Caleb in all things from now on. The truth was that she wanted him. The truth was that she wasn't sure of his feelings about what had happened to her. And the truth was that she had no control over the terror that came over her when she tried to give herself to him.

Was she brave enough to tell him all that?

Regarding the death of Winston Parker, Sheriff Fox sent word to Caleb that Benjamin had acted in self-defense and that no charges would be laid.

Caleb told Ellie the news over supper one evening.

Flynn, who'd been told of the incident in the simplest of

terms, piped up. "The kids at school called Benjamin a hero."

"Well, he is a hero," Caleb replied.

Ben flushed and ate a slice of Ellie's apple pie.

"Guess who came to see me today?" Caleb asked.

Ellie picked a slice of cinnamony apple from Nate's bib and fed it to him. "I don't know."

"Mabel Connely."

"Is she ill this time?"

"She's decided to listen to my advice and follow my suggested diet."

"Oh, my goodness! Your reputation has convinced her you know what you're talking about."

"I don't know if it's that or the fact that her niece is getting married next spring and has asked Mabel to be in her wedding. Seems her own mother is dead. Mabel wants to fit into the dress she wore to her sister's wedding."

"Is that possible?"

Caleb grinned. "Anything is possible. But the dress she wore then would still hold *two* of you, so she doesn't have to lose that much to fit into it."

Ellie laughed. "Well, that is good news. You were concerned about her."

He wiped his lips and laid down his napkin. "That I was. Do you boys have schoolwork?"

"Yup."

"Yes, sir."

"Help Ellie clear the table, so you can get to it."

They jumped up to obey.

Caleb took Nate outside while Ellie did the dishes. Finished, she found him on the front porch. The sun had gone down and fireflies dotted the yard.

"Is he about ready for bed?"

"I think so."

"I'll help you." Caleb got him a bottle of milk and fed him. Ellie changed him and placed him in his cradle. He snuggled down with a sleepy smile.

"Was your wife very beautiful?" Ellie asked as she studied the baby.

"She was lovely," Caleb replied. "She had fair hair and blue eyes."

"Like Nate's."

"Yes."

"Do you miss her terribly?"

An odd expression crossed his face. "I felt terrible about her death. I regretted that I couldn't save her, but I knew in my heart that no one could have. It was just one of those things."

He hadn't answered her question, but she waited.

"I loved her," he said. "I thought we could be happy together. But I never made her happy. She wanted to live in the East where there were more exciting things to do. She loved the parties and the theater and the whole social whirl. She never forgave me for setting up my practice here in Newton. She'd hoped to get away from here."

"Maybe she wanted to get away from her father."

Caleb's expression showed the thought was a new one. "Maybe she did. Her mother died the year before we were married, but she never had anything bad to say about her father."

"Do you think he…?"

"What?"

"Is it possible her father…" Ellie couldn't make herself ask it.

Caleb understood, however. "I don't believe so. She was a virgin on our wedding night."

Ellie flushed with shame and embarrassment. "I'm sorry

I asked. Most people would never think of something so awful."

"You couldn't help but wonder. It's okay."

It would do no good to regret her lack of virginity. If Ellie was going to accept herself the way she was, Caleb would have to, as well. "Caleb. Do you have any…I mean is the idea of making love to me spoiled by what you know?"

Nate had fallen asleep and they were speaking in low tones. Caleb took her hand and led her to sit on the foot of the bed beside him. "Ellie, it makes me sick to know what he did to you. I hurt for your pain and for the child that you were. But it doesn't change the way I feel about you…or the way I want you. You had no choice. You are still innocent."

"I've begun to believe that, too," she said. "Caleb, you truly don't get disgusted when you think of me like that?"

He touched her cheek. "No, I don't. How can you even wonder?"

"Because I thought it of myself for so long. But having you love me has changed the way I feel. I can see myself through your eyes now, and I don't have to hate the person I see."

"I love you, Ellie."

"Caleb." The time for honesty was long overdue. "I love you."

He smiled, a smile that touched her heart. He was glad.

"And I want you. I don't want us to sleep apart. But I'm so afraid of what happened the last time we tried. I have no control over that."

"You have nothing to be afraid of. That time I didn't know what had happened to you. Now I do. I won't do anything to make you uncomfortable…and we can talk about it. But I can wait, Ellie. Until you're ready."

How would she know when she was ready unless she tried?

"Why don't we give Nate his own room?" Caleb suggested. "You and I can share a bed. I want to have you close. If you don't feel comfortable with more, we'll be patient. There's no hurry."

His words set her mind at ease. And she wanted to be near him so badly. The night he'd stayed with her had shown her how much she craved the closeness. "All right," she agreed eagerly. "Which room?"

"We'll give Nate your room. Tomorrow you can bring your things in here. But for tonight we'll sleep in your bed. If that's okay with you."

She nodded and they went downstairs to send the boys up and lock the house. Ellie carried water up and washed. She'd just slipped into her nightgown when Caleb tapped on the door and entered.

She gave him a welcoming smile.

In the lamplight he removed his shirt and she didn't look away. He washed his face, chest and arms, then turned and cocked his head questioningly. "Want the light off?"

"No."

He unbuttoned his trousers and removed them, tossing them over the back of a chair. He wore his knee-length drawers, just like Ben's. She smiled. "You sleep in those?"

"Not usually."

"Are you uncomfortable taking them off?"

"I thought it might make you uncomfortable."

"Not yet."

With a grin, he pulled them off, then moved to turn the wick down.

Ellie enjoyed the view of his backside. "No. Don't turn it out."

He paused, obeying, then turned and got into bed beside

her, giving her only a glimpse of the rest of his mysteriously sleek and long-limbed body. He leaned back against the pillows and raised an arm over his head.

Ellie studied him, the smooth skin of his muscled arms, the dusting of hair that covered his chest and arrowed downward. Her gaze stopped at the sheet at his waist. Her attention traveled to his eyes: warm, brown, loving.

Caleb didn't see fear in her eyes. That fact pleased him more than anything. He had hoped to earn her trust. He'd done everything he knew how to show her he meant her no harm and that he only desired to express his love.

By understanding her fears, he could set them to rest. He had made it clear that he didn't want her to do anything merely to please him. The choice had to be hers—because she wanted it. Because she loved him. Oh, Lord, that knowledge warmed his heart.

Ellie had had no choices in her life growing up. She'd had no choice over her body when Winston had forced her and given her a baby. But she had choices when it came to their marriage.

"Ellie?"

"Yes?"

He explained the methods of preventing her from having a baby as directly and as thoroughly as he knew how. She accepted the information with fascination and a few discerning questions.

"The choice would be yours, of course," he added. "Whatever you were most comfortable with. I'd be pleased to assume the responsibility."

She gave him one of those smiles that made his toes curl and looked at him with huge violet eyes that reached a place in his heart no one had ever touched.

She seemed perfectly comfortable talking about this and she'd been looking him over with appreciation in her expression. Ellie had to have choices. She needed to be in control of her body and her desires.

And Caleb planned to give her that control. No matter how difficult it would be for him to use restraint when he wanted her so badly, he would do it.

"You can touch me," he said. "Any time…anywhere you like."

She appeared to think about it. "Would you like it?"

"Yes. But we're going to concentrate on what you like, and what's comfortable for you."

"You have to like it, too."

He smiled. "I'll let you know if I don't like something, but I wouldn't hold my breath if I were you."

She propped her head on her hand, her elbow on the bed, and used her other hand to trail her fingers across his chest and over his biceps. Her fingers came back and curled into the hair on his chest.

"That feels good," he said.

She scooted closer and leaned up to kiss him, a hesitant and uncertain brush.

"That felt good, too," he told her.

She smiled and kissed him again, this time a little more boldly, indulging him in the sweet taste of her lips and the feel of her lush breasts flattening against his chest.

"There's a little more to this kissing stuff that we've never done," he said.

"More? Like what?"

"Like getting tongues involved."

Her eyebrows rose in disbelief.

"You might like it," he added.

"Show me."

"All right. Kiss me again."

She did, and he ran the tip of his tongue along her lower lip until she opened to him. At first she accepted the kiss hesitantly, but then she returned it, moving closer and pressing her palm to his cheek. Her sweet innocence touched him anew.

She ran her hand down his neck, across his chest, and her touch set him on fire. With great restraint, he kept his own hands curled in loose fists, one at his side, the other at her back.

She ended the intimate kiss, but her lips lingered, almost touching his.

"Did you like it?" he asked.

"Yes. Did you?"

"Oh, yes." It came out as a half laugh, half groan.

She leaned back and ran her palm over his chest, down his stomach, studying him in the golden glow of the lamp. "I like looking at you."

"Go ahead."

Her gaze moved to his hip, partially covered by the sheet, then rose to his eyes.

"Go ahead," he said again. "Only if you want to."

She caught her lower lip between her teeth, thoughtfully, making him want to grab her and kiss her. He concentrated on relaxing his limbs.

Her hand twitched at his hip. "I can't."

"You don't have to."

Regret filled her luminous eyes.

"But if the sheet just happened to fall away, you wouldn't mind?" he asked.

She shook her head in agreement.

Caleb stretched, flexing one leg, and pulling the sheet downward with his foot. Ellie's eyes widened, but she didn't look away.

He had been aching for her since she'd leaned against him and given him that first tentative kiss; he was throbbing with arousal now, but he acted as though having this woman stare at him didn't make him want to flip her on her back and bury himself inside her.

That was exactly what he wanted to do, but even more than that, he wanted her to learn she could trust him and that neither he nor his body was anything to be feared.

Her expression showed more wonder than fear, but he asked, "Are you thinking I could hurt you?" he asked.

"It does seem…that way."

"It only hurts some the first time," he told her. "Because a woman has a tiny piece of flesh that is torn. But after that it shouldn't hurt again…unless the woman is forced. That would hurt no matter how many times she's done it before. When she's ready to accept the man into her body, it doesn't hurt."

"So it wouldn't hurt this time?"

"I don't think so. Maybe a little uncomfortable since it's been a long time, but nothing like what you knew then. I promise, Ellie."

"Did they teach you this stuff at school?"

"Some of it."

"A bunch of men in suits sit around discussing this?"

"No, they assign reading material, then ask for questions."

"Did anyone ask questions?"

"Not as many as you do."

She laughed and lowered herself to his chest again, bringing her legs to twine with his. "How would I know if I was ready?"

"I could show you how to know." And he explained arousal of both sexes to her, finding it the most erotic thing he'd ever done. He didn't know how he'd survive if this was just a warm-up and she wasn't ready to move forward.

But she seemed eager to experience all he'd just explained. She sat up and unbuttoned the tiny buttons at her throat and slipped her nightgown off over her head, watching his eyes, gauging his reaction.

Her breasts were full and lovely, with darkened nipples that stiffened when he feasted his gaze upon them. Her waist was narrow and her hips flared becomingly, but that was all he could see because of the way she knelt beside him.

She studied his face. Her gaze flickered to his hands. He read the message clearly. "Do you want me to touch you?"

She nodded.

"Show me where."

She took his hands and brought them to her breasts. Her eyelids drifted closed as he cupped and tested the delicious weight of her, ran his fingers over her budded nipples.

She was lost to the magical sensations and the reactions of her body. Caleb forced himself to wait for her spoken or implied demands before he did the things he ached to do. And slowly, but surely, she showed him what she liked and requested more.

He held himself in rigid control, her enflaming touches and entreaties setting him on fire. If she wasn't ready to go through with this, he would live, he assured himself. All that mattered was Ellie.

Ellie.

Ellie was consumed with her need for this man. She loved him with every ounce of her flesh and wanted to show him—wanted to be whole and complete within his love. His words and his patient tutoring gave her a new-found courage and confidence that made her head light and her body tingle. With him she felt so beautiful, so good and so right. Love made the difference. Loving him and knowing he loved her in return.

She wanted to consume him. She wanted to envelop him. She wanted to have that elusive something that would bind them as surely and as securely as she desired.

"Now, Caleb," she pleaded. "Will you take me now?"

Chapter Eighteen

She expected him to turn and pull her beneath him. Instead, he took care of the promise he'd made, then urged her astride, his eyes adoring her body and adding to all those signs he'd told her would prove she was ready. "You do it, Ellie."

"I can't…I don't…"

"I'll show you. Easy. Like this."

"Oh, my…"

"Stop if it hurts." Passion showed on his face and made his body tremble. His guiding hands were sure, but gentle as always.

"Oh, Caleb…"

"Does it hurt?"

"No-o." The word slipped out as whispered pleasure. "I didn't think…I didn't know.…"

"You don't have to think." He urged her with his words and his body. "Just enjoy. Take your pleasure, Ellie."

She did, losing every last shred of self-consciousness and doubt at the indulgence and love that she read in his eyes. He had explained each physical detail, so she would understand and not fear. But he hadn't been able to explain the wonder and the passion…the love…. She wanted to weep with the beauty of it. She was going to cry.

"Ellie, my sweet, what's wrong? Stop if you want."

"No. I don't know. You didn't tell me it would be this way."

He brought his hand to cup her cheek. "What way? What's wrong? Just tell me."

"It's…" She dropped her head to his chest. "It's too good…it's too hard…it's *frustrating*." Her body quivered beneath his hands.

He chuckled. "Trust me?"

She raised her head and nodded. He kissed her until her toes curled. Reaching between their bodies he touched her until she gasped, then he took hold of her hips, and as she welcomed that demanding, firm grasp, he guided her—raising her body until they nearly lost contact—and then pulling her back down against him with rapturous jolts.

Waves of sensation throbbed from the center of her being outward, pleasure as intense as any pain she'd ever known, as all-consuming and severe as she'd needed to make her understand—to make her forget—to make her new.

Caleb's body convulsed in shudders as hers had, and he loosened his grasp on her hips and stroked her thighs gently. His skin glowed damp, his chest heaved with exertion.

Ellie collapsed forward, her legs trembling, and rested against him. He brought his arms around her for the first time, and she relished his embrace.

He brushed the hair from her face and kissed her. "I love you, Ellie."

"I believe you do. And I'll never let you stop telling me…or showing me."

He shifted her to his side and they lay in each other's arms while their breathing slowed and their bodies cooled.

"So." He drew circles on her shoulder with his finger and spoke against her hair. "You didn't say. Did you like it?"

She pulled away and looked into his smiling eyes. "Did you?"

"Oh, yeah."

They laughed and hugged. And laughed and hugged a few more times before they fell into exhausted slumber.

"I have a surprise for you." Caleb had dropped the boys at school and returned home.

"I like your surprises more and more all the time." She moved into his arms and gazed up at him.

He kissed her indulgently, then drew away and held her at arm's length. "You're going to have your clothes on for this surprise, so let's get going. I told Mrs. Swensen we'd drop Nate off early."

Ellie smoothed her hair and her skirt. "Goodness. What have you planned this time?"

"You'll see. Come on. I'll get his things. Grab your coat."

Ellie bundled Nate in his cap and jacket and Caleb ushered them to the buggy. A few minutes later she kissed the baby goodbye and waved to the Swensens. "I think she's practicing to have one of her own," Caleb said with a sidelong smile.

He flicked the reins and headed away from the grocery.

"They're going to have a baby?"

"Well, she made an appointment for next week, so I can't say for sure yet, but she has that look about her."

Ellie considered the Swensens for a few minutes, imagining the prospect of having a baby with someone you loved. "Where are we going?"

"You'll see."

He'd headed toward Florence, and thinking that might

be their destination, her stomach fluttered nervously. The closer they came, the more apprehensive she grew. "Are we going to Florence?"

"Yes."

Her heart skipped a beat. "Caleb, people will recognize me there."

"Maybe. If they do, they'll see that you have a husband who loves you now."

She'd been worried about his reputation. He obviously didn't think the fact that he'd married a Foster would reflect badly upon him. Or he didn't care.

"This town is my past," she said finally.

"Yes," he agreed. "You're right. But there's one part of your past that still needs to be resolved."

Winston was dead. Caleb had taught her the beauty of physical love. Her body still tingled with the fulfillment and pleasure they'd given each other. The only remaining memory that still had the power to hurt was—

Ellie grasped the edge of the seat. "Caleb, where are you taking me? What are you doing?"

"We're going to visit the Mastersons. I wrote first. Then I came and spoke with them in person. They had a few concerns, but they welcome the opportunity to meet you and discuss them. And they have some things they want to tell you."

Ellie's heart tripped painfully. She grabbed his arm. "I can't do this! What were you thinking?"

He slowed the buggy just outside Florence. "I was thinking that you've spent years torturing yourself over whether or not you did the right thing. And if I'm guessing correctly, you've spent that time wondering whether to love or hate a child who was created under such horrible circumstances."

Ellie flushed beneath the piercing truth of his words and drew her hand back to her lap.

"I was thinking that you've put the rest of your childhood behind you. This needs to be opened and cleaned out, too. Like infection drawn from a wound."

She would have laughed at that physician's analogy if she hadn't been terrified to the tips of her toes.

She clutched her reticule. "What do they think of me?"

"They think you were very brave. And they want to tell you what you've done for them."

She studied the buildings that lay ahead. She did wonder if she'd done the right thing. She'd never dreamed she would be able to know. She hadn't wanted to know if she'd done the *wrong* thing. But Caleb wouldn't take her there to show her something that would make her unhappy. His surprise was obviously a good one.

She rolled her eyes. "You're always right, you know. Don't let it go to your head."

He drove the horses onward and pulled up to the house Ellie remembered. A scattering of fall flowers bloomed near the porch and the rosebushes beneath shuttered windows had been clipped back. In the side yard a tire swing hung from a gnarled oak tree. "They know we're coming?"

He nodded and tied the reins. "Mr. Masterson works at the rail station, but he stayed home this morning for your visit."

"Caleb, I'm scared."

"I know. But not any more scared than you were that night you threw a rock at their window."

She drew a fortifying breath. "No."

He clasped her cold hands and brought them to his lips. She gave him a feeble smile. He came around and lifted her to the ground, then held her hand as they walked through a gate and up to the house.

Children's voices reached them from somewhere inside, and suddenly Ellie couldn't wait to see the little girl—her little girl. She stepped forward, lifted the brass knocker and rapped it against the wood.

The door opened immediately. A small, dark-haired woman with freckles sprinkled liberally across her face and neck opened the door. A genuine smile of pleasure and recognition revealed small even teeth and charming dimples. Tears glistened in her wide gray eyes.

"Dr. and Mrs. Chaney," she said. "Please come in."

They entered a small foyer, and she led them to a sitting room with nice, but well-used furniture. Ellie sat on a divan with Caleb beside her, and Mrs. Masterson seated herself on the edge of a chair so her knees almost touched Ellie's.

She leaned forward. "Mrs. Chaney—"

"My name is Ellie."

"Ellie. Please call me Marissa. You don't know how pleased we are that you've come."

A man entered the room. He was as tall as Caleb, but more slender, with chestnut-brown hair that lay in waves against his head.

"This is my husband, Jack."

"How do you do?" Ellie shook his hand. "I'm Ellie."

"Your husband told us you were very young when you had Mary Michael," Marissa said.

She grasped the first bit of information eagerly and stored it away like a treasure. "Is that her name?"

The woman nodded. "Yes."

Ellie ran the name through her mind a few times.

"Did you know we'd lost a child?"

Ellie nodded. "I'd heard someone in town talking about it." It had probably been someone outside a saloon, but she didn't mention that.

"A little boy only a few months old," Marissa clarified.

"At first—when I saw the bundle on the porch—I thought someone had played a cruel joke on us. I didn't realize it was a real baby for a few minutes. Jack picked her up and she moved. I was so confused. I was going to make him take the baby to the sheriff, but she was so tiny and helpless. I realized right then that she was a gift—from heaven. From you."

Ellie's throat grew thick with tears. "You loved her?"

"We love her very much," Marissa said, choking back tears of her own. "So many times I have wanted to thank you. To tell you that your trust in us was valid and that we welcomed her. She has been such a joy. I can never thank you enough."

A remarkable solace settled over Ellie. She glanced at Caleb and he smiled encouragingly.

Marissa placed her hand over Ellie's, and Ellie clasped it in both of hers.

"We sure have wondered," Jack said and cleared his throat, "about you."

Ellie looked into Marissa's eyes. "I was fourteen years old with no food and no money. I couldn't keep her. I was frightened and I didn't know what else to do. I have wondered all these years, too…if I'd done the right thing."

Marissa's gray eyes darkened. "Your husband said seeing her and talking to us would set your fears at ease. But, well, we're a little worried now that—that you might want to take her away from us."

Ellie's heart went out to this woman who had raised her child. "Oh, no," she said, clasping her hand tightly. "I wouldn't do that to her—to you. You're her family. Family is everything."

Marissa smiled through her tears. "You can see her anytime you like. Someday, when she's old enough to understand—or to wonder—we wouldn't mind if she knows the truth about who you are.''

"I'm not prepared for someday yet," Ellie told her honestly. "But I would like to see her now."

"Girls!" Jack called over his shoulder. "Come greet our guests."

Two girls skipped into the parlor, both dressed in ruffled pinafores and dainty black boots, both wearing their hair in braids.

The smallest of the two had freckles scattered over her nose and two dimples winked playfully when she smiled. Her intelligent eyes were wide and gray.

The taller of the two had delicate ivory skin, hair a shade darker, and finely cut features. A fringe of dark lashes surrounded pansy-dark eyes, which were an astonishing and familiar shade of violet.

"This is Dr. and Mrs. Chaney from Newton," Marissa said.

"Is somebody sick, Daddy?" the older girl asked, her abashingly lovely eyes widening. She moved a little closer to…*Jack*…*her father*. Her *daddy*. He wrapped his arm around her waist and drew her close. "No, darling. They've just come to visit."

"Oh." She smiled shyly. "Pleased to meet you."

Tears stung Ellie's eyes. "I'm pleased to meet you, too. Mary Michael?"

The enchanting child nodded.

"This is Nancy." Marissa tapped the daughter she'd indicated on the shoulder.

"Pleased to meet you," Nancy said at the prompting, then huddled against her mother's skirts.

Ellie absorbed all the enlightenment she could hold. Her child was healthy and well dressed, obviously well cared for and secure within her family. She had two parents…and a sister.

She had everything Ellie had ever hoped for her to have. She had everything Ellie had craved for herself and for her brothers. "You are such pretty girls," she said. "Do you go to school?"

Mary Michael replied, and the sisters vied for attention, relating stories of their classmates and occasionally running into another room to bring something one of them had made to show their visitors.

Ellie looked at the plaster-of-paris molds each had made in Sunday school. She allowed her fingers to trail over the imprint of Mary Michael's hand.

"Perhaps you'd like to give those to the Chaneys," Marissa said. "I'll bet they don't have anything quite like them."

Ellie met the woman's kind gray eyes and recognized a love and an unselfishness she would never have appreciated before Caleb had taught her that it existed in the world. The gesture touched Ellie and meant more than these girls could imagine. Maybe someday…

"I'd like that very much," she said in a throaty voice. "That is if you girls could bear to part with them."

"We can make more," Nancy said.

Mary Michael agreed.

Jack brought paper and Ellie wrapped them carefully.

Marissa brewed tea and served it from a silver service. She and Jack and Caleb sipped the sweetened refreshment, but Ellie drank in the reassuring details of Mary Michael's life.

The girl became so at ease with Ellie that she invited her upstairs to see the room she shared with Nancy.

"If it's all right with your parents?" Ellie raised a brow.

"Of course," Marissa supplied.

"I'll show you, too," Nancy piped up.

"But you were going to show Dr. Chaney how you play your scales, weren't you?" her mother asked, distracting her.

"Oh, yes!" She reached for Caleb's hand and drew him over to the upright piano beneath a leaded-glass window.

Ellie followed Mary Michael upstairs and admired the cheerful room. A patchwork quilt in various shades of yellow covered the feather bed. Bright curtains matched the ruffle on the edge of the quilt.

A row of dolls lined a window seat, and the window overlooked the side yard. Ellie listened to the child tell her each doll's name and something about the birthday or Christmas when she'd received it. From beneath the bed, she drew a flat case that held changes of clothing—for the dolls!

Ellie fingered the tiny garments in awe. "Your mother made these?"

Mary Michael nodded.

It couldn't have been chance that had drawn Ellie to this house that night so long ago. It had to have been divine guidance. This child had grown up secure and loved in a warm home with attention and food and the good things all children deserved. The things Ellie had never known and had tried to give her baby.

Ellie had loved her enough to let her go. And the Mastersons had loved her enough to accept her as their own.

Ellie had done the right thing.

As they walked down the stairs together, Ellie knew satisfaction and pride of a new and serene kind. Caleb met her gaze, and she smiled, loving him even more. He had given her yet another gift this day—the gift of closure.

"You'll come again?" Marissa asked as they said their

goodbyes and stood on the front walk.

The girls had dashed over to the swing and stopped squabbling over who would use it first long enough to wave.

"I'd like that," Ellie said. "Thank you."

"And you'll bring the boys?"

"We'll bring them," Caleb replied.

Caleb helped Ellie up to the buggy seat. She waved at the Mastersons, who stood together in the shade of their porch.

The horses pulled away. Ellie leaned against Caleb and he caught her in one arm and drew her to his side. "How was that for a surprise?" he asked.

"As surprises go, it was probably one of the best I'll ever have." She tucked her head against his shoulder. She gazed up at him. Goldie had been right. The day Ellie had fallen off that platform at the railroad station had been the luckiest day of her life. Caleb had not only known how to heal her arm, but he had known exactly what she'd needed to heal all the hurts and misgivings of her former life.

Because of his love and his strength she'd been able to put her past behind her and could now look forward to her future—their future—a concept she'd only dreamed of, a future as a family. Because of Caleb she had her brothers, a newly adopted son, renewed faith in people and a new-found acceptance of herself.

She had survived and started over. Ellen Foster Chaney was a woman of character and stamina, and she had a lot of love left to give.

"I just might surprise you one of these days, too," she said to her husband.

"How's that?"

"Now if I told you, it wouldn't be a surprise, right?" She smiled to herself, trying to recall—and not remembering—all those good reasons she'd had for not wanting a baby.

*   *   *   *   *

If you enjoyed what you just read,
then we've got an offer you can't resist!

Take 2 bestselling love stories FREE!
Plus get a FREE surprise gift!

"This book is DYNAMITE!"
—**Kristine Rolofson**

"A riveting page turner…"
—**Joan Elliott Pickart**

"Enough twists and turns to keep everyone guessing… What a ride!"
—**Jule McBride**

See what all your favorite authors
are talking about.

Coming October 1999 to a retail store near you.

HARLEQUIN®
Makes any time special ™

WIN A DREAM

In celebration of Harlequin®'s golden anniversary

Enter to win a *dream!* You could win:

- A luxurious trip for two to
  The Renaissance Cottonwoods Resort
  in Scottsdale, Arizona, or

- A bouquet of flowers once a week for a year
  from **FTD**, or

- A $500 shopping spree, or

- A fabulous bath & body gift basket, including
  K-tel's *Candlelight and Romance* 5-CD set.

Look for **WIN A DREAM** flash on
specially marked Harlequin® titles by
Penny Jordan, Dallas Schulze,
Anne Stuart and Kristine Rolofson
in October 1999*.

FTD

RENAISSANCE.
COTTONWOODS RESORT
SCOTTSDALE, ARIZONA

K·TEL

This season, make your
destination Great Britain with
four exciting stories from

In October 1999, look for

LADY SARAH'S SON #483 by Gayle Wilson
(England, 1814)

and

THE HIDDEN HEART #484 by Sharon Schulze
(Wales, 1213)

In November 1999, look for

ONE CHRISTMAS NIGHT #487
by **Ruth Langan, Jacqueline Navin and Lyn Stone**
(Scottish Highlands 1540, England 1193
and Scotland 1320)

and

A GENTLEMAN OF SUBSTANCE #488 by Deborah Hale
(England, 1814)

**Harlequin Historicals
Where reading is truly a vacation!**

This season,

COMING NEXT MONTH FROM

HARLEQUIN HISTORICALS

DON'T MISS THESE FOUR GREAT TITLES AVAILABLE NOW!